BEYOND THE

A novel

AYESHA EJAZ

Tellwell Talent
www.tellwell.ca

ISBN
978-0-2288-1438-2 (Hardcover)
978-0-2288-1437-5 (Paperback)
978-0-2288-1439-9 (eBook)

DEDICATION

T o Amee for having faith in me and Aboo for all the hours spent playing Scrabble and going through "A Student's Companion".

For my best friend, anchor and husband, Ejaz Farooqi, for his love and support.

ACKNOWLEDGEMENTS

I am grateful to Kathy Hatter and Heather Todd from FirstEditing and especially to my editor, Tereza for all the effort she put in reviewing my manuscript.

Special thanks to Asim Haider for his time, support and faith in me. Thanks to Daoud Hassan and to Rukhsia Waqas. This book would not have been possible without Saima Raheel Khan pushing me forward until I had no choice but to take the bull by the horns. I am indebted to my son Zain Farooqi for his valuable suggestions and to Fatima Ejaz for keeping things interesting while I worked. Amanda Young, thank you for the photography.

I am indebted to Michel Anderson and Redjell Arcillas and the team at Tellwell for their hard work.

I thank Dr. Aksan for all the lectures she gave on Turkish history and being one of the inspirations to write this book.

I have seen the movement of the sinews of the sky,
And the blood coursing in the veins of the moon.

Sir Muhammad Iqbal (1887-1938)

CHAPTER 1

A chill wind was blowing from the South, which seemed to creep into my bones and freeze the marrow within. The forecast called for fifteen degrees below freezing. I couldn't even take a full lungful of breath, fearing the wind would form icicles within my chest. Anything was possible in this Godforsaken land. My mouth was covered with the scarf you gave me, but even then, breathing was an ordeal. I kept my steps short; I didn't want to get breathless with exhaustion. Trudging slowly up the hill, I could see the outline of the house and quickened my pace. The house was bound to have a fire burning in the grate and hot soup on the stove. The thought of food kept me occupied. It had been almost half a day since I had had a full meal. Dry biscuits and half a packet of pretzels was not enough for a man of my appetite. The big oak loomed in front of me. I was only a few minutes away from being with you.

I half-expected you to be standing by the window, but you weren't there. I opened the door expecting the familiar gust of house smells to greet me. Two things happened simultaneously while I stamped the snow off my boots and opened the door. First, the anticipation of meeting you and finding a warm house with hot food was quickly replaced with a foreboding and dread, which was settling fast in the pit of my stomach. Within seconds, the feeling was growing rapidly.

Second, as I crossed the threshold to the place I called home, a metallic, corrosive odour assaulted my senses. It was taking far too long for my eyes to adjust to the dark. I groped for the light switch, then stumbled and fell on the carpet we had bought last year in Turkey. A strange, dark wetness covered the intricate pattern. I lay still for a minute or so, trying to get my bearings. One thing was certain: you were nowhere to be seen and something awful had just taken place in the house.

Holding onto the coffee table, I force myself to stand. I could see you now. You lay face down near the settee. Your hair was wet and spread on the wooden floor, and your head was covered in blood—I could tell by the wetness that surrounded it. A sob escaped my throat when I saw Petsy with her throat slashed; lying on the side of the carpet I was standing on. One of her paws covered most part of her bloodied face but I could still see her lifeless eyes staring stonily at the ceiling. She had been with us since the day we had moved to the countryside and had been your devoted companion especially on the days I had to be away.

Later, when the police asked why I had not checked whether my wife was alive or not, I could only say I knew you were not by the angle you lay at, and more so, by the sick foreboding I felt the moment I reached for the doorknob. Initially, I was the prime suspect. Later, after investigating that I had been away on business, the police decided to change their opinion. The fact that other people corroborated the evidence that you and I were madly in love and had been blissfully married for the past eight years, forced the police to close the case and leave it as a random act of violence. Nothing had gone missing and there was not much evidence to continue the investigation. The officers probably thought it boring to come to such a remote area to investigate an incident which didn't excite the public beyond our small community, or perhaps they found the farmland too cold and inhospitable. Nevertheless, the case was closed as inconclusive.

With the children gone several days after the funeral, there was not much to occupy me with. Sympathetic neighbours visited infrequently and some of your friends politely dropped by with an occasional pie, but I was not in the mood for company. An uneasy thought rankled somewhere in the back of my mind. A few days of deathly quietness and sorrow made me decide to sell off the farm and leave—leave the house we had made a home and hoped to die in. At least you had kept that part of the deal. But, each day spent on the farm after you left was unbearable.

Every tree, window, and turn reminded me of your presence, or the lack of it.

Joel McCutcheon wiped his teary face with the back of a grimy hand after putting the last of my suitcases in the train compartment. He had been kind enough to buy the farm he had helped run and now stood looking miserable at being separated from me. We shook hands and bravely looked into each other's eyes. A million words passed between us in the silence. The train's whistle forced us to part and gave Joel reason to jump off and stand by the window. I smiled and waved as the train pulled out of the station, out of the town, and out of the memories that shrouded the place.

I don't know what brought me to the cosmopolitan humdrum of Toronto so soon after you left me. I kept myself busy for the first few days by looking for a small apartment on Victoria Street and then furnishing it with the few articles I had had delivered from the farm. The apartment looked cheerful enough. It was clean, and had all the bare necessities. Only one framed picture adorned the house—the photograph of the two of us on our dream vacation to Turkey. It stood on the kitchen counter. It has always been my favourite picture. In it, your hair is pushed away from your face by the slight wind and you're turned toward me, looking into my eyes. My left arm is around your shoulder, and I'm looking down at your upturned face. It was a random picture taken by a friendly waiter on the ship—a picture that captured our happiness together.

I placed the coffee and ashtray on the table. The card with the address and the earrings were already there. The diamonds glittered under the kitchen light. Thoughts were filtering through my mind. I am looking through your drawer for my cufflinks, and come across the fancy blue box under some scarves. You quickly pull the box out of my hand before I can look inside it. Looking at my distressed face, you pull me into your arms and we sit on the bed. You open the box to reveal crisp pink paper and only one sparkling diamond earring. It's a striking piece of jewellery and I marvel at its beauty. It is an unusually large teardrop diamond with gold and silver claws holding it.

"It is beautiful, where's the other one? I've never really ever seen you wear any jewellery," I ask, while admiring the earring you are holding up for me to see.

"It got lost," you reply. "I'm keeping it safe for someone." The earring remained in the box for all that I could remember.

I get up to make another cup of coffee and empty the ashtray. Some habits die hard. You never liked to see a full ashtray and would always empty it after every few cigarettes I had.

The other thought that came to mind was the way I found you that day, sprawled on the floor with your face turned to the right. When the police were taking you away, I let my eyes stray to the face I had adored for so many years. Apart from an unattractive, bluish-black bruise on your forehead, your face was unblemished as usual. Loose strands of soft brown hair hid most of the discolouration. What did not register at once was the fact that the earrings lay on the carpet, almost mocking me. That was the thought that kept rankling in my mind. It was an elusive thought—it did not stay for long, but kept on recurring like a bad dream. And then, I knew what was bothering me. There were two earrings on the carpet, not one.

I didn't know how cold it could get in Toronto. With the leaves changing from green to yellow and orange, winter was around the corner. With my raincoat pulled tightly around my neck, I walked briskly to the police station and was told Chief Krenos would be at the prison that day. I insisted that the officer call the Chief; I had to see him.

Upon hearing my story, Chief Krenos initially took me for an aching husband, mourning the loss of his wife and seeking retribution. However, the earrings took his breath away. The information was collected from the jewellers and the earrings were taken into custody, and a detective was assigned to the case.

The first snow had fallen. I stood by the open window, inhaling the crisp air and a cigarette. The words of Krenos, from so many months ago, reverberated in my ears. "Your wife had a scuffle with the perpetrator, possibly a burglar, and hit her head on the table and died. They probably had an argument before you found her and in a fit of fury, the assailant pushed your wife."

I stubbed the cigarette and went to the kitchen to empty the ashtray. I switched on the television and saw your hand-cuffed murderer being led away. For a moment, when he looked at the camera, it seemed our eyes met. There was tight-lipped anger and hate in his blue eyes. I switched off the news.

Lights had come on outside, dotting the eerie silence of the winter. My last thought was of your windblown hair and the taste of sea salt in my mouth.

CHAPTER 2

She could only walk another few steps before collapsing on the grass. Zaheer Khattak urged her to get up.

"If we don't cross the woods within the hour, we are bound to get caught. You have a plane to catch tomorrow. Sitting down here isn't going to help you get to Canada."Safina looked into Zaheer's eyes. The eyes of a young man who had given her more love than all the people in her life put together. A man who was risking everything for her, trying to unite her with her mother in a faraway land. How Zaheer had managed to go to the Canadian High Commission in Islamabad and get her visa and air ticket, was beyond her. Now, all she had to do was reach Islamabad airport where the representative from the Canadian High Commission would be waiting, and get on the plane and out of Pakistan. Had she escaped the prison she was living in? Was her tribal father going to pursue her all the way to Canada? She shuddered when an image of her father crossed her mind—his handsome face and neatly trimmed beard, and his piercing blue eyes that had the capacity to look right through you and into your soul. No wonder her mother, Samantha, had fallen in love with him.

Little did Samantha know when she first met her husband that he hailed from the harsh and constrained life of the North of Pakistan, an area untouched by development and where civil jurisdiction had very little say. When the young Canadian came across Khodadad Wali Khanzada in London, she was not just taken by his looks, but by his chivalrous manner as well. Samantha had observed him for the first time from afar, while he stood thumbing through a magazine at a bookstore. There was something about him which set him apart, and she felt drawn to him. The way he walked into the store, with long, easy strides, and his raincoat draped casually over his shoulders. The way he talked to the cashier, asking about something and her taking him to the history section and extracting a large tome off the shelf, while he stood away at a short distance and smiled thankfully at the girl; there was no superfluous chit-chat, just a respectful distance. Samantha had sat on the couch intended for reading, and observed him with interest from the moment he entered the store. There wasn't anything singular about his clothes, but it was the way he carried himself that set him apart. His bearing spoke of discreet affluence and understated modesty. There was an almost regal bearing to the breadth of his shoulders or the way he lowered his head slightly to speak to the girl, with his head tilted to the side. Samantha had gotten up from her point of vantage, and going around the couches, had stood across from where the pair stood browsing through the shelf.

The second time, she spotted him sitting in a café talking animatedly with someone. Although she only caught a glimpse of him through the glass while hurrying towards the Museum of Natural History, she knew it was fate that had chanced her upon him again in a city teeming with tourists at that time of year. Instead of continuing on, she stood across the street waiting for the mystery man to come out of the café. She must have waited for almost twenty minutes, with no sign of him coming out. Then, laughing at her own silliness, she decided to head towards the museum.

"I am wondering if it is my beard or my accent that interests you, or do I remind you of someone?" The words took her by surprise. The man from the café stood across the glass display table where she had her head bent, observing the fossilized prehistoric insects. He was smiling and there was amusement in his eyes.

Samantha looked up, embarrassed and unable to answer. Realizing she was being rude, she offered her hand and apologized. "I'm terribly sorry, I'm Samantha," she smiled, "and I like to observe people I find fascinating. I've been trying to place where you could be from."

"Khodadad Wali Khanzada," he replied, with a twinkle in his blue eyes, and took her small hand in his large ones, "and I'm guessing you're trying to decide if I'm from Turkey or some Eastern European country." Blushing, Samantha had to concede that that was indeed what she had been trying to reckon since she first saw him. She did not want to admit anything further, like the fact that she found his laid-back yet imposing personality rather distinctive within the fast-paced cosmopolitan city or the fact that she found him terribly attractive. She could tell he was not an ordinary man; despite his slight accent, where he emphasized the "th" sounds, his words sounded poetic, and were spoken in an almost lyrical manner. And the way he addressed her, smiling, almost reverently, was gracious and gentle, and she couldn't help being drawn to him. After learning she was visiting England for the first time and was a student in her second year at a university in Canada, Khodadad offered to show her around the city. He was visiting from Pakistan on business and knew his way around from years spent there in school, and later at university. What started as a casual friendship, with daily visits to museums and parks together, soon turned into hours on end spent in each other's company discussing art and music. Despite their growing friendship, Khodadad always treated Samantha with utmost respect and an unpretentious deference. He was chivalrous to the point of being awkward, and this was something new for her. It did not take long for the two to realize that the closeness they felt went beyond long walks and talking about culture. The attraction was mutual and soon, Khodadad asked Samantha to be his wife and move to Pakistan with him. If Samantha had any doubts about accepting the proposal, they were short lived. She knew life would not be the same if she did not have Khodadad in it. However, the thought of moving from the world she knew to an unknown territory overwhelmed her. The fact that she would have to conform to a conservative lifestyle crossed her mind for a fleeting moment, but when she looked at Khodadad's easy and westernized bearing, her fears seemed ridiculous. Their quick marriage in London's Regent's Mosque was followed by a long honeymoon across Europe, filled with lavish hotel suites and first class travel and dining. After a lazy two months, she felt just a mild tremor at the thought of moving to Pakistan with her husband. Was life going to be very different from now? She had no friends or family there. It would almost be like starting life on a different planet.

Islamabad proved to be a pleasant surprise. The couple moved into Khodadad's sprawling house hidden behind lush trees at the base of The Margalla Hills. Samantha quickly made friends with people from all parts of the world living in Islamabad, just like her. Her days were filled with endless dinners and tea parties and picnics. Her parents also made a trip and visited her in her new home and were awed by the splendour and comfort they found their daughter in. Khodadad was a devoted husband, of that Samantha had no doubt. The few days each month he went away to his village were the most difficult to bear.

Life was perfect until her husband made the decision to move to his tribal village in the northern region of Pakistan. Samantha, or Saman now, felt strings of apprehension tug at her. The thought of leaving the comfortable life she had spent living in the country's capital for the past four years, and of meeting her in-laws for the first time worried her. She wondered if they would approve of her, and she clutched baby Safina to her chest as the Range Rover made its way across the bumpy mountain road. Khodadad sat at the front with the driver and spoke little.

1963, Islamabad, Pakistan.

Saman tightly held onto sleeping Safina. The uncivilized territory of the north and her increasing apprehensions were weighing her heart down. Why did Khodadad seem distant so suddenly? They had hardly exchanged a dozen words during the long ride to the village. Alighting from the four-wheel drive, Saman was momentarily mesmerized by the pictographic beauty around her. Small wooden huts dotted the territory. Green hills surrounding the valley gave it a strange, silent appearance. It almost seemed as if the firs surrounding the valley stood as sentinels guarding escape, and the gushing river was there to drown out the sound.

The Range Rover stopped outside massive limestone walls with an unimposing wooden door, which suddenly opened to let the travelers in. If the village outside appeared meagre and humble, the house looming ahead was anything but. The colossal structure was washed in pink marble and surrounded with blossoming beauties of all kinds. Saman had never seen such a splash of colour before. Huge trees lined the walls of the house. These trees were so different from the ones outside. Later, Saman would marvel at the fact that despite her unease, she had noticed tiny details while walking up the narrow cobblestone path which led to the house. For instance, she noticed pecan and walnut trees. She noticed the dahlias were of the dinner-plate variety, and that the wooden bench placed under the cherry tree was crooked. She didn't mind the fact that besides the ancient gardener who had opened the wooden door, no one seemed in sight.

"This is Mumtaz Bibi. She will take care of you and Safina," Khodadad pointed to a middle-aged woman who did not meet either of their eyes. Strangely, without a word, Khodadad walked out the same door they had entered only moments ago. Mumtaz Bibi took the now awake Safina from her mother's arms and took them to their room. It seemed she had been preparing for their arrival. Saman's luggage, which had arrived earlier, was neatly put away in closets and drawers. Her toiletries were already laid out in the washroom. A connecting door revealed a cheerful room for Safina with a crib near the window. All Saman wanted to do was lock herself in the room and weep. She felt miserable. How could her husband leave her in a strange place with a strange woman without saying a word? What about the ordeal of meeting his family? Where was his family? And where did he take off to so suddenly? These thoughts swirled in Saman's head.

"I will have the maid bring tea for you," Mumtaz Bibi spoke for the first time. Saman was startled to hear her talk in perfect English, and noticed her swollen, red-rimmed eyes for the first time. She had obviously been crying for a long time. Saman let herself drop on the sofa and raised questioning eyes at the kind face.

"Mumtaz Bibi, is everything alright?" Saman asked the woman, her own misery quickly being replaced by concern for the older lady.

The woman sat next to her and held Saman's delicate hand in her rough ones.

"Khodadad Wali's father and two older brothers were killed by our rival tribe," she informed her gently. "Everyone is in mourning. My husband, son and his family were also butchered mercilessly. Your husband will not come back for a few days," she added. All this information was too much to assimilate in just a few minutes, and Saman felt her body go limp.

Mumtaz Bibi was Khodadad's uncle's daughter. After her son and husband had been killed in the tribal encounter, she had lost everyone except her youngest son, who was studying in Islamabad. Khodadad had asked her to come and live with his family not only because she had no one to go to, but also because she spoke English, thanks to her days at the Murree Convent School. Saman was thankful for the lady's presence but didn't know at the time how Mumtaz Bibi would become an important part of her changing life.

It was Safina's eighth birthday and her father had promised to be home. There was a lot of excitement. For the first time, Saman's friends from Islamabad were also visiting. Wrapping the peach chiffon sari around her, she felt alive for the first time in a long time. With a dab of Madame Rochas behind her ears and wrists, and a peach rose in her coiled brown hair, Saman made her way to the garden where colourful lights had been strung up. Viola was plucking at the strings of a guitar under the cherry tree, while some of the younger guests sat in a semi-circle at the tutor's feet looking up at her with awe. Khodadad's jeep stopped outside and there was a flurry to open the small wooden gate. Safina ran to greet her father, while the guests rose to welcome him. "Make way, he's been shot. Please move." Khodadad's driver spoke in the local Darri dialect as he supported his master with one arm. A horde of servants and guests rushed to assist the driver. Khodadad was taken inside the house and laid on a settee in the lobby.

Safina watched in horror as Mumtaz Bibi pushed a tea cloth to Khodadad's stomach. Blood gushed through the cloth and onto Bibi's hands. Her fists clenched to her mouth, and Saman stood near the settee watching her husband's blood spill onto the smooth floor. The Russian exile, Dr. Yakov, who was also a guest staying at the house, rushed inside and ordered the room to be cleared. Viola took the guests outside, with Safina clinging to her skirt, and ordered the food to be laid out on the tables. She thought it was the best way to distract everyone. However, no one seemed to be interested in food. Everyone looked at each other with dread and unanswered questions in their eyes. Khodadad's fleet of gunmen stood guard against the walls of the house.

Mumtaz Bibi rushed around the room, shouting orders and pushing people out, and mostly, comforting Saman. Khodadad had been moved to the table in the breakfast room, while Dr. Yakov and his wife, Katarina, began to organize the room into a make-shift operating area. The doctor's medical bag and supplies were fetched from the guest annexe next to the big house. Mumtaz Bibi stayed in the room, holding her cousin's hand. Even though the morphine had dulled the pain, Khodadad fiercely clutched Mumtaz Bibi's left hand to his chest. The old woman had seen too much pain and suffering in her years to squeal at the sight of blood and was therefore able to keep a level head through the ordeal.

Dr. Yakov and Katarina worked with incredible speed and dexterity, pulling out first one, then two and finally three bullets from Khodadad's abdomen. Bandages were wrapped around the neatly stitched wound and the patient was moved to Safina's room with the connecting door to the master bedroom.

Over the weeks that followed, Saman had become drawn and quiet. The pink scars on her husband's body reminded her of the harsh reality she lived in. She had started to fear for herself, her daughter, and her unborn child. On the other hand, Safina was overjoyed to have her father all to herself. The fact that Khodadad was convalescing in her room was a source of pride for her. She spent all her free time with her father, leaving him only at night to sleep with her mother in the adjoining room. Mumtaz Bibi and Safina were with Khodadad constantly, while Saman avoided him. She couldn't bring herself to look at him, lest he see the fear in her eyes. The pride in the man did not ask for his wife's presence, but grieved inside for the chasm which now loomed between them.

Safina woke to the howls which reached into her sleep and woke her with a jolt. Her mother was nowhere to be seen and neither was her father. She ran to the foyer looking for Mumtaz Bibi, and then stopped in her tracks when she heard another howl. The girl ran to the back of the house to the guest rooms and saw her father beaming near one of the closed doors.

The tribe had an heir. Khodadad's son would now carry the family's name forward. Had Khodadad died in the encounter, his leadership would have passed onto the rival tribe. Not so anymore. Adam Wali Khanzada was going to carry on his father's blood and heritage. The brand-new baby's arrival was heralded with pomp and glory befitting a future tribal chief. Food and money were distributed to the poor, feasts for all surrounding tribal elders and chiefs were held, and drums were beaten to announce the baby's birth. Where Khodadad was ecstatic, Saman was listless and indifferent. The birth of a boy meant fear. She was aware that Adam would grow up to be like his father, like all the men of the land. She would live in constant terror for her son's life. Life in the mountains was getting claustrophobic and she had to get away.

A soon as he could walk, young Adam spent all his time with his father. He would accompany him on his daily rounds and sit by his side when he went to his meetings with the villagers or visited the quarries and the lumberyard. As soon as he could lift a gun, the boy was seen on the back of an open jeep going on hunting trips—some lasting for days. Saman felt helpless as she could not stop her son, who was fast becoming aware at a young age that he was a future leader of land and men. "When will Adam start his schooling in Islamabad?" Saman asked her husband one day, knowing well what the answer would be. "He is going to be four this year."

Khodadad looked wearily at his wife. He was annoyed that all these years had not educated her in the traditions of the land.

"He will not go to school in Islamabad," he answered, running a hand through his hair. "He will go to a private boarding school in Europe after he learns his roots here. He will follow in the tradition of his ancestors." Khodadad's tone did not encourage further debate.

Safina, on the other hand, loved her life in the mountains. Each month, she would go to Islamabad with her mother and Viola and visit shops, libraries and her mother's friends. However, no matter how much fun she would have, she always longed to return home after a few days. She stayed because her quiet mother seemed to come alive on their shopping trips, and chatted incessantly with her white friends. Khodadad and Adam rarely accompanied them. A lack of conventional schooling did not deprive Safina of an outstanding education. At fourteen, she was fluent in English, French, Urdu, Pushto and Darri. She played the violin and sketched magnificently. Adam, on the other hand, could hunt, fish, ride, handle ferocious dogs, read stars, and showed promise in mathematics. He refused to learn an instrument, but like his sister, had a flair for languages.

Returning after a trip to Islamabad, Saman was impatient to see her son and show him the gifts she had brought. Adam was nowhere to be seen and upon inquiring, she was told he had left with his father for a polo tournament and wouldn't be back for a few days. Later that evening, Mumtaz Bibi came and sat next to Saman on her bed and held her hand. Saman knew something was wrong.

"What is it Bibi?" she asked of the older woman, alarm bells ringing in her ears. Mumtaz's broken voice seemed to come from far away. She was trying to tell her that Adam was fine; he had a small accident and had been taken to a hospital in Islamabad. Mumtaz left Saman's side and rushed around the bedroom, hastily packing Saman's suitcase.

"The jeep is waiting outside. You are leaving in half an hour with Viola. Safina will stay with me. Hurry!" the woman told Saman without looking at her.

Saman got up and changed into a pair of slacks and a lilac cashmere sweater. Her bags were already packed. Before leaving the house, she went back to her room and opened the safe behind the Saqeduain calligraphy. Stashing several bundles of American dollars and her passport into her handbag, Saman quickly left the house in the deep darkness of the night.

"Why didn't she take me with her?" Safina asked with reproach.

"My peach, she had to go in a hurry to Islamabad. Someone needed here there," Mumtaz placated the young girl. Safina couldn't understand how her mother hadn't woken her to say goodbye. She could tell something was utterly wrong.

The little boy was heavily sedated when his mother walked into the hospital room. Bandages covered his head and right leg, and all sorts of monitors were beeping to show he was breathing. Saman ignored her husband and rushed to the bed, her pent-up anger and fear manifesting in tears that coursed down her cheeks.

"He will be fine, my love. He will be fine." Khodadad's raspy voice was lost in the sobs that racked from Saman. Getting up, Khodadad pulled his wife to his chest and let her cry, his own ashen face was wet with tears.

Adam was recovering quickly. Apparently, the fall from his horse was not going to deter him from asking when they would return so that he could get back to his guns and horses. The more Adam spoke of returning, the more nervous Saman would get. She did not want to go back. She wanted to take her children away from the madness.

"You can leave right away, Saman, but you can't take the children away just like that, "the man at the Canadian High Commission informed her. "You would need your husband's consent. I would suggest you leave without the kids and file a complaint against Mr. Wali Khan, stating he was keeping you hostage against your will. Canadian law will help you get your children safely out of the country."

Saman was desperate to get her daughter to Islamabad, but was told she had the mumps. There was no time to waste. Leaving her sleeping husband in their hotel suite, Saman pulled the already-packed small case out of the other room. The taxi took her to the hospital where she looked at her son for the last time before leaving for the airport.

CHAPTER 3

Saman rushed to make it to the bus stop. Balancing her purse, a knapsack, and a bag full of groceries was not easy. She should have let her sister help her move stuff to the tiny rented upstairs room in the rundown house. She did not have too many possessions to move and this was going to be the last trip she made. The wind was making it difficult to fish out her keys from her purse and make her way in. Even though the outside of the house was neglected, the landlord, an old Chinese widow, kept the indoors spotlessly clean. Mrs. Chung was out at the moment. Saman eventually located her keys and quickly opened the door, and became enveloped by a fresh pine smell. Mrs. Chung must have recently mopped the floor. The smell brought Saman back to the home she had left behind. The scent reminded her of a sunny day when Khodadad took her and Safina for a picnic. He drove the jeep himself, with Saman sitting next to him in the front and Safina and Viola in the back. Another jeep followed with armed guards and food. The jeep stopped in a beautiful clearing of pine trees. Freshly cut logs had been stacked in piles of varying heights all around the clearing, and a strong smell of resin and pine wood filled the air. The jeep with the guards parked itself behind a clump of trees, giving the family privacy. "I wanted you to see this place," Khodadad said, looking at the trees. "My father made my brothers come to his lumber yard and chop wood. He believed a man should be able to handle an axe just as skilfully as a gun. I was too small to split wood, but I always came along to watch my brothers work side by side with the wood cutters."

"Where are the wood cutters today?"asked Saman.

"I gave them the day off so that I could bring you here," replied her husband. It had been a perfect day. Safina and Viola sat on the logs and practiced on the guitar, while Saman dozed off on the carpet laid out on the pine needles. Gunshots in the distance woke Saman with a start. Her husband was nowhere to be seen and Safina and Viola, both holding large pinecones, were rushing towards her. One of the guards came running towards them and keeping his eyes to the ground, told Safina in Darri that they had to leave. "But where's my Baba?" Safina asked the men, keeping in check a surge of emotions that was rushing to her head.

Saman had gotten up and covered her jeans and hoodie with a long chadar. The women were being rushed into the guards' jeep.

"I'm not leaving without my Baba! Where is he? I won't go!"Safina told the guard fiercely. Viola pulled the frenzied girl into the vehicle while Saman, in a daze, was unable to speak. The jeep drove through the wooded area, away from the route they had taken earlier. The ride was uneven and bumpy.

She tried hard to push back the flood of memories. She was not going to let her emotions consume her.

"You will have to be very practical now," her lawyer's voice of reason echoed in her ears. "If you want to see your children, you will have to be realistic and try to build a life for yourself. After the divorce is final, there will be no going back."

As she made her way up the wooden staircase, the steps dented in the middle from years of use, Saman entered her room and put down her load on the bed. She had come earlier and organized most of her belongings. The room was tiny but crisp. A white bedspread with a pattern of tiny blue herons embroidered in the middle adorned the twin bed. There was a desk facing the single window, which overlooked a red maple tree. A chair and a screen with the picture of a Chinese girl painted in fading hues of blues and lilacs stood near an empty wall. Opening the closet door, Saman looked at her meagre wardrobe. She had already spent a lot of the money she had brought on lawyer's fees and the rent deposit. Buying more clothes was out of the question.

When she heard Mrs. Cheung entering the house, Saman made her way downstairs. The old lady was carrying grocery bags and was grateful when Saman took them from her.

"I brought lots of food before you came," Mrs. Cheung beamed, holding up a can of peaches. Saman almost told her about how sweet and luscious the peaches were where she had lived for the past eleven years. Or how juicy the apricots and plums were, and how fragrant each flower and fruit had been. She pushed back a memory of Khodadad holding a bowl of dark red cherries close to her just when she was opening her eyes to a beautiful spring morning in Islamabad. "These just arrived from the village. Once you eat these, you will forget the ones you had all your life," he said, as he held one from the stem and deposited it in her mouth. The explosion of juice and flavour woke Saman with a start. Sitting up in bed, she emptied the bowl in no time, while her husband lovingly watched his young wife.

The whistle of the kettle brought Saman back to the present. Mrs. Cheung was saying something, and Saman looked away before the woman could see the ache in her eyes.

Just when she thought life was taking shape, a call from her lawyer disrupted her peace. "I had to call you on short notice because your soon to be ex-husband is being very generous," the lawyer informed Saman. "You understand that Canadian law does not apply in Pakistan and according to their norms, he gets to keep the children. Get the divorce finalized, and we will figure out getting your kids later." Saman was dazed to see the amount on the draft Khodadad had sent. There was no letter, no form of communication, no questions asked—just a fat deposit for her bank account. She had hurt him. She understood that. But what about the constant hurt and fear she had been living in? Fear for all their lives, and fear that she might lose her family to tribal rivalries? She did not want to become another Mumtaz Bibi. The reality smacked her when she realized that she had lost her family, and there was no going back. She knew Khodadad would never forgive her. He would never let her have the kids either.

Finally, life slowly began to take shape. Saman, or Samantha as she liked to call herself once more, was taking baby steps. Now that she was settled in a place of her own, she had to find a job to initiate the process of bringing her children to Canada; she wasn't going to give up. But everywhere she applied, it seemed she was not qualified to work in an office. Her degree in social sciences had been abandoned halfway when she decided to marry Khodadad on her vacation in her freshman year. Now, at thirty-two years of age, she did not want to pursue what she had left so abruptly.

Walking out of the dentist's office after her fourth job interview, Samantha was met with a torrent of driving rain. That morning, Mrs. Cheung had advised her to take an umbrella with her, but Samantha had utterly forgotten with all that was occupying her mind lately. Now, water squelched in her nice heeled pumps. With shoes in hand, Samantha entered a tiny bookshop thoroughly soaked. It was a used book store, and the first thing that caught Samantha's eye was a set of old leather bounds sitting on the counter. A short, bald man was bent writing something in a ledger and did not bother looking up when she entered. Samantha dropped her shoes to the floor, moved closer to the counter, and picked up the first book from a set of five. Looking up, the clerk, or perhaps the owner of the store—judging by his suit—gave her a questioning look. "These have already been sold, I'm sorry," he said in a soft voice.

"Oh, I was only looking. They look very old and I have read translations by this poet before," Samantha replied in her soft voice. Drying her hands on her trousers, Samantha picked up one of the books. It was a translation of selected verses from Iqbal's poetry, most of which she had memorized by heart. Khodadad used to recite the poet's work to her whenever he was in the mood for it, and would then explain to her the deeper meaning behind the words.

Viola looked at the cake through the glass insert of the oven. Khodadad had state-of-the-art kitchen appliances flown in from Italy when Mumtaz Bibi suggested Safina learn some cooking. So far, it was only Viola and the ancient cook who used the equipment. Safina seemed least interested. It was Adam's sixth birthday and Viola was busy with all the preparations. Safina walked in through the kitchen's back door, her windblown brown hair indicative of her increasing forays into the woods behind the house. Since her mother's departure, the young girl spent more and more time in the outdoors, tending to her mother's exotic flowers and reading under the giant walnut trees. Despite the fresh air and sunshine, Safina's eyes lacked sparkle and Mumtaz Bibi could see the sorrow in them. Khodadad mostly kept to himself in the library or was either out hunting or holding durbar with his tribals. Safina reminded him too much of Saman, and he was quickly growing distant from his first born. Mumtaz Bibi felt helpless in the face of the growing distance between them. She reminded Khodadad time and again to spend time with Safina, which he dismissed with an injured look. "Safina needs you more than ever, Khodadad. She misses her mother and you cannot overlook her presence. Start reading with her again. She is getting so quiet and hardly talks to anyone. Either that or just send her to boarding school to Murree. I can't sit here and watch the girl wither away," Mumtaz Bibi said on a rare occasion when she was able to get Khodadad alone in the breakfast room. Rather than respond, Khodadad took his coffee and walked out the French window and onto the veranda overlooking Saman's rose garden. The gardener was tending to the plants and looked up when he saw the chief. His backhand salute and toothy grin was met with a nod. Saman would have waved and said hello, asking about his family. Everyone missed the mistress of the house. She was friendly and concerned about everyone. The gardener was reminded again of her when he looked at his hands clad in the thick, protective farming gloves she had given him from one of her shopping trips to the city.

"*Cherie*, the cake is almost done. Would you like to decorate it?" Viola asked Safina hopefully.

"Umm, I think I will go and tell the gardeners about the lights outside," Safina quickly responded, and before the governess could protest, she hurried out back from where she had entered.

Viola sighed and pulled the cake out of the oven and set it on the cooling rack. These days, it was getting impossible to get a hold of her ward. She had approached Khodadad several times regarding the girl's disinterest in her lessons and asked if perhaps her time as tutor was done in Pakistan and she should return to her village in Provence. Lately, all she had been doing was keeping Mumtaz Bibi company and reminiscing about Saman. Adam, like before, spent most of his time with his father, and was getting hopelessly unruly. Khodadad would not hear of it. "Give the children some time. They are probably going through growing pains. Tell Bibi to talk to Safina and I will have some more books sent in from the

British Council," Khodadad responded. Viola couldn't understand why he wouldn't acknowledge that the girl missed her mother. He seemed to have blocked the whole episode of Saman taking off so suddenly completely from his mind. It was almost as if she had disappeared into thin air! The children never cried openly about it, although she knew Safina wept in bed at night. However, no one ever talked about how life had changed in the two years since she had left. Only Mumtaz Bibi seemed to care and bring up Saman with Viola, but again, never in front of the children or Khodadad.

Viola felt a pang when she remembered how special birthdays had been for Saman. The preparations started days in advance, where Viola used to take out her calligraphy pens and personally write the invites to be sent. Depending on whose birthday was being celebrated, the menu and guest list were carefully drawn up. Since it was Adam's sixth birthday, his friends from the surrounding villages and their parents were duly invited. He had declared earlier that he wanted a vanilla cake with a candied horse on top. Nothing from Islamabad had to be ordered because the things he liked were all available in the village. His tastes were fastidiously local— hunter's beef, stuffed game, oven baked chicken, and egg sandwiches. Mumtaz Bibi had added pudding and cherry punch, knowing full well that the guests would expect a more interesting carte du jour.

Mumtaz Bibi was bustling with joy at the prospect of seeing her son after almost a year. Zaheer's room had been prepared next to his mother's and a new shalwar kameez suit had been laid out on the bed. His course in Islamabad had come to an end and he was coming to discuss his future options with his uncle. Mumtaz hoped he would stay for a long time, although she knew it was not safe for him to be around. Her husband's murderers were still not comfortable with Zaheer's presence. Khodadad had been able to pacify them and had accomplished some sort of truce with the rival tribe. Zaheer was Mumtaz's only living child and she feared intensely for his life.

Safina was being chided by Viola for taking so long, and was being rushed into her room to get changed before the arrival of the guests when Zaheer walked into the foyer. There was an awkward silence while the two cousins met after such a long time. Safina briefly looked into his electric blue eyes and lowered her gaze, while Zaheer was struck by her sharp resemblance to her mother, the woman who always engulfed him in her perfumed embrace and lavished him with gifts whenever she visited him at his hostel. Before he could say anything, Mumtaz Bibi rushed into the room, shrieking with joy and with tears of happiness streaming down her face. Zaheer scooped his mother in his arms and held onto her.

Safina went off with Viola to get dressed. She rejected the pink shalwar suit picked out for her and pulled out a pair of jeans and a yellow sweater from her closet instead.

"*Cherie*, wear the shalwar suit tonight. You know your father's friends will be coming and they don't like girls in western clothes," Viola suggested.

"I know Dad doesn't mind, and I don't care. And please, Viola, I don't want you to wear the sari either. You always end up tripping on the grass. Just wear your silk pants. If someone doesn't like it, that's their problem." It was true that Khodadad never objected to what the women in the house wore; as long as they were modestly dressed while out of the house, he did not mind. The only person who had any issue with Safina's clothing was her brother. For a mere six-year-old, Adam had his own ideas about how women were to conduct themselves. In his father's absence, he had recently started to act like the man of the house. If Safina wanted to go to Islamabad, Adam insisted on accompanying her and Viola. And when there, he would limit her shopping forays, objecting on all western clothing she chose. Over time, Safina gave up on leaving the village and would just give a list to her father of the things she wanted whenever he was going out of the country. Adam dared not object to the jeans and blouses and magazines Khodadad brought back for his daughter. He would just look at his sister with disgust to let her know of his disapproval.

A few days after Adam's birthday, Khodadad told Mumtaz Bibi to set up a few rooms in the annexe. Fathe Khan, a local chief of a neighbouring village, who had long ago sworn allegiance to Khodadad, had died in a car accident and his second wife had sent a message to Khodadad that her late husband's grown sons—from his first marriage—would harm her son. Not wanting to start another tribal conflict, Khodadad offered Rabia and her son a safe place under his wing until the woman made arrangements to move to Islamabad to the house under her name. Rabia's son, Babar, had occasionally visited the Khodadad household with his father, and accompanied them on hunting trips. Even though he was closer to Safina in age, he was friends with her brother.

Rabia kept to herself in the annexe and was hardly ever seen outside, while Babar and Adam were seen together throughout most parts of the day. Babar joined Safina and Adam for their daily lessons with Viola and it was evident that the fatherless child had been raised very differently. For instance, his proficiency in English was limited and he preferred to speak in the local dialect. He never looked at Viola straight in the eye, and ignored Safina. Adam had finally found a companion who preferred tribal traditions to western culture. Babar's presence inside the house or in the garden gave Adam the chance to practice more manly activities. Now, instead of sitting down and reading, the boys could be seen climbing trees or chatting about guns with the house guards.

Both Mumtaz Bibi and Viola were somewhat relieved to have the boy around—finally there was someone with the same interests to keep Adam company. Zaheer's time in the village was coming to an end, which was evident from Mumtaz Bibi's listless demeanour. The woman wondered for her son's safety and was not sure when she would see him again. In the few weeks that he had been there, Zaheer had befriended Safina. They could both be seen sitting under the cherry tree playing chess or reading in companionable silence. Mumtaz Bibi would look at the pair sitting outside and couldn't help but nurture a hope that the two would get married one day. Safina was as close to Mumtaz's heart as her own son was, and she could see that they were developing closeness.

Mumtaz had been too busy packing for Zaheer's departure that evening to notice that Safina was nowhere to be seen since the morning. It wasn't until Viola interrupted Mumtaz, who was in the middle of cramming some books into a cardboard box, and asked her if she had seen the girl. "What do you mean she went out after breakfast? Doesn't she always do that? Maybe she fell asleep under the walnut trees." Mumtaz Bibi replied without looking up.

"I am worried because she did not show up for her lessons or come in for lunch, and I have searched the house twice already," the French woman responded in a firmer tone.

Mumtaz let M. M. Kaye's *The Far Pavilions* drop into the box and grabbing her dupatta from the bed, rushed past Viola and into the foyer.

"Adam, Adam! Where is your sister? Babar, where is Safina?" she asked the boys who were glued to the T.V screen, while in the middle of a Mario Brothers game on their Nintendo. When she could not elicit any response, Mumtaz marched up to the T.V. and pulled out the switch from the electrical outlet, causing the game to come to a premature end. Seeing her glaring at them, the boys knew Mumtaz meant business, and any sort of disregard would mean either a thrashing or worse, telling Khodadad about it. "Where is Safina?" the woman asked in a roaring voice.

The boys looked at each other and shrugged their shoulders. "I saw her walking in the woods this morning after breakfast," Babar replied helpfully. "I haven't seen her since."

If Safina had walked too far off into the woods, God knows what could have happened. Not only were there wild foxes and coyotes abounding, but poachers and some unruly fugitives who hid amongst the thick foliage as well. Khodadad walked in with Zaheer just when Mumtaz was marching towards the kitchen, with Viola in tow. "Bibi, what's going on? Where is Safina?" Khodadad asked the women, the blue of his eyes turning a dark shade.

"*Marra*, we don't know where Safina is," Mumtaz said, wringing the corner of her dupatta between her hands and breathing heavily, "no one has seen her since breakfast."

Without asking any more questions, Khodadad slung the bandolier back onto his shoulder and asked Zaheer to get him a pistol from the study cabinet. Within minutes, the Range Rover and two more jeeps with guards took off into the woods. It was getting close to dusk and would be dreadfully dark soon. The men had to leave without delay.

The typically frolicsome Labrador Retrievers in the back of Khodadad's Range Rover were still, sensing a quest at hand. Hustling the jeep through the open iron gates and onto the unpaved dirt track, Khodadad drove with a ferocity that did not match his usual calm composure. Zaheer's throat felt dry when he recalled Safina's crestfallen face after he told her he would be leaving the next morning. Upon Khodadad's counsel, Zaheer had enrolled in a preparatory course to sit for the Foreign Service entry exams. His classes were to commence in two weeks' time. But the fact was, he wanted to stay here, amongst his family, and near Safina. The jeep was tearing through the brush on either side of the track and Zaheer bumped his head twice when the all-wheel drive went over deep ruts. The dogs were let out the moment the jeep stopped, while the other two vehicles circled the woods in opposite directions. It was not long before the dogs seemed to catch a scent and eagerly took off in the direction of the river. Zaheer and Dilnawaz, who was Khodadad's most trusted guards, went after the Labradors whereas Khodadad followed at a slower pace, looking for tracks. Safina's book lay open near the river bank and the dogs excitedly sniffed at their discovery, simultaneously letting out yelps of triumph and recognition. Moving further, Zaheer could see from the tracks on the road that the girl had moved closer to the gushing river. "She's here!" Dilnawaz shouted over the roar of the water. Both men and the dogs running ahead of them, reached the lip of the river. Safina lay comatose face down over a branch, with one leg stuck between a fallen tree and a boulder and the other dangling precariously over the water, almost touching it.

The village doctor was already waiting when Khodadad carried his daughter into the house. At the sight of the two entering the house, Mumtaz Bibi let out a series of shrieks and started beating her chest with clenched fists. Their faces white with fear, the boys stood huddled in a corner of the room, looking guilty. The ancient cook hovered in the background, wringing his hands and clicking his tongue inside a toothless mouth. Viola was the only one who was composed. With surprising alacrity, she had prepared the guest room in advance. Safina was laid on the bed and Viola swiftly changed her into dry clothes. The doctor, a local who had studied medicine in Peshawar, took her temperature and checked for any broken bones. Safina was in a concussion and aside from an ugly gash on her forehead, she had a sprained ankle. "She will be awake soon. I have given her painkillers. Miss Viola (which he pronounced as Wee-o-la), please continue icing her foot," the middle-aged doctor advised, while putting away his instruments after stitching up the cut.

The days that followed were bliss for Safina. Her father came each day after his breakfast and sat in the guest room where she was convalescing. Both father and daughter read like they had in the past. Even Adam was being nice for a change and brought her all sorts of bugs from the garden trapped inside empty jam jars, and made cards with Babar, which were lined up over the fireplace. But to Safina's greatest delight, Zaheer spent most of his time with her. They played endless games of chess and draughts, chatted, or read books. Zaheer insisted on feeding her with a spoon and stopped awkwardly one day, when Viola remarked—with a raised eyebrow—that Safina had hurt her foot, not her hand, and was therefore quite capable of feeding herself.

The first time Safina brought up her mother was with Zaheer. She sensed understanding and compassion in his blue eyes. They had both been very quiet the whole afternoon because Zaheer was finally leaving the following morning. "I miss her perfume the most," Safina said, suddenly breaking the silence. "She always smelled so good. I have some of her sweaters, which I keep in my closet. They still smell of her." If Zaheer was surprised with this bit of confession, he did not show it. "My mother always wore Madame Rochas. Baba used to bring the perfume and matching cream each time he visited London."

Zaheer moved his chair closer to the bed on which Safina lay with her leg propped up on a cushion. "I think of her often, Safina. She was always full of excitement and cared for everyone. It's okay for you to miss her, and I'm happy you're talking about her." Zaheer said in a calm voice. When Safina looked up at him, her hazel eyes were brimming with tears. Slowly, the tears came cursing down and Zaheer sat on the bed holding both her hands in his. No words of consolation were needed to convey Zaheer's sympathies to Safina. She found balmy comfort in the warm hands and the heady citrus cologne he wore.

With a promise to write, Zaheer said his goodbyes to her and left early the next morning.

In the weeks that followed Zaheer's departure, Safina tried hard not to think about him. After her mother, Zaheer was the only other person who could see inside her soul. She felt if she allowed herself to think about him, he too would leave one day. For now, she felt it was better to remember how his hands felt on her skin, rather than think of how her days had been filled with their conversations, or how Zaheer knew exactly what to say to cheer her up. Safina had gotten used to the concern in his eyes and his subtle gestures to make her feel more restful. If she started missing his presence, like she did her mother's, she would not be able to endure the feeling of loss and abandonment for a second time. She had tried to find peace and solitude by the river, hoping the crash of the gushing water would drown the sound of the storm that was brewing in her heart. In trying to get away from everyone, she had ended up losing her balance and almost fallen into the river.

As soon as Safina could walk, Khodadad planned a trip to Islamabad with the family. Mumtaz Bibi did not want to join them as she wanted to visit her sister in another village, but Viola was to accompany them. It had been a while since the Frenchwoman had spent time with any of her friends from the French Consulate, and she looked forward to a change of surroundings. They were not going to stay at the house they owned in Islamabad, but rather, Khodadad had booked rooms at The Serena Hotel. The boys had a room to themselves, as did Viola and Safina, while Khodadad had a room on his own. For the ladies, being in the multi-ethnic city meant endless trips to the malls and book stores. Adam and Babar preferred to spend their days swimming in the hotel pool and ordering infinite servings of ice-cream. Viola visited several of her French friends and Safina always accompanied her. The light skinned women in heels fascinated her and reminded her of Saman. These excursions to visit Viola's acquaintances brought back recollections of when, as a girl, Safina would accompany her mother to drawing rooms with floral patterned upholstery and coffee served on dainty tea trolleys. After a while, one of the ladies would clap her hands to silence the animated group and take up playing dance music on the stereo. Furniture would be quickly cleared to make room and Saman would be the first to take the floor. On such occasions, Safina would be captivated by her mother's slim body swiftly moving across the room. The laughter, music, and the exotic strawberry and vanilla pastries, as well as the flush on her mother's face were all so mesmerizing.

On the fourth day of their trip, Khodadad remarked that Zaheer would be joining them for lunch that day. Safina tried not to look interested at the news but she could not stop the sudden spread of colour to her cheeks. If Khodadad noticed it, he made no mention of it. Viola helped Safina pick a beautiful peach and cream blouse to go with her white trousers and suggested she apply a bit of mascara and lip-gloss. "I've never used make up. What would Baba say?" Safina said, looking at Viola with flushed cheeks. She did not want her governess to know how she felt about Zaheer. Viola just clucked her tongue and replied mischievously that mascara was not make up, but rather, part of a young girl's outfit. She also put her hair up in a messy knot with a few wisps of hair escaping from the sides.

Dressed in jeans and a sport shirt, Zaheer was already sitting with Khodadad when Safina came down to the hotel's lobby. For a fourteen-year-old, Safina had the poise and charm of a young lady. A few feet away, Viola watched the girl with affection and unmasked admiration. Safina was quickly blossoming into an exceptional beauty and she had her mother's elegance, as well as her father's pride. Her dark brown hair with copper undertones was swept up from her smooth temple to form a widow's peak. The cut from her accident in the woods had healed, leaving a pink blemish disappearing into her hairline. Like her mother, she had deep hazel eyes with thick lashes tipped with gold. Her arched eyebrows, which naturally winged out on the outer edges, gave her an ethereal, waiflike beauty. Despite the fluttering in her heart, Safina walked towards the men with unhurried steps and graciously asked about Zaheer's wellbeing. Zaheer's throat felt suddenly dry and he answered her in abrupt responses. Their hands briefly touched when Safina handed him the package Mumtaz Bibi had sent for her son, and Khodadad did not miss Zaheer's quick reaction when he pulled his hand away, almost as if he had been stung. The assembly walked towards the dining area and were ushered to a table. Leaving her place of vantage, Viola made her way to the table. She had wanted to give the family time to reunite and especially to Safina. Viola felt pleased to note Safina felt close to her cousin. After shaking hands with Zaheer, Viola sat down, smoothing her dress. An awkward silence was taking over the group. Without looking at anyone specifically, Viola observed everyone at the table. Khodadad had one arm slung over the back of the leather seat and the other rested on the table, his hand drawing patterns on the table-cloth with a fork. Zaheer and Safina were concentrating on the menus, with Zaheer stealing glances of Safina sitting across from him. The uncomfortable calm was thankfully disrupted when Adam and Babar waltzed into the dining hall, their hair slick with freshly showered dampness. "Sorry we're late, Baba. It was the final for the water polo today and we won 6 to 4." Adam enlightened everyone. "What's for lunch?" Khodadad signalled for the waiter to come and take everyone's order.

"Why do we have to leave so soon?" Safina asked Viola for the second time. Viola was tight lipped and pale, and was already packing their things. The lunch had ended with Khodadad announcing they would be leaving the next day. Only Adam and Babar were happy to hear this announcement. They were getting bored of swimming all day and longed to go back to their hunting trips and tree climbing and looking for frogs in the woods. Besides, Babar's mother had called twice, feeling nervous about her son accidentally encountering anyone from his father's side of the family, and had asked Viola on numerous occasions when they would return.

Viola was enraged at the words Khodadad had spoken to her in the elevator as they both made their way to their floor. "I entrusted my daughter to you to keep an eye on her, not to encourage her to display herself like this. What is the meaning of allowing her put so much paint on her face? She looked like a grown woman today, not a twelve-year-old," he spoke in a voice that was gradually rising. This was the first time Khodadad had lost his cool with Viola, and she was taken aback.

"First of all, your daughter is not twelve, but fourteen. And secondly, she was not displaying herself. All normal girls her age make an effort to look pretty and appealing. Safina's life right now is anything but normal. The girl has no company except Bibi and I, and you are hardly ever home, leaving behind a nine-year-old boy to boss her around. To make matters worse, her mother took off when she most..." Viola left the sentence unfinished, realizing she had said too much. The thunderous look in Khodadad's eyes left no doubt in Viola's mind that she had crossed a precarious line. She also knew that Khodadad's blinding rage was such that he would never understand what she was trying to convey to him. He was unable to see how much his daughter was suffering inside. The girl was given all the liberties of the West within the four walls of her house, but when it came to making friends or socializing, her father expected her to follow traditional norms. Unlike the local tribesmen, Khodadad was clear about how he wanted his children to be raised. They could take up any sport or learn any instrument or for that matter, dress in western clothing. But, when it came to building relationships or interacting with the outside world, Khodadad had separate standards for Safina and Adam. Adam invariably accompanied his father on his rounds to his lands—the boy was always with him on most social visits and hunting trips. He was fast learning the importance of tribal loyalty and etiquette. For instance, as a tribal chief's son, he understood the significance of honour, allegiance and alliance. No matter how many years he had spent abroad, the tribal values were essential for Khodadad. However, where Khodadad accepted most western ways of life, his son was turning out to be a die-hard tribal.

CHAPTER 4

Samantha got off the bus and turned at the intersection to get to the bookstore. She had been entrusted with the keys to the store and made sure she arrived at least half an hour before it was time to open. Going to the back of the store, she took off her coat and put away her purse in the tiny office. Chance had brought her in Walter Pridmore's path a year ago and she felt lucky to have found work when she did. At least, she did not have to worry about her expenses anymore. Walter was astonished to hear her quote from the Persian book that wet afternoon when, shoes in hand, she had stumbled into his shop. Before long, Samantha was offered a job there and tonight, Walter had invited her for dinner. Unlike their previous engagements, which took place at various coffee shops, they were dining at his house and despite Samantha's protests, Walter insisted on cooking for her.

The evening progressed pleasantly enough. Walter was eager to show Samantha his rare book collection, which was housed in his study and contained several more titles in Persian. Dinner consisted of roast duck, mashed sweet potato, a steaming loaf of artisan bread fresh out of the oven, and baklava. For drinks, Walter had a chilled bottle of crisp Sauvignon Blanc. Samantha twirled the glass stem between her thumb and index finger. The glow from the candles on the table glinted in the clear liquid. "You are not in an uncivilised village in Pakistan anymore. Please try to enjoy the evening and don't let the past spoil what's ahead of you," Walter said softly. Samantha had given up drinking alcohol when she married Khodadad as it was prohibited for Muslims. Now, as she found herself mentally trying to accept that her previous life was over, she knew it was not going to be easy picking up where she had left off fifteen years ago. Travelling alone on the bus at night after closing the shop, or lugging groceries in her arms to Mrs. Cheung's house, Samantha would wonder if she really had lived the fairy-tale life of comfort and indulgence. "Uncivilised village" Walter had said. Samantha's lips twisted in a grimace. How misrepresented the under-developed world was in the West and how little Walter understood her. If anything, she had experienced the most incredible life in the village. Of course, a lot of it had to do with the fact that her husband had the money to indulge her with. Had she been married to an ordinary man, life would have been very different. But Khodadad was no ordinary person. He was the most refined, big-hearted and tender man she had ever known, and it sounded almost comical to her when well meaning, sympathetic people automatically assumed she had been oppressed in her life in Pakistan and was lucky to have escaped a patriarchal prison.

All aspects of Samantha getting her children back looked bleak. Since both her children were above seven years of age, according to Pakistani law, they could choose to stay with their father. Canadian law was useless because the children did not have Canadian citizenship and were Pakistani citizens by birth. The only option which Samantha had was going back and begging Khodadad's forgiveness. The desire to be reunited with her children was so strong that she was even willing to do that. She would appeal to Mumtaz Bibi's motherly instinct; she would fall at Khodadad's feet—anything. What she could not do, and what everyone suggested, was to forget her children. Everyone said her children belonged to the tribal land and would never want to leave their roots. They would be misfits in Western society, and it was a good thing they were with their father. It was time, they advised, that Samantha put the life she had lived behind her and move on; to forget it like a horrible dream.

On the other end of the world, Safina lay in bed looking at the stars through the window. As a child, Khodadad had taught the family how to navigate the territory using the stars as their guide. On many warm summer nights, they had sat on the wooden bench in Samantha's rose garden and looked up at the sky, tracing patterns with their fingers and learning the names of the stars. Safina would cuddle next to her mother, while Adam would be perched up on Khodadad's shoulders. Despite his four years, Adam surprised everyone with his knowledge of the sky—knowledge which came in very useful during his hunting trips with his father.

"I will be back in 20! Have to make a quick stop down the block," Samantha shouted over the sound of the radio playing soft music. Walter looked up from his desk and before he could suggest they take a bit longer than twenty minutes and have lunch together somewhere, Samantha was out the door.

Weaving her way through the crowded street, thronged with winter-weary people outside on a rare sunny day in April, she headed towards the post office. Samantha had been coming to the post office every single day, hoping Khodadad had written back to the numerous letters she had mailed him over the past six months. Each day, she came with expectancy and left empty-handed and defeated. Today, the lady at the counter was waiting for her and looked up when she entered the building, giving Samantha a wide smile. Before she could ask if there was anything for her, the post woman reached under the counter and held up a thick manila envelope for Samantha. "I will need you to sign right here to receive this as it arrived by registered mail," she said, pointing to a form, and handed Samantha a biro attached to the counter with a synthetic spiral. With an unsteady hand, she signed on the dotted line and almost snatched the packet from the smiling woman. Samantha rushed out the glass door and into the sunshine and sitting down on a stainless-steel bench in a bus shelter, she broke the seal of the thick brown envelope. The letters which she had written, all twenty-one of them, spilled onto her lap. None of them had been opened. Crestfallen and too choked up to cry, Samantha dragged her feet back to the shop. Walter saw something was terribly wrong the moment she entered. Flipping the window sign to display "Closed for Lunch", he promptly followed Samantha to the back of the shop. "Samantha, will you please tell me what the matter is?" He asked anxiously, his eyes making large saucers behind his thick spectacles. The envelope dropped from Samantha's hand, and picking it up, Walter noticed the sender's address: Jamal, Mehmood and Murtaza, Solicitors was printed in the top left corner of the envelope, addressed to Samantha White, P.O. Box 44563, Toronto, Canada.

Samantha had let herself drop on the sofa in the tiny office, her face in her hands, and was sobbing uncontrollably. Unsure what to do, Walter left the office to get Samantha a drink of water. Upon returning, he found her wiping her face with a bunch of tissues. "Thank you," she said gratefully, taking the cold glass from Walter. "I'm so sorry for all this, I think I needed a good cry."

"You don't need to apologise, Samantha," Walter said, sitting down next to her and reaching for her hand. Perhaps it was the need for physical touch or maybe it was the kindness in Walter's voice that made Samantha reach out to him and put her arms around his neck. Emotions which Walter had chosen to keep dormant since the death of his wife, and which he felt tug at him since the day Samantha quoted Persian that wet afternoon, surfaced with a surge of passion. In a feverish rush of sensations, the pair sought each other's lips and gave into their pent-up feelings.

Samantha refused Walter's offer of a ride back home. She wasn't even sure if she wanted to see him again. Letting her guard down had been a mistake, she reflected, and made her realize that even if he ever did let her back into his life, she would never be able to look into Khodadad's eyes again without remembering what took place that afternoon. She could still feel Walter's breath on her neck and the aftermath of his hurried lovemaking clung to her like the reek of cooking pungent spices in hot oil. In just over three years, life had distorted itself into a repulsive picture, and Samantha knew there was no going back. She would have to give up her job at the bookstore and distance herself from Walter. She could not let herself go without remorse and wanted to hold onto Khodadad's memory.

Mrs. Cheung answered the door and was surprised to see Walter standing there, clutching a large bouquet of peach roses. Samantha had not gone to work since almost two weeks and had refused to receive calls from Walter. Now, the old lady wondered why he was here.

"Mrs. Cheung, please, I must see Samantha. You have to let her know I'm here." Considering his words for about a minute, Mrs. Cheung shrugged her shoulders and moved aside to let him in. Upstairs, Samantha could hear the exchange and came down before the land lady called for her. The strained silence between the two was enough for Mrs. Cheung to understand that they needed privacy to sort whatever needed to be sorted. Samantha asked Walter to seat himself at the kitchen table, while Mrs. Cheung went into the laundry room, with an excuse that the clothes were piling up. She made sure to leave the door slightly ajar, partly out of curiosity and partly for Samantha's safety.

Walter lost no time in coming to the point. "Samantha, I think both of us need each other. You can't hold onto a life you had and it's about time I let go of memories of Johanna. We both have ghosts from the past, and we need to purge ourselves of them." Samantha listened impassively. "What I'm trying to say is can we be friends again? I cannot think of not having you in my life anymore. And it was a mission to find peach roses at this time of year, so could you please just..." Walter's sentence was cut mid-air and Samantha covered his hand with hers. She had spent the past two weeks trying to figure out her life and could understand that living with ghosts was exactly what she was doing. The fact remained that she missed her children, and she hoped that one day they could reach out to her. However, it was not fair on Walter to take all responsibility for what happened between them that afternoon. She had wanted to be touched, to be held and comforted. It was unrealistic to expect she would one day go back to her old life with Khodadad and things would be as they were. The only way from here was to let go of the past and move ahead with whatever life had in store for her.

Zaheer rarely visited the village anymore. Firstly, he had gotten busy with work and secondly, Khodadad had given a tacit signal that he was to stay away from his daughter. The rare occasions on which he visited were family events, such as weddings and funerals, or when his mother asked for him to see her. Zaheer had cleared his Foreign Service entry test and was now working as a junior member of staff for two years. "It has been quite some time since you visited last," the driver, who had been with Khodadad for ages, remarked casually, while collecting Zaheer from the bus stop. Now, sitting in the passenger seat of the jostling jeep, Zaheer could only think about what he was going to say to Safina. Almost three weeks ago, he had received a letter forwarded by the Canadian Consulate from Saman Aunty. The first thought he had after getting the letter was to mail it to Khodadad. However, after long deliberation, he decided to talk to Safina about it first. Saman—or Samantha, as she had signed her letter—missed her children and despite writing to Khodadad many times, had elicited no response from him. Saman wanted to get in touch with her children and wanted Zaheer's help. Since Adam's departure to boarding school in England, and shortly after Viola's return to France, the only companions Safina had were Mumtaz Bibi and Babar. Rabia had remarried and was living in Lahore, while Babar continued to stay under Khodadad's protection. The past five years had seen a lot of changes. Khodadad was now the undisputed leader of the area and its surroundings, and his influence extended far beyond the hills and forests. As such, matters related to the land and its development were his responsibility. People came to him for advice, to settle disputes, and to reinforce allegiance. Khodadad's word was law. Safina, now a seventeen-year-old girl, rarely left the village and spent her days with the aging Mumtaz. Babar, also seventeen, and who now occupied the annexe which formerly housed his mother, was a kind of aide to Khodadad and took care of petty matters related to the house and outside. His lack of interest in further schooling had forced his mother to leave him there, so that he could keep himself busy, as well as stay under the shelter of the tribal leader's guardianship.

Mumtaz Bibi was sitting under the cherry tree waiting for Zaheer. Holding her son in a tight hug, she remarked that he had lost weight. Zaheer was somewhat relieved to hear that Khodadad was away until the weekend, and after dinner with his mother and Safina, he asked Safina to join him outside for a walk. There was no awkwardness between the pair despite the long break between their reunion. It felt comfortingly natural for them to be in each other's presence. It was chilly in the late October evening, so Safina put on a pair of Ugs and wrapped a cashmere shawl around her shoulders. Lately, she had been troubled because she had overheard her father and Mumtaz Bibi discussing two very suitable boys whose families had approached him for her hand in marriage. In the discussion that ensued, Mumtaz expressed her wish for a marriage between her son and Safina, but her father had refused. However, on what grounds, she could not tell. She hoped that perhaps she could talk about this gloomy subject with Zaheer, and solicit advice.

Safina had to sit down on a nearby garden seat when Zaheer told her about the letter. A surge of emotions passed through her body and despite warm clothing, a cold stole up from her feet, immobilizing her. Zaheer was saying something which Safina could not comprehend. She was trying to process the fact that her mother had tried reaching out to her, that she missed her children and had not forgotten them. When Samantha had left so suddenly, both Safina and Adam had expected their mother to eventually return. After a year, Adam, who never let on that he missed his mother's presence, let go of the hope of seeing her again and channelled all his time and energy towards his father, striving to please him. Gradually, the love for his mother was replaced with a fervent revulsion for anything that reminded him of her. On the other hand, Safina refused to believe that their mother would abandon them. She held onto anything that was dear to her mother and lived with a hope that she would return as unexpectedly as she had left. In silence, Safina tended to her mother's roses, strived to excel in her lessons, and kept up with learning French and music so that when she came back, Samantha would find everything just the way she had left it. When weeks turned into months, and months into years, with no sign of return or any form of communication from Samantha, even Safina had to concede and relinquish the dream of ever seeing her, and a feeling of cold rejection wrapped itself around the young girl's heart. Now, listening to Zaheer, the frost was slowly beginning to melt. The image of her mother, which she kept locked in the deepest recesses of her mind, came to life with lucidity and she knew what she had to do.

Zaheer and Safina's arcane meeting did not go unnoticed. While the two sat on the bench thinking they were alone, a pair of eyes was trained on them from a window in the upper storey of the annexe. Unobtrusively observing them, Babar was experiencing his own set of emotions; a rage was choking him and he had the urge to go down and physically hurt Zaheer. His growing obsession with Safina was such that he had feigned apathy for college, and had chosen to stay back in the village with Khodadad. The idea of moving away from her was unthinkable. Now, looking down at her so engrossed in conversation, Babar was finding it difficult to contain his loathing for the glossy city boy. He hated how the two of them could discuss music and art and conversed effortlessly in English. Whenever Safina addressed Babar, which was rare to begin with, she automatically switched to Darri, unwittingly rubbing in the fact that he struggled with English, which everyone in the house spoke with ease. *How could Safina talk to him? Where was Mumtaz Bibi and why had she let them be alone together?* thought Babar. He felt their togetherness was unacceptable. Safina was not a child anymore, and she belonged to him.

Zaheer and Safina decided to keep Samantha's letter secret from Khodadad and Mumtaz. Safina had made it very clear that she wanted to get in touch with her mother, and judging from the fact that her father had refused to respond to Samantha's letters, she would keep this desire undisclosed from everyone. Zaheer devised a plan for them to communicate. Safina would have to smuggle letters to Islamabad in the parcels of fruit, nuts, and clothing which Mumtaz regularly sent to Zaheer and their relatives. Zaheer in return, would send back books to Safina through the same driver coming back; books with coded messages in them. It sounded like a shaky plan, but it had to do.

"I heard Zaheer was here. Was he just visiting or did he have some work?" Khodadad asked Mumtaz over tea a day after his return. Ever since she had suggested a match between her son and Safina, Mumtaz noticed an edge to Khodadad's voice whenever she mentioned Zaheer. Khodadad had made it relatively clear that he did not want his daughter marrying into the family, and even though it was permissible, he did not believe in cousin marriages. When the time came, his daughter would marry into a strong family settled in Islamabad.

Mumtaz deliberated before answering her cousin. "Zaheer is my son, Khodadad, my only living child. If he's not welcome here, I can go live with my sister, so that he can come and go whenever he wants," Mumtaz replied with her chest heaving and on the verge of tears.

Looking at his older cousin, who was like a mother to him and his children, Khodadad moved forward in his seat and reached out to place his hand on hers. "Bibi that is not what I mean. I don't want the two to start having feelings for each other and then be unable to get married. I'm trying to save us all from heartbreak. If it makes you happy, tell Zaheer to visit often, but also keep in mind that he cannot think of Safina, except as a sister," he said by way of apology.

The carton that arrived from Islamabad with various kitchen supplies also had two hard cover books wrapped in plastic, which Kaka Manju, the cook, brought to Safina while she sat sketching in the breakfast room. The room had been a favourite of Samantha's because of the wide windows overlooking her prize rose garden and the bamboo gazebo covered in a flowering vine. This is where she answered her correspondence and gave instructions for the day to the house staff. Kaka Manju startled her when he placed the packet on the table. After waiting for the man to leave, Safina took the books to her room and unwrapped the plastic. There were two books, one was Natalie Zemon Davis's *Le Retour de Martin Guerre* and the other was an Anthology of American Poetry. Safina opened the book in French. It was a new book and like most foreign books sold in Islamabad, it was sealed in clear plastic to inhibit customers from thumbing through the titles without buying them. Safina knew Zaheer must have found a way to slip a letter in and reseal the wrap. True enough, there was a letter for Safina; however, it was not from Zaheer, but from her mother. Safina's hands trembled when she carefully let the letter opener slide through the corner of the envelope, cutting it open. The hand was not as neat as she remembered. *Perhaps she was also experiencing the same emotions as she was right now,* Safina wondered.

"*Mon Cherie,*" the letter read, "I know when you read this you will have many questions in mind. First, I want you to know there has not been a single day I have not thought about you or your brother since I left. I wish things were different and we were together, but life has a funny way of taking unexpected twists and turns. Circumstances forced me to leave so hastily when I did and I won't say that I don't regret that day. I have wanted to speak to you and Adam, to hold you and feel you close to my heart for such a long time. I hope one day you can forgive me for leaving you both behind. I also hope we can meet one day soon. You are and always will be my most precious darling and I love you with all my heart. Your loving mother."

Safina sat at the desk for a long time after reading and re-reading her mother's note. She was awash with conflicting emotions. The feeling of abandonment and rejection was being replaced with the assurance that she was not forgotten. At this moment, she did not care to reflect on the reasons why her mother left her, but focused on how she could reconnect with her beyond the piece of paper she held in her hands.

In the weeks that ensued, a periodic communication developed between mother and daughter. Safina was heartbroken for days to learn that her mother had remarried and was living in Toronto with her husband. Meanwhile, Samantha was happy to learn that her son was safe in school in England, away from the treacherous life he had with his father, and that Safina had completed her A Levels and had blossomed into an accomplished young woman. On Zaheer's next visit to the village, he informed Safina that the letter business was getting too risky. Before long, someone was bound to find out and he did not want to affront either his mother or Khodadad. Adam would be home soon for his summer break and it was likely he would want to visit Islamabad whenever the car came to pick up supplies, and it would be impossible to smuggle any more correspondence.

"I want to see my mother, Zaheer. Please, do something. I don't want to live here and end up getting married to a stranger. Please, help me!" Safina implored Zaheer the day he was about to leave. Zaheer looked intently at the big, brown eyes entreating him. Apart from that one instance when she was bedbound, Safina had never been very expressive about how she felt about her mother, so watching her speak like this was distressing for Zaheer. Babar walked in through the back door of the kitchen where the two were talking, while Safina packed some snacks for Zaheer's journey back to Islamabad. Looking at them engrossed in conversation, Babar could not contain his resentment. He rolled up his sleeves and folding his arms against his chest, leaned back against the kitchen counter. "Did you want something, Babar? Kaka Manju is with Bibi," Safina said to him in Darri, feeling irritated.

"I'm watching how the city boy is trying to impress you with his English. Wait until Adam comes back; he will not like the fact that the two of you are always alone and talking," he retorted back, looking at Zaheer with a snarl.

"I don't know about that, but I do know that Uncle Khodadad would not like it if he heard how you talk to his daughter," Zaheer answered in a calm, measured voice. At the mention of Khodadad's name, Babar wavered for a second before shifting with alarming speed to strike Zaheer with a closed fist. Zaheer was quick to dip and counter with his own fist closing in on his burly assailant's wrist, and twisting his arm, he held it locked behind him. Safina watched horror-struck at the fierce exchange between the two. Physically, Zaheer was no match to Babar and even though the latter was younger than Zaheer by more than eight years, his natural life of hunting and roaming the hills had carved his body into resilient toughness. However, where Zaheer was lighter in bulk, his years of martial arts training had made him quick and supple and as he held onto Babar's arm twisted behind him in a tight lock, it was evident that Babar was defeated. Letting go of his arm with a final jerk, Zaheer left the kitchen, leaving the two behind. Safina was too shocked to move or make a sound. No matter how harsh the environment outside, in contrast, life in the Khodadad house was always peaceful. With his ego squashed, Babar could not bring himself to look at Safina, so he left through the back door, rubbing his wrist.

The mention of Adam's name rang alarm bells in Safina's mind. No matter how many years he spent in England, he returned each year even more set in his conformist ways. He would spend all his time visiting his father's territory, with Babar sitting beside him in the jeep. During his time in Pakistan, he wore the traditional shalwar kameez and waistcoat, with Peshawari sandals, a turban on his head, and a gun belt slung smugly across his chest. He presented a sharp contrast to his sister who only wore jeans and blouses within the house. If Adam could have his way, he would have done away with all the furniture in the house and decorated it in the traditional style of carpeted floor seating, with low carved wooden tables. He would also have preferred his sister to be in loose clothing, with her head covered. At home, Adam made a point of speaking in Darri, and much to the annoyance of Mumtaz and Safina, he would respond to their questions in the local dialect. So steeped was the indigenous way of life in Adam that it seemed as if the boy had never lived anywhere but the village. The only person with whom he spoke in English was his father. Adam dared not challenge the way things were run in the house because that was how his father wanted his lifestyle to be. He would have meetings about mining and logging and the neighbouring tribes with his father, and throughout their discussion, they would stick to English. It amused Khodadad to watch his son embrace his own culture with so much ownership, but he was also impressed when Adam demonstrated a keen understanding of the dynamics of both the area and the world. When Khodadad was not home, Adam would have his meals with Babar in the annexe, sitting cross legged on the carpet and eating with his fingers.

Adam arrived home for his summer break ten days after the exchange between Babar and Zaheer. Khodadad, along with the boys, returned early one day from their hunting trip and Safina was roused from her nap by the barking dogs, happy to be let out of the jeeps. Hunts usually lasted about four days, and everyone was surprised to see the three vehicles pulling into the driveway. Khodadad and Adam seemed pleased about something, while Safina could clearly see that Babar, who had abruptly headed towards the annexe, had a long face.

"Where is Bibi?" were Khodadad's first words upon entering. Draping the dupatta over her head, Mumtaz came from her room and into the foyer, wondering what the commotion was that had disrupted her siesta. "*Asalamo alaikum* Bibi, please have Kaka send some tea for both of us into the library. I need to speak with you." Safina froze hearing these words. As a rule, her father always showered and changed after coming back from a hunt, but today, there was urgency in his voice and he had called Mumtaz into the library with him. Safina's first thought was that he had found out about her connection with her mother and was so enraged he wanted to let Mumtaz know about it before confronting her.

The moment the door to the library closed, Adam looked at Safina with a grin on his face. "Don't look so worried. You are getting married, so cheer up," he said to the startled girl.

"What do you mean" Safina whispered, her initial fear replaced with another.

The hunting party had to return early because their father's friend and his wife from Islamabad were coming today to see Safina for their son who had returned from the States after getting his degree in law. The family also belonged to the northern area and were tremendously well off. "So, now you will finally wear normal clothes like you're supposed to, and not go around in these tight jeans all the time," Adam added self-righteously. Safina walked unsteadily to her room and sat down on the bed to process all the information. She did not want to get married to anyone, she loved Zaheer. And right now, she wanted more than ever to be with her mother. How her father could just let some strangers come and see her like that and force her into a loveless marriage...were muddled thoughts turning in her head. The door opened and Mumtaz walked in and sat on the bed next to her. The older woman's face was flushed and Safina could see she had been crying. "Safina *jaan*, you must get ready and put on a nice shalwar suit. Uncle Jibraan is coming with his wife. They want to see you," she said, while smoothing Safina's hair.

"Bibi, I don't want to get married. Please, tell them not to come. I'm going to talk to Baba to stop them. How can he do this to me?" Safina asked with incredulity, her own eyes flooding with tears.

"My baby, you have to get married one day, and I think moving to a big city will be good for you. You can go to university, the library; you can go shopping, meet new people..." Mumtaz's voice trailed off as she tried to console the girl, despite not being convinced herself.

Jibraan ul Kareem and Fareeha arrived with their son and two daughters carrying gifts of clothes, fruit, and jewellery. Khodadad and Adam greeted them at the gate, and Mumtaz seated them in the formal drawing room. When Safina entered the room, she was pleased to note that both daughters were in western attire. *At least, he had not picked a traditional, strict family to wed her into,* she thought with some comfort. Khodadad looked with affection as his daughter walked in. He was proud of the way she carried herself. She walked in, with her head held high and candour in her eyes. The resemblance to her mother was striking, except that Safina was much taller and had her father's stride. Mumtaz also looked pleased and both Fareeha and she looked at each other with a smile. Adam, on the other hand, was not so happy with the way things were going. For starters, when his father had said the Kareem's were also from northern Pakistan, Adam had assumed they would be entrenched in native culture. He was taken aback to see the two sisters come out of the car dressed in casual pants and loose shirts, which barely covered their rears. Mrs. Kareem had no dupatta on her. In fact, sitting in the drawing room, he realized with disdain, that he and Mumtaz were the only ones dressed traditionally. Mumtaz was in her typical loose shalwar suit, with a dupatta covering her head and he was in his full northern gear, complete with a turban, waistcoat and gun belt. He did not want to make a further fool of himself by speaking in Darri, while everyone else conversed easily in English, with a few phrases in the local dialect thrown in for effect. The second thing that he found annoying was that he had expected his sister to walk in a little demurely. Rather, she had walked in the way school girls in England sauntered around on the streets. His sister had been raised all wrong, he mused. And even though Safina wore a shalwar suit for a change, she had not covered her head, and now sat talking with the two girls as if they were long-lost friends.

After a sumptuous dinner, Khodadad and Kareem withdrew to the library for cigars, while Mumtaz suggested that Safina and Rameez go out for a stroll and get to know each other. As discussed earlier, Khodadad and she had agreed that they should be given some time together. Fareeha, who was worn-out from the long journey, called it a night and accompanied by her daughters, left for one of the two guest rooms arranged for them.

Adam paced the foyer, annoyed at Khodadad. There were hundreds of perfectly eligible, tribal families to choose from, and what does his father do? He goes and picks the most inappropriate and non-conventional family to wed his daughter into. Adam's life had been limited to the hills surrounding his village, where he felt most at home, and England, which he only tolerated until he could finish his schooling. He could not wait for the day he finally came back home and took the reins of his father's responsibilities. What Adam did not realize was that there were people in Pakistan who chose the middle ground and had embraced a life which was relaxed and modern in its approach, yet loyal to their traditional values.

When earlier that day during the hunt, Khodadad suddenly announced—after receiving a message from his aide—that they had to cut short their trip because guests were on their way, Babar had been positive the guests were his uncle and mother coming on his behest to ask for Safina's hand in marriage. He had asked his mother countless times, alarmed at the easy friendship between Zaheer and Safina, to visit the village. However, Rabia had been hesitant, saying that Khodadad would never agree to the match. Financially, Babar had nothing to his name, and it was pointless to expect a man like Khodadad to hand over his daughter with no guarantees to the kind of life she was accustomed to. However, he believed his mother must have had a change of heart because she was finally giving into her son's wishes.

Babar's euphoria was quickly replaced with wretchedness the moment he heard father and son talking in the back seat of the jeep. "I kept delaying this family from coming because I was waiting for their son to finish his education in the States. They still have some land around here but are now based in Islamabad. I can't think of a better family for Safina." It was not possible to hear the rest of the conversation over the noise of the gushing river they were crossing, and sitting in the front with the driver, Babar suddenly felt like an outsider. He saw his world come crashing over his head, and the rest of the ride home was torture. He already hated the family that was coming over and prayed in his heart that one look at Safina and her non-conventional ways of behaving, would be enough to send them back, empty handed.

Now, Babar watched the pair walk out of the foyer together. He stood amongst the shadows of the maple tree in front of the annexe.

Safina had changed into jeans and a pullover, while Rameez had borrowed Adam's jacket to keep warm in the chill evening air. It was a clear night, and like most nights in the north, the sky was dotted with a million stars. "I was fourteen the last time I came to the village. My maternal grandfather had passed away and we had all come for the funeral. I don't remember noticing the sky at that time. This is such a beautiful place and so peaceful," Rameez remarked. The pair walked on near the side of the house, close to the hedges, and Safina didn't know what to say. Rameez was trying to draw the girl out of silence and tried again. "I heard you telling my sister that you know French. I find that incredible. I've always wanted to learn a foreign language, but never had the chance."Safina noted that Rameez was careful not to patronize her. He could have easily said he was surprised that despite growing up in a rural area, Safina could learn a language he only dreamed of learning while living in a cosmopolitan city.

"One of the positive aspects of living here is that you are close to nature and learn to use it," Safina spoke for the first time. "My brother and I were taught to look beyond the beauty of the landscape and let it be part of our lives. Take those stars, for example," Safina raised an arm and pointed to a cluster of stars forming an arc directly above them. "We know that those four stars are close to the river that runs behind the woods, and where the arc bends, is where this house is." Rameez looked at her with awe. "Not only do these stars guide our way, they offer inspiration to what I write or the music I play," Safina continued. The pair strolled to the side of the house and moved towards the rose garden. Sitting down in the gazebo, Rameez thought it best to come to the point. He could see that Safina was no average village girl; rather, she was refined and mature beyond her age.

"Safina, you know why we are here. My parents forced me to come today even though I told them I did not want to get married yet. At this point, when I've just come back to Pakistan after six years, I'm still in the process of deciding where and with whom I want to spend the rest of my life. But meeting you has taken me by surprise. I never expected you to be so eloquent and knowledgeable. You are so easy to talk to." Safina smiled inwardly, as Rameez did not use cliché terms to describe her. She half-expected him to say that he found her beautiful or that the stars reminded him of her eyes, or something equally banal and poetic. Instead, Rameez had appreciated her inner traits and looked beyond appearance. "I wasn't planning on sharing this with you, but talking to you, I realize I must be honest," Rameez said in a rush of words, looking directly at her eyes. "I am already committed to a girl in New York and with time, will talk to my parents about her. I just want you to know that it will not be possible for us to get married. Would it be too much to ask that you please play along and let our parents feel we are getting to know each other?" He had realized, after speaking with her, that she would not break down at this piece of news, but the reaction he got was not at all what he was expecting.

As she listened to him speak, a strange weight lifted off Safina's shoulders. In fact, she felt ecstatic, and one could hear the buoyancy in her voice. "Rameez, thank you for sharing this with me. I am relieved to hear you are totally uninterested in this match. I think you and I will make very good friends," she said laughingly.

Mumtaz smiled, watching the two of them sitting and laughing under the flowering vines. Thinking of Zaheer, she felt that perhaps it was just a dream she nursed that could never come true.

Another set of eyes also looked on keenly. Watching the two sitting under the gazebo in comfortable camaraderie, Babar longed to hear what they talked about. He was outraged at both Adam and Khodadad for letting Safina walk around unchaperoned with a total stranger, and angry at his mother for not coming first and speaking about a match between him and Safina. It was obvious the couple sitting under the vines were getting along, while he was left alone to sulk and nurse his misery in silence. He had not been invited to the dinner or introduced to the guests. It was almost as if he did not exist. There was a fire burning in him and he could not bring himself to look away.

The next morning, after a breakfast of slow-cooked game, pancakes, eggs, and cakes, both families bundled into cars and jeeps to take a tour of the village. Leading the way in his Range Rover, Khodadad sat with Jibraan, his wife and Mumtaz, while Adam drove the other jeep with the rest of the group. Judging from the sparkle in Safina's eyes and the ease with which she chatted with Rameez, everyone blissfully assumed the two had hit it off well and the older ladies mentally started making lists of things that had to be done for the forthcoming wedding. The guests left the next day with plans to meet in two weeks' time in Islamabad, with an implicit understanding that Safina and Rameez should spend some time together to get to know each other better.

CHAPTER 5

With trembling hands, Samantha put down the phone. She had spoken to her daughter for the first time after leaving Pakistan. Not much was said in the five minutes they were connected, but both knew what the other was trying to say with tears soaking their faces. Walter handed her a glass of wine and with a hand on her elbow, guided her to the living room. Samantha pulled her feet up on the sofa and cuddled next to Walter. "You hardly said a word. What did Safina say? I'm sure she sounds different now," Walter said, pushing Samantha's hair away from her wet face.

"She sounded like a grown up; not a little girl anymore. Walter, she's missed me so much all these years," Samantha said between a fresh wave of tears. "She wants to see me, Walter; my daughter wants to see me."

Zaheer had informed Samantha that Safina would be in Islamabad to meet up with her prospective husband, and had arranged for a clandestine phone call from his room for Safina. "Samantha Aunty, she will only be here for a few minutes to pick up my mother. I will make sure my mother is in the other room and you can talk to Safina. But please, keep it short."

Samantha was tremendously grateful for the huge risk Zaheer was taking on her behalf. She was sad to be told that Adam would not want to talk to her as he avoided every mention of his mother and therefore, was totally unaware of the connection between her and Safina.

From Zaheer, Samantha also learned that Khodadad never spoke her name. Khodadad's first reaction when Samantha disappeared was that she had had been abducted or worse, had been in an accident and was lying unconscious in some hospital. He could never guess that the woman he loved with so much passion, and who reciprocated with the same ardour, could just walk out of his life without a word. In the process, not only his love had been taken for granted but his honour had been trampled on. He found it impossible to believe that his wife, who cared for their children above anything else, would abandon them so heartlessly. With her departure, a door firmly closed in Khodadad's heart, and he evaded any mention of her.

Over the months that passed, Safina made frequent trips with Mumtaz to Islamabad under pretext that she wanted to meet Rameez and shop around. Mumtaz, who as a rule avoided going to the city at all costs, never refused to accompany her niece. Khodadad made no objection to these trips, but invariably, Adam opposed these excursions. Fearful of his father, he only voiced his opposition to Mumtaz Bibi. "Bibi, do you think its right for her to go to Islamabad every few weeks? What does she do there all the time? Last time, she only met Rameez's sisters for lunch and went around the malls without buying anything. What's the point of leaving the house so much? She should be staying here and learning something useful, and wait until she is officially engaged or something," he said one day.

"If it bothers you, why don't you talk to your father about it?" Mumtaz, who was busy packing for the three-day trip the next morning replied, and put an end to the discussion.

The truth was, even Mumtaz couldn't understand why Safina wanted to go down to Islamabad so much. When there, Rameez or his mother and sisters would occasionally visit them at their Islamabad house. On the other hand, Zaheer spent most of his time after work with Mumtaz and Safina, offering to take them around. It seemed to Mumtaz that Safina seemed happier with her son and both spent most of their time together, with no sign of the prospective fiancé. Watching the two in such easy companionship was alarming for her, as she had given Khodadad her word to keep them away from each other to avoid the possibility of any romantic notions between the two. The quicker her niece became formally engaged to Rameez, she mused, the better. Besides, these trips to the city were proving quite unproductive, with no sign of any wedding preparations or meetings between Safina and Rameez, and it was about time both families sorted out the details for the marriage.

On one of these trips, after a phone call to her mother from a payphone in the mall, Safina sat down for coffee with Zaheer at a nearby restaurant.

The two had volunteered to collect some suits from the tailor, which were ready for pick up. As always, Safina was subdued after her interaction with her mother. "I don't want you to be sad each time you speak with Saman Aunty. Please cheer up," Zaheer said to Safina with concern in his blue eyes.

Safina stared into her coffee, cupping it with both hands. There were so many things which needed to be said to the only friend she knew. If she didn't say them now, it would be too late. "Zaheer, the reason I want to leave is not only that I want to see my mother. If I stay, I will end up marrying some stranger. Rameez likes someone else. When Baba finds out, he is bound to marry me off to the next best candidate," she paused and took a deep breath before continuing. "I've only loved you, Zaheer. I cannot think of marrying anyone else."

Hearing her words, Zaheer's hands felt cold, despite the hot coffee he was drinking. When she looked up, she could tell she had upset him. The blue eyes were averted and looked troubled. Zaheer did not speak for a long time, and when he did, his tone was measured and low. "Safina, there is nothing I've wanted more than to have you in my life. You are the reason why I went to the village so much. But I also love your father like my own. He took me and my mother in when people were after our lives. What I am today, I owe to him and the fact is, your father does not want us getting married. He looks upon cousin marriages as unethical or something. I don't know. And the fact is, my mother and I can't go against him," Zaheer said, looking at Safina for the first time.

If Safina had expected Zaheer to respond to her with ardent confessions of passion, she was wrong. Instead, Zaheer was making it clear to her that regardless of how he felt about her, a union between them was not possible. His sense of indebtedness to her father forbade him from crossing a fine line.

He also made it clear that he was going against Khodadad's unspoken rule by setting up her telephone calls to Samantha. "I have spoken to my contact in the Canadian consulate. You have to wait until after you turn eighteen to apply for your passport," Zaheer told Safina on the drive back from the mall. "Safina, you have to understand that we cannot let Uncle Khodadad know about any of this. I will come to the village next month and give you the details of how we are going to do this," he added, with a worrisome frown creasing his forehead. Safina listened very calmly. She was certain she wanted to leave; especially now that Zaheer told her they could never be more than good friends. If she told her father about wanting to see Samantha, she had no doubts he wouldn't let her and would instead tie her down without delay in a marriage to whoever he deemed appropriate. She was thankful that Adam's summer break was coming to an end and he was due to head back the next week. With all that was on her mind, adding her brother's questions and criticism to everything she did was more than she could take.

As promised, Zaheer showed up unannounced at the village the weekend after Adam's departure. Khodadad was in the library with Babar discussing the shipment of a load of lumber due to leave the next day, when Kaka Manju announced, while placing a cup of tea on the table that Zaheer Sahab had arrived. Shortly after, Zaheer came into the library and after embracing his uncle and with a curt hello to Babar, sat down. He waited for Babar to leave before starting. "Uncle, I've been given my first assignment from the Foreign Office," he said seriously, "and I will be leaving for West Africa in less than two weeks." Khodadad's initial response was of happiness for his nephew, but was quickly replaced with a feeling of loss at his departure. Zaheer had been like a son to him, in more ways than Adam could ever be. Unlike his son, Zaheer shared Khodadad's guiding principle of keeping a balance between western and traditional ideals and was not inflexible in his attitude towards life. Adam, on the other hand, was a tribal to the core; years of schooling in England had done nothing to loosen his rigid, tribal framework. If anything, Adam came back each summer more set in his ways, and left for another year determined to let it be his last.

The next day, soon after breakfast, Zaheer signalled to Safina to meet him in the garden. It was a beautiful morning in September and the gardener was pruning the rose bushes. Casually strolling to the bench under the cherry tree, Safina opened her sketch pad. She was thankful that Babar had left in the early morning and later, her father, to oversee the timber shipment. Moments later, Zaheer joined her, holding the chess box under his arm. "I thought we could have a last game of chess before I leave," he said, sitting down next to Safina. Putting her sketching aside, she noted that Zaheer had changed into his travelling clothes, indicating that he would be leaving soon.

As he arranged the chess pieces, Zaheer spoke in a muffled voice. It was obvious he did not want to risk being heard. "I want you to start taking walks along the river from now on. Get to know the area. Make up an excuse that you are sketching or something," Zaheer said. Safina listened, careful to keep her expression neutral. Moving a chess piece as the game opener, Zaheer continued, "I know what your father said about not going into the woods after your accident. But it is important you learn the terrain, do you understand?" Zaheer said, looking up, his eyes a very deep blue and his tone firm. Safina had never seen him so stern; she could almost see her father in the person that sat across from her. "Remember the spot where you fell?" he continued, "follow the river south for about two miles from there. There is a rope bridge that goes across the river where it narrows to a bottle neck." Zaheer paused when he noticed his mother approaching them, with Kaka Manju following with a tray.

Safina took the cue from Zaheer and pretended to be engrossed in the game. "It's such a pretty day! I thought we could all have some halva and enjoy the sun," Mumtaz Bibi chirped and lowered her heavy frame on the garden seat, while Manju set down the tray on a folding table.

Zaheer took the plate of warm halva and samosas from his mother and smiled at her. "I've been asking Safina why she doesn't draw anymore. After Viola left, she's just put away her guitar and sketchbook. Amma, you should tell her to continue because she's got so much talent," Zaheer said, trying to keep the conversation light.

"Yes Safina *jaan*, you should do as Zaheer says. You hardly sketch anymore. I was so proud of the pictures you made for me last year. Here, have another samosa," she said, putting another one on her plate, not realizing the girl had not even touched the first one.

Zaheer was getting impatient, and wanted his mother to leave. "This halva is delicious Amma, and I can tell you made it yourself. I grew up eating this stuff almost every day I was here and just couldn't get enough," Zaheer remarked light-heartedly to Safina. "Do you know what else I miss?" he added, "I miss the hot milk with almonds and pistachios that you used to make, and you added honey and figs to it," Zaheer rolled his eyes upwards and rubbed his stomach for effect. This was all the prompt

Mumtaz needed. All motherly instincts came to the surface, and getting up hurriedly, she disappeared into the house to go make her son the hot beverage he craved.

The moment she was out of sight, Zaheer became serious once again and continued with the outline of his plan. "During the next full moon, which is exactly ten days from today, you will take a walk through the back gate into the woods to where you almost fell into the river. Leave a dupatta or something of yours there to mislead the dogs. I'm praying it doesn't come to that, but just to be on the safe side," Zaheer was rushing his words. Safina listened intently, mentally noting down all he said. "Go south about two miles; you will notice the river narrowing at one point. Get on the rope bridge and cross to the other side. I will be waiting there." The rush in Zaheer's voice prevented Safina from interrupting, although she had a million questions that needed answering. Seeing his mother re-emerging from the house, with Kaka Manju in tow with a tray, Zaheer hurried on. "In a backpack, bring a few clothes, sensible shoes, and as much cash as you can lay your hands on. Wear gloves because the rope will cut into your hands and make sure you have a flashlight," Zaheer finished just in time before his mother reached them, and beaming, poured them steaming, frothy milk from a porcelain teapot.

CHAPTER 6

Her hair was getting caught in the branches and slowing her down. Wrenching her hair free of a limb, Safina ran through the woods towards the river. What she thought was the sound of the gushing water, quickly turned into the baying of dogs. She ran faster, heedless of the whiplashes on her face from the overhanging branches. There were people close behind, shouting above the dogs' barking. What were they saying? Safina couldn't make it out. The river was close by; she could tell from the taste of the musky air and the dampness on her face. Just when she thought she had reached the water's edge, somebody scooped her off her feet and brought her down on the hard earth with a dull sound, and straddled her body. When she tried to turn to get up, she saw Babar looking down at her, his chest heaving and his eyes ablaze. Safina clawed at his rowdy, smirking face, while he looked on laughing, not bothering to shield himself.

She woke up suddenly, the sweat encircling her neck like a hot band. For a moment, Safina just lay there, unsure if the heaviness on her body was Babar weighing her down or something else. Her fingers hurt and her throat felt sore. Safina turned on the table lamp and pushing the quilt that was bunched up on her body to the floor, sat up in bed. Looking at her hands, Safina noticed paint from the wooden head board under her nails. She had scratched the wood with her fingernails in her sleep.

Nightmares woke Safina up each night. She would dream she was running breathlessly through the woods, trying to overcome one obstacle after another. She would hear the river and of the dogs in pursuit. Sometimes, she would see Zaheer trying to reach a hand out to her but she could never touch it. In the end, however, Babar would always suddenly obstruct her and bear down on her. Shuddering with terror, Safina could not get his hot breath or sneer out of her mind.

Six more days and she would have to make her get away.

"It's good you are drawing again, *jaan*. Your father was asking me where you go each morning, and he was so pleased when I told him you are working on a set of sketches," Mumtaz said over breakfast one day. Each morning, at about ten o clock, Safina could be seen in her running shoes heading for the woods behind the house. She would chat for a few minutes with the gardener and take one of the dogs with her, then head straight down to the river. Sitting down on a nearby log, she would sketch, and while doing so, she would also try to memorise the terrain. She had not ventured as far as the bridge she was to cross in a few days, but she had a general idea where the river narrowed.

Coming home from her exploration one day, Safina stood near the back of the kitchen, stomping the mud off her shoes when Babar suddenly opened the door and stood staring at her. Seeing the person from her nightmares looming in front of her startled Safina and she moved to the side, trying to let the boy pass. However, Babar had no intent to pass and instead, reached out and held her arm in a tight grasp. "Let go of my hand! What do you think you're doing?" she let out, trying to twist her arm free and dropping her drawing supplies.

"Why don't you look at me the way you look at the city boy, huh? What do you both talk about? Am I not good enough for you?" Babar said between clenched teeth. Safina knew she needed to overcome her fear from her nightmares of Babar, and stopped writhing in his grasp. She stood still and looking straight in his eyes, warned him that if he did not let go of her arm, she would scream and gather all the servants and would also tell her father about his brutish behaviour. Hearing Khodadad's name was enough for Babar to come to his senses and letting go of her, he left the kitchen and headed for the annexe.

The incident had shaken up Safina and while she stood rubbing her wrist, Manju Kaka walked into the kitchen. One look at her and he could tell Safina was upset. Safina refused to answer any questions he asked, and kept insisting that it was nothing. Manju bent down to pick up her fallen sketch pad from the kitchen stoop and noticed Babar making his way up the incline leading to the annexe. "Did he do something to you?

Was it Babar? What did he want?" he asked the girl through his gums, trembling with rage.

Safina walked out of the kitchen and into the main house, clutching her sketch pad. She did not need any distractions at this point. If she made a big deal out of this, Mumtaz was bound to call her father, who was away for a meeting with the village elders. She prayed she did not come across Babar for the rest of her time there.

Mumtaz knocked on Safina's door just when she was getting ready for bed. "Are you awake, *jaan*?" the older woman asked quietly. Mumtaz rarely came into Safina's room, and only did so when she had something important to tell her. Safina froze, afraid that Kaka Manju had told her about the episode with Babar this morning, and she had come to investigate. What she started to talk about, however, completely took Safina by surprise. "Safina *jaan*, you know that I love you, Adam, and Khodadad very much. After Zaheer, you all are the only family I have," she said solemnly, while sitting down on the bed and pulling Safina close to her. Safina was not accustomed to her aunt making declarations of love; neither could she recall Mumtaz ever displaying any physical affection. The woman expressed her feelings in the things she did for the family. There was adoration, verging on the point of worship in her eyes for Khodadad and her devotion to both the kids was evident in how she made sure they were comfortable and taken care of. Mumtaz hardly ever left the house, not even to visit her only sister who lived in Peshawer, afraid that by doing so, she would be neglecting her household duties.

Safina sat close to her aunt, and felt nervous about what Mumtaz was trying to say. "*Jaan*, you are a woman now, and will be starting a new life soon. After you leave, your father and I will be here all by ourselves. I just want you to try to be a little more understanding of Khodadad. To this day, he has not gotten over your mother leaving him." Safina listened with concentration at what her aunt was trying to tell her. Mumtaz had ceased to mention her mother, and Safina always wondered with a pang if she was the only one who missed her presence. Looking at her aunt now, sitting on the bed and holding her close to her ample body, she felt a surge of sorrow at the woman's heartache. She noticed, with surprise, the wrinkles etching intricate lines on her face and the hair which had almost turned completely white. She had been so wrapped up in her own mourning, she never noticed that in her own way, the older woman suffered just as much. All these years, just like her, Mumtaz had kept the pain of losing Samantha locked in her heart.

Between heaving melancholy sighs and a catch in her voice, Mumtaz reminded Safina that it would be twelve years the next day since her mother walked out. Her absence had created a vacuum in all their lives, but more so in Khodadad's heart. He hadn't remarried even though there were countless efforts from various tribal chiefs offering their daughters in marriage for him to choose from. The reason he did not remarry was because he wanted the essence of his house to remain unchanged. Bringing a tribal woman or someone from Islamabad would have meant the fading away of the way of life he valued so much, which included the raising of his two children in a certain way, and of which Viola had been a key role player in maintaining. He wanted music and art and a particular ambiance to adorn his house. Mumtaz wanted Safina to try to understand her father and ease his ache before she left the house to get married.

Safina lay in bed long after Mumtaz left, thinking about all she had said in a rare moment of admission. Until now, she had not looked beyond her own feelings of abandonment and hurt. Perhaps Adam's rigid attitude was also a kind of coping mechanism, which had kicked in when he suddenly felt lost and unloved. He was very young at the time, but not so young that he couldn't remember his mother's presence, or the lack of it.

When her father returned the next afternoon, he found Safina with her sketch pad sitting under the cherry tree. The Labradors were frolicking around her, chasing butterflies and happy to be out in the sun. Looking at her father getting off the jeep, Safina could tell he had spent the past few days at the lumber yard; he had on his big safety boots and instead of the shalwar kameez he wore around the village, he was in his khakis and hunting vest. He was such a handsome man, Safina thought. Even though his dark brown hair was now dappled with a bit of silver, he still had the clearest blue eyes she had ever seen; eyes that could abruptly change from turquoise to a deep indigo, depending on his mood. Her father walked with squared shoulders and long strides and wherever he went, seemed to fill the space with his presence. It would have been so easy for him to have remarried and lived a normal, cheerful, warmth-filled life. Instead, he had chosen a life of celibacy and unceasing isolation, and continued to nurse his wounds under a facade of indifference and hard work. It was impossible to believe this humourless, stern man was the same person who quoted poetry to her mother and used to whisper things in her ear to make her blush and laugh. For the first time, Safina noticed her father and for a fleeting moment, she almost hated her mother for ruining all their lives.

As was his habit, Khodadad was in the library after dinner, outlining tasks to Babar for the next day. Safina sought to bridge the gap between herself and her father and felt emboldened after hearing Mumtaz's words the previous night, she knocked on the door. "Come in!" she heard her father's deep voice, probably thinking it was Manju Kaka bringing his coffee. Babar went white as a sheet when Safina walked into the room. Looking at Babar pointedly, Safina spoke, "Baba, when you are free, I would like to talk to you."

"Yes, what is it, Safina? Have a seat," he said, while motioning for her to sit on the chair across from him.

"I want to have a private chat with you. I will wait until he leaves the room," she replied, without looking at Babar. Meanwhile, Babar's discomfort was evident from the deep red his face had turned and being a sharp man, Khodadad noted this with some surprise.

"I think Babar and I are done here. Babar, I will meet you tomorrow at the office. You can go and rest now," Khodadad dismissed the boy with his words, making him more aware of the disparity between Safina and himself.

"Baba, I want to talk about something that is very important," Safina started. "I don't want to get married yet," she continued with her head bowed and hands clasped in her lap, not looking at her father. "I think you have some idea that I've always liked Zaheer, and if I was to marry someone, it would be him," she said, looking up at her father's cloudy face. She was not sure how he would react to her daring confession.

After a lengthy pause, Khodadad answered his daughter, his brow furrowed and a sorrow in his voice. "Safina *jaan*, I've known how both of you feel about each other. And there is nothing wrong with Zaheer. I've always wanted my children to be strong, capable individuals but Zaheer is too close in the family for me to marry you to him. You would be making our family's lineage weak and diluted if you were to do that. And I will not consent to letting my daughter do something which she might later regret."

Safina was not willing to give up so easily, and said, "But Baba, I love him. How can I live with someone else if I have Zaheer in my heart?"

Before his daughter could continue, Khodadad raised a palm, dissuading her from continuing and said in a very unmistakably firm and decisive tone, "You will stop thinking of Zaheer as a future husband. If you do not like Rameez, I can find you some equally worthy man and with time, you will eventually get to love him. I want you to stop thinking otherwise. We will not discuss this further." There was finality in his voice and his jaw was set, discouraging any further discussion. The meeting was obviously over and Safina got up. She did not want to look up for fear of her father seeing the tears in her eyes. At this moment, she despised her father. How could he be so open about most things and rigid about something so natural? He was not even willing to listen to her. It was probably his unyielding, inflexible temperament that made her mother run away. Well, good for her! Safina's mind was full of these seditious thoughts as she left the library and went to her room, ignoring the startled look on Bibi's face as she crossed her in the corridor.

The next morning, Safina overheard her father talking to Mumtaz Bibi in the breakfast room. "If she does not like Rameez, I think there is no need to encourage them into believing we are interested in their son. I will talk to another family who have asked me several times to come and visit us here," her father was saying to her aunt. "She doesn't realize that I want her to get married and move to a big city where she can go to university and get on with her life. It is my responsibility as her father to make sure she is settled and taken care of...." her father was going on.

Unnoticed, Safina turned back; she did not want to listen to her father's rant about what he wanted for her. Maybe, for a change, he should start seeing what people around him wanted.

The Swiss Army backpack was hidden behind Safina's winter outfits in her closet. It had a few changes of clothes, a photo album and her jewellery, which consisted of small pieces given to her by her father and Mumtaz on birthdays and special occasions. She also had a parka, flashlight and a pair of sturdy gloves nicked from the gardening shed behind the house. When Khodadad had left for work, Safina stole into his bedroom, looking for the keys to his safe. They were nowhere to be found. She opened his closet and while rummaging through the section of his western outfits, came across an old box she remembered from her childhood. It was her mother's hat box. Safina remembered her father bringing it back from a trip to Paris and her mother squealing with delight when she pulled out the dainty cream-coloured hat from layers and layers of light pink tissue paper. A few days later, Samantha had left with her father for a Christmas party at the Canadian Consulate, wearing the hat and a fawn coloured satin gown. Viola had arranged Samantha's hair in a French knot, with the hat balanced on top, giving her mother a classy air. Khodadad's mother's string of pearls with a diamond catch completed the outfit. Seeing his wife come out of their bedroom, Khodadad had whistled playfully in admiration, and Viola and Samantha had burst out laughing. Safina had sat sulking in a corner, annoyed why she was not invited to the party.

The box had obviously been moved from the Islamabad house and brought here. Safina could only imagine what memories her father must associate with the box. Gingerly lifting the top, Safina looked inside it and found old photographs of her mother. Some were from their honeymoon in Europe, when both her parents were very young. There were others of her mother in her rose garden, a few from different parties they had attended or held, and several others of Samantha with the kids or with Mumtaz. Lifting a few more pictures out of the box, Safina found a tiny blue box within the hat box. It was from a jewellery store. Opening the cover, she found a pair of the most dazzling diamond earrings she had ever seen. She could not remember her mother ever wearing them. Perhaps her father had bought them for her but never got a chance to give them to her. *Who knew what ghosts the hat box housed*, Safina wondered. A door banged shut somewhere in the house, and panicking, Safina put the box away. She did not get a chance to close it and quickly left the room, clutching the photographs and the box with the diamond earrings.

Mumtaz Bibi yawned noisily and saying good night, asked Safina to turn off the lights when she was done watching the movie. Every Saturday night, they snuggled together on the day bed and watched a comedy together. Safina had put on "Monty Python" because Mumtaz was in the mood for some British humour. She waited for the older lady to go to her room, then turned off the home theatre and headed for the kitchen. She prepared herself a thermos of strong coffee, then went to her room and waited until she was sure everyone was asleep.

The light from the night clock read: 1:28 a.m. Another two minutes and she would head out through the breakfast room windows. Taking the main doors was too risky because there was always a night guard patrolling at the front of the house. The October night was bitter cold, and Safina was glad for the parka and thick socks under her runners. Flashes of her nightmare kept distracting her. She almost felt that Babar would appear from nowhere. "Focus, focus, Safina," she remembered her father's words when he would take her and Adam for target practice to the make-shift firing range in the logging area. But surprisingly, Safina was not nervous. She knew Babar was in Lahore visiting his mother and her father had long gone to bed. The knapsack was tied securely to her back and putting on the gardener's worn gloves over her mother's leather ones, Safina set off for the woods at a brisk pace. The dogs, which were left to roam the periphery of the house at night since the time Safina almost fell into the river, were used to her leaving for the woods. However, tonight, Safina did not encourage them and told them to stay put. Whimpering with disappointment at not being invited for a walk, the dogs went off in another direction.

Even though it was night time, the looming trees did not seem so intimidating. Perhaps, it was the fact that Safina had memorised each bend and pothole over the past few days, or perhaps it was the conviction that she would go insane if she let her father decide her life, which led her to move with such sure footedness. After about twenty minutes of brisk walking, Safina could hear the roar of the river. Without breaking her pace, she pulled out the flask and drank a few mouthfuls of coffee straight from the thermos. She remembered Mumtaz Bibi used to give Adam and her a spoonful each of brandy on cold winter nights to keep chest infections at bay. Right now, she wished she had some of the Bodegas Torres, which Mumtaz kept locked in her cupboard to warm their insides. Looking at her watch in the moonlight, she was pleased to note she had reached the river in record time. Safina headed south, keeping her speed brisk and her stride firm; she could make out where the river narrowed.

The rope bridge looked very makeshift and for a moment, Safina wondered if Zaheer had been serious she take it to cross the river. However, when she put her foot on the first wooden plank and tried to budge it to test how strong it was, she was relieved to know that it was sturdier than it looked. Safina flashed the light towards the opposite end of the bridge.

Instantly, another light flashed in reply, signalling to her that Zaheer was waiting at the other end. The bridge was secured firmly alright, but it was the swinging movement that Safina was not prepared for. Each step she took set the lines in motion, making Safina grasp at the ropes even more tightly. Inwardly, she thanked Zaheer for asking her to wear gloves, because even though her hands were covered in the thick industrial cotton, she could feel the bite of the lines in her palms, making them ache miserably. It took longer than the twenty minutes Safina had estimated it would take to cross the river. When she reached the other end, she was thankful to have Zaheer's strong hands take hold of her. It was a bright night, and she could see the clear blue eyes that met her. Looking into them, she saw the apprehension Zaheer was experiencing. "I was not sure you would make it," he said, pulling Safina onto solid ground, "The bridge was moving so much, I was afraid you would fall over." Safina was trembling, partly from her frightful flight and partly from the biting wind that crept into her despite her protective clothing. Zaheer had left the engine running in the jeep, and Safina was grateful to jump into the snug comfort of the vehicle. Driving carefully, trying to keep to the compact part of the road, Zaheer headed the jeep towards the highway, which would take them to Islamabad.

It was almost seven in the morning when Safina woke with a start. The jeep was not moving anymore. "It's okay. No need to panic, we're safe," Zaheer answered her troubled look. "We are at the airport. A Mr. Kirby and Rachel DuBois from the Canadian Consulate will be here around eight thirty with your travel documents. You will wait for them near the AVIS Car Rental kiosk. They will recognize you and see that you clear immigration and will make sure you board your flight. Your plane leaves at eleven a.m.," Zaheer said in a rush, not looking at Safina. He was aware he was putting them both at risk. If they were discovered by Khodadad or any of their acquaintances, they would be in a lot of trouble. It would put an end to Khodadad's trust in them and in his eyes, would bring humiliation and dishonour to his name and family. In short, he would never forgive them. Already, Zaheer reminded himself with some discomfort, he had led his mother and Khodadad to believe he had left for West Africa.

Safina got off the jeep on stiff legs and swinging her bag over her shoulder, waited to say goodbye to the only person she trusted. Zaheer took her hands and turned them over. There were blisters where the rope had rubbed in. He traced his thumbs across both palms and looked up at Safina. At this moment, Safina was not sure she wanted to get on that air craft to join her mother. She wanted to be here with the man she adored, she wanted him to not let go of her. The eyes that looked so much like Khodadad's were moist, and the early morning sunlight glinted on them, making the dark blue turn into a cerulean shade. Tears slowly made parallel pathways down Safina's smudged face and she held onto the hands that were soothing her blisters. "Safina, there is nothing in this world I want more than to keep you with me. But I told you before that is not possible. I would be going against Uncle Khodadad's wishes; I feel I have already betrayed both my mother and your father by bringing you here. We have to forget each other," Zaheer said, looking deep into Safina's eyes. With a catch in his voice, he continued, "You have a whole new life ahead of you. At least now you won't have to get married to someone you do not love, and you get to see your mother." Safina did not trust her voice at this moment, and where words did not come to her lips, she clung onto Zaheer's hands unmindful of the soreness in her hers.

CHAPTER 7

The cafeteria was never crowded at this hour and that was when Safina liked to come and sit by the window overlooking the football field. At this time of year, the field was covered in eight inches of snow. Her appointment with the guidance counsellor wasn't for another hour and she had to write the sample letter of intent during that time. Opening her laptop, Safina started to write the 1500-word document that would make it possible for her to gain entrance to McMaster University's post-graduate program. Writing came easily for her, and when she put her heart to it, Safina could write with an intense clarity of thought and expression. She remembered the day, almost four years ago, when she came to Canada and visited the University of Toronto for the first time. She immediately knew she belonged amongst the students rushing to classes. The energy and joie de vivre in the young people there, dashing off to lectures and tutorials or languidly browsing through libraries opened a skylight of prospect and possibility in Safina's mind. She completed a four-year degree in three and in those years, she developed a strong yearning for historical research. She now hoped to qualify for the master's program at McMaster University, learning about tribal dynamics, especially in the Ottoman Empire.

The woman who sat in the book-lined, tiny office on the fourth floor in Chester New Hall looked at Safina from the top of her reading glasses. Her straight black hair was cut in a wedge that fanned her jaw, and she had piercing, dark eyes. Safina had expected a much older person, but the woman who sat there was probably in her late thirties. Dr. Virginia Ambrose, head of the History Department at McMaster University, was an expert on Turkish history and amongst the hundreds of letters of intent that had dropped into her mailbox from prospective students all over the world, Safina's had caught her interest the most. She found it intriguing to work with a student who had been raised in a tribal culture, had no formal education and yet, whose GPA provided evidence that she had an exceptional flair for writing and languages. Safina had secured a straight 93% in her undergrad and besides being fluent in French, she had taken up German. Accepting her in the special grad program for research on tribal society would be an asset, Dr. Ambrose considered.

Safina had moved in with Walter and Samantha when she arrived in Canada four years ago. Walking out of the arrivals exit, she saw her mother standing next to a man in thick glasses, whom she assumed was her husband. Her mother was wearing a woollen coat that came down to her ankles, while holding a thick winter jacket in her arms. Samantha rushed forward the moment she saw her daughter come out the doors, leaving Walter behind. Safina had pictured this meeting countless times; she had dreamed about this day since the time Zaheer showed her the letter in the garden. The reunion was not as she had imagined it would be. Right now, she felt flat, like a soda drink minus the fizz. She did not feel the rush of affection or the urgency to drop her bag and bury her face in her mother's neck to inhale her lemony scent. Instead, what she felt was a strange indifference to the woman reaching out to her with tears heedlessly falling down her face and making unsightly streaks on her powdered cheeks. There were fine lines around her mouth and the red lipstick she wore was smudged in one corner, which gave her a lopsided, droopy grin. Her hair that poked out from under the wool cap was a bleached blonde, not the rich, lustrous brown Safina remembered from her childhood. Her mother was saying something to her, but Safina was finding it difficult to understand the words coming out in sniffles. "You must be freezing my darling; I hope it's the right size. We can always change it if it doesn't fit, don't worry. We will go to the mall tomorrow and get you lots of winter clothes," Samantha said, as she tried to drape the coat over her daughter's shoulders with trembling hands.

Walter had walked towards the pair and introduced himself. "Welcome to Canada, Safina! We are so glad you finally reached here. I'm Walter, by the way," he said, extending a hand.

Safina looked at the man standing in front of her. He had four capped front teeth, which looked strangely white in contrast to the rest of his yellowing ones. Safina seemed to tower above him and could see his shiny scalp under the sparse hair carefully arranged to cover the balding middle of his head. Speaking for the first time, Safina shook Walter's proffered hand and replied with a bland, "I'm pleased to meet you, Mr. Walter."

Sitting in the backseat of the Prius, Safina felt too tired to notice the landscape hurtling by and fell asleep. She woke up to Samantha turning in her seat and trying to wake her up gently. Walter was at the front door, shaking the snow off his boots and taking them off at the entrance inside the house. Samantha and Safina did the same before going onto the tiled floor, which had been mopped sometime that day; Safina could tell by looking at the streaks of water that had dried on it. Walter already had an apron on and pulled out a casserole and put it on the table. There was bread, butter and mashed potatoes, and Samantha was microwaving a large side dish of vegetables. The house felt unusually warm, and Safina pulled off the knitted scarf from around her neck. The light pink cashmere scarf was weightless and exquisite and was a present from Mumtaz Bibi; it reminded Safina of the contrast in the surroundings she found herself in, to those in which the scarf had been given. *The scarf does not belong here*, Safina thought with an inward shot at humour.

Mumtaz was excited that Zaheer was coming back after more than six years. His work had taken him from one country to another and the times he was stationed in Pakistan, he barely left Islamabad. It would be quite a houseful, with Adam also back for good since last year and Babar's mother, Rabia, visiting her son in the annexe. After Safina had left, life had come to a sudden halt in the Khodadad household. It was six years ago when returning from a polo match, Adam was called to pick up the dorm extension in the hallway. He could hear his Aunt crying at the other end. His first reaction was that something had happened to his father. Despite Mumtaz telling him not to come back, Adam was on the first available flight to Islamabad and later that same evening, to his ancestral home in the village. Babar met him at the gate, and as he hugged him, Adam thought his childhood friend's eyes looked swollen, as if he had been crying. Kaka Manju stood in the foyer, wiping his damp eyes on his sleeves, waiting to take Adam to Mumtaz and Khodadad, who were in the library. On entering the room, Adam felt his father had aged at least ten years since he saw him last, which was only sixteen days ago. Looking at his father, with the furrows deep on his forehead and his eyes a lifeless grey; he was filled with a desire to strangle his missing sister. Mumtaz let out a series of wails the moment she saw Adam, and cradling his head on her chest, she held onto him and sobbed uncontrollably. Surprisingly, Adam was the most rational and level-headed one in the room. He caressed the aging aunt's head, and spoke to her in a soothing voice. "Bibi, calm down, don't tire yourself, please. I am here now. We will find Safina, don't you worry. There, let me get you something to wipe your face with," he said, while reaching for the tissue box on the table next to him. The village doctor had to be called and Mumtaz was given a shot to calm her and put her to sleep. Adam settled his aunt in her bed and sat with her, holding her hand until she drifted off into oblivion.

The next task was going to be more difficult, Adam thought with unease. Where Mumtaz had been expressive of her suffering, he knew his father was keeping his grief locked inside. Only the lamp on his father's desk was turned on when Adam entered the library. Khodadad was reclining in his easy chair near the fireplace and there was a cigar resting in an ashtray on the table next to him, sending up swirls of lazy smoke towards the ceiling. Pulling a chair next to where Khodadad sat, Adam tried to make out his father's face in the soft glow from the smouldering coals. For a very long time, neither of them spoke. "Baba, you cannot let this break you. I won't let you destroy yourself," Adam said, breaking the silence. "I look up to you for everything, and if you break down, I will not be able to continue."

Khodadad stirred in his seat and turned to look at his son. "I broke when your mother left us, Adam. Safina's departure has shattered me," said Khodadad. Getting up from his seat, Adam did what he had not done in a long time. He bent down and hugged his father tightly. Khodadad's arms slowly came around his son's tall frame and the tears, which had stayed locked inside him, coursed down his face. Father and son stayed this way for several minutes and when they parted, there was gratitude, respect and realization in the older man's eyes. The loss of his daughter had turned his son into a man.

Dry eyed, Adam silently said, "I'm here for you, Baba. I won't ever leave you."

The house was bustling with activity since morning and Mumtaz, who rarely ventured out of the house these days, was in the garden shouting instructions at the incompetent men putting up the lights. Today was a big day. Her son was coming home after so many years and had just been appointed some very important task in the Foreign Office. He had become a prominent person, and she was so proud of him. The day was also special because it was Khodadad's fiftieth birthday. Up until Viola had been around, birthdays were given a lot of value and were celebrated with due pomp and ceremony and now, after a very long time, someone's birthday was going to be celebrated within the walls of the tribal chief's house. "Bibi, can you please let me do this? You will be too exhausted to even look at Zaheer when he gets here," Rabia said, taking a stack of tablecloths from Mumtaz's arms.

The older woman had been on her feet since morning and was firing directions at the staff hired for the evening. She was finding fault with just about everything. The crème brulee was not the way Khodadad liked, the flowers that arrived were the wrong colour and to make matters worse, the guests arriving from Islamabad were at least two hours early. "Where is Babar? I can never find him when I need him the most." Heedless of Rabia's admonitions, Mumtaz kept panicking and looking for Babar at the far end of the garden, calling out to him in a booming voice. This was not a day to cross paths with his aunt, Adam thought with amusement while getting out of the jeep. It was a long time since he saw so much activity in the house, and he wanted to indulge Bibi and let her do whatever pleased her. It was, after all, a big day for the whole family.

Rabia had been right. When Zaheer finally arrived, Mumtaz was worn out with exhaustion. One look at her pale face and heavy breathing, and Khodadad asked Zaheer to take his mother to her room to rest until the evening. Unable to refute her cousin, Mumtaz left for her room, leaning on Zaheer's arm without protest.

After the fireworks signalled the end to the long day, and after the last of the guests had been either seen off or settled in their rooms, Khodadad asked Adam and Zaheer to join him in the library. Mumtaz had long gone to bed after a much-needed foot rub from her son, and the men could now discuss matters more serious than how the food tasted, without interruption. Kaka Manju had left a teapot on the table, and after pouring cups of steaming coffee for the three of them, Khodadad settled in his favourite leather recliner. "Zaheer, I am leaving the running of the Rawalpindi cotton mills under your supervision. And I also want you to keep the revenue from the orchards to fund your project," Khodadad told Zaheer. This bit of news came as a relief for him because up until now, Zaheer had no idea how he was going to finance the rural water purification venture he was working on. His work at the Foreign Office was impressive but unfortunately, came short in terms of money to support his undertakings in social work. Adam had taken over most of his father's responsibilities and was equally respected among the tribal population. He shared his father's vision for improving the lives of the locals and providing opportunities to their children. However, where Khodadad had been regarded as a rather unsociable leader, respected for his fairness, Adam liked to intermingle with the people. He was hardly ever seen in anything but the traditional *shalwar qameez*, and unified with the community. He knew people by name and attended any family gatherings he was invited to. Adam was overseeing the building of a charity hospital, which was being done in collaboration with the government. He had also funded education for those interested and qualified to study in university.

Safina looked at the calendar on her desk. The date had always held so much significance in her life. It was her father's fiftieth birthday today and she was finding it impossible to ease the dull ache in her heart. When she left her rented house this morning, which she shared with two other girls, she was determined to make a call to her father. However, sitting at her desk in the corner of Dr. Ambrose's office, Safina could not gather the courage to make that long-distance phone call and wake up old ghosts. Hearing her father's voice would break her and right now, she needed more than anything to be strong. Moving out of Walter and Samantha's house had been the initial step towards her salvation. Her initial days in the new country had first been filled with disappointment at her mother. She found it unbelievable how a woman could leave a man like Khodadad and the lifestyle he provided and live with a feeble and pathetic person like

Walter in such mundane conditions. The other emotion which Safina had to combat was heartbreak. She understood that Zaheer had his sense of loyalty to Khodadad, which prevented them from getting married. What she could not comprehend was why her best friend refused to respond to any of her attempts to connect with him. Safina had written countless letters, all unanswered and had called the embassy in Sierra Leone, knowing well that Zaheer was stationed there, but was frustrated when she was told each time that he was not free to talk, or was out, or some other such excuse. The least Zaheer could do was ask how she was coping, or let her know how the rest of the family were doing.

The woman Safina remembered from her childhood as her mom had been a woman of refined taste and culture. A woman who, despite being born and raised in the West, had accepted and adhered with pride to the life of her husband and adopted country. The woman, who now stood at the kitchen stove hurriedly frying eggs for her, while she sat at the breakfast table, was anything but refined. The oil splattered everywhere from the frying pan, and her mother was still in her house coat, with her hair sticking out in all directions. Safina could see that she was trying to make up for all the lost years in the things she insisted on doing for her, and making breakfast was one of them. In any case, Safina was useless when it came to culinary skills, and let Samantha spoil her. The woman with the dull yellow hair was not her mother, she wanted to believe. Samantha had been so particular about taking care herself. The person sloppily lathering butter on her toast had clearly let herself go. There were ugly sun spots on her face and hands and one could notice the fine blonde hair on her arms glistening in the early morning sun. A sad attempt had been made at a manicure and the dull red nail polish, chipped and at least three weeks old, glared at Safina. She could not help it. Safina just couldn't bring herself to look at Samantha and feel what a daughter was supposed to feel. It was almost as if the woman of her childhood and the woman standing in front of her were two different people. Watching her mother and Walter live the unexciting life of a middle-aged white couple whose highlight of the day was sitting down to dinner, while watching Alex Trebek give answers to contestants in Jeopardy was too much to bear. They seemed to complement each other, fitting together like a hand in glove. Where formerly, Samantha had embraced the life of a tribal chief's wife, she seemed to have embraced her life with Walter as well. She drank wine with her meals and even though she was careful not to give any to Safina, Samantha enjoyed her bacon and pork ribs. As she watched her mother and Walter eat things which were taboo amongst Muslims, Safina knew she had to get out of there and find a place of her own.

After two years of living with Samantha and Walter in their tiny semi-detached home, Safina saved enough money from two part-time jobs to find a room in a rundown house a few blocks away from the university. Samantha insisted on furnishing it with a bed, desk and chair from her house and gave Safina some essentials for the shared kitchen. "You should have let me bring the rug as well," said Samantha, pulling the chair from the back of the rented pick-up truck. "You will need it in the winters. I wish your room was not in the basement. I hope there's no mildew on the walls. How much more did you say the rent was for the upstairs room?" she continued, while Safina ignored her worrisome questions and picked a box to take downstairs. There were a million things she could say to her mother, but refrained from uttering them. Amongst other things, her mother had become very talkative since she moved back to Canada, Safina thought wryly.

Samantha insisted on arranging the room with Safina, and kept voicing her displeasure at how abruptly she had forsaken her mother and opted to live on her own. "I will constantly be worried about you, Safina. What if you're hungry and have nothing to eat, or fall sick? You did not have to leave Walter and me so suddenly. You know how much we both love you and Walter is trying so hard to be like a father to you," Samantha said in a reproaching tone, exasperated that her daughter was giving no straight answers.

Safina could not believe how her mother could blame her for leaving. When would she understand that living with her was like being locked inside a box with no air or light? When she could not take any more of the unwarranted accusations hurled at her, she turned around abruptly from arranging clothes in the closet and glared at Samantha. "You talk about abandonment? Do you even know what the word means? Abandon is what you did to Adam and me when you left us without a trace. Why should you worry about me getting sick?" she answered, unable to stop herself from the rush of words that were coming to her. "Do you know how many times my brother and I fell sick and who took care of us and sat through winter nights holding pans against our mouths so that we could wretch? Mumtaz Bibi and Viola were there for us. Who do you think worried about our food and who do you think I went to with all my problems? Who do you think talked to me when I was lonely or noticed that for the longest time, I cried myself to sleep, or even that I would bury my face in your clothes just to get a feel of you? Where were you then, mom? Tell me, where were you? I will tell you where you were. You were here, in Canada, depending on Walter to fill the gaps in your life. Gaps that were left because of the mistakes you made." By this time, Samantha who had abruptly sat down on the bed, was lost for words. She looked at the fierce eyes staring at her with so much scorn. At this moment, Samantha thought she sat facing Khodadad instead of the quiet, pensive girl she believed her daughter to be. Safina was not done talking yet, and continued, "You keep telling me how wonderful Walter is, or how much he helped you when you first came here. Do you know who is truly wonderful? It's my father! He sacrificed all his life for his children. He did not chicken out and got married the moment he was lonely and wanted comfort, so please tell Walter not to bother trying to be a father to me because he never will be one!" Samantha shook her head in denial but no words came out of her mouth. She looked at Safina with a mixture of fear and dismay, unable to answer in her defence. Drained of all pent-up resentment, Safina sat down on the only chair in the room, and looking at her mother's appalled face, regretted letting her emotions get the better of her. She had said too much, but there was no going back. There was nothing to do or say anymore and picking up her purse, Samantha left the room, blinded by the tears welling up in her eyes.

Now, staring at the phone, Safina was reminded of the day she had said all those things to her mother. She was realizing that she had done exactly what Samantha had done so many years ago. Without saying a word, Safina had left her father, her brother, and everything she loved and had run off. Like Samantha, she was just as much to blame for abandoning the people who mattered most in her life. The telephone sat untouched—a sad reminder of her weakness and shame.

The door opened and Dr. Ambrose walked in with a man behind her. "This is Dr. Russo, a very old friend and colleague. He was fascinated to read your paper on the trade alliances between the French and the Italians." Dr. Ambrose introduced the man. Shaking hands with him, Safina realized she was talking to the famous Dr. Eugene Russo, who had recently been in the news because of his sensational book on anthropology.

"Miss Khanzada, I found your theories in the article very interesting. You wrote about the disparity between regional and cultural ethics based on economic standards. If you have read my book, you will note these are some of the facts I based my research on." Safina was flattered that a person like Dr. Russo found her small paper interesting enough to comment on and draw similarities from. Previously, she had spent most of her time doing research for Dr. Ambrose but recently, Safina had started to also do research on topics that interested her, and had written several remarkable papers.

Over the next few days, Safina saw quite a lot of Dr. Russo as he had agreed to teach for one year at the university. His friendship with Dr. Ambrose frequently brought him to her office and he always made a point of talking to Safina when he was there. It was interesting listening to the man speak, especially since he was also part of a National Geographic series about the cultures of the world and would regale everyone with stories of his adventures during the filming of the series. One evening, just when Safina was leaving the office, Dr. Russo walked in. Safina told him that Virginia had already left and she would be happy to take a message for her. Eugene shut the door and told Safina he had come to see her and not Virginia. Not letting her surprise and annoyance show, Safina led him to the sitting area. She sat in a chair and motioned for him to take the sofa opposite her. "What is it, Dr. Russo?" she asked in a calm voice.

"Please call me Eugene and just hear me out. Safina, I find you very intriguing. It has taken a lot of nerve for me to come and say this to you. I've wanted to do this for quite a while now," the famous professor was saying to her, leaning forward in his seat and looking at her earnestly. "You are the reason I'm in this office so often, and please listen to what I have to say," he continued, preventing Safina from interrupting him, "but could you try to give us a chance to get to know each other better?" Safina was not prepared for this speech and for a moment, was lost for words. For the longest time, she had kept waiting to hear from Zaheer. Unless her father had found out about his involvement in smuggling her to Canada and had forbid him to have any contact with her, Safina found no reason why he would disregard her attempts to connect with him. She had never thought of anyone romantically except Zaheer, and being ignored by him was hurtful beyond words. She was beginning to feel that anyone she loved moved away from her. Her reunion with her mother was not all what she had envisioned, and it almost felt like she had lost her for the second time. On the other hand, her association with Zaheer went deeper than friendship between two cousins. Zaheer was her friend, her confidante, and the only person who could see through her, reaching the depths of her heart.

As she looked at the man sitting in front of her, who was much older than her in years and wisdom yet unable to express his feelings eloquently, Safina was almost filled with pity. She could see how awkward this confession must be for Eugene and how unfortunate it was that she could not reciprocate his feelings. He would experience the same rejection which she had felt with Zaheer's refusal to respond to her. "Eugene, I am touched to know you feel like this about me. I truly am. But the fact is, I'm not ready to commit to anyone," she said by way of refusal.

"Safina, I just want to get to know you better, I won't ask for more. I find you fascinating and can't keep you out of my mind. You're the first woman I have met who has not been swayed by my accomplishments or tried to wheedle her way into my life, and I find that so refreshing," replied Eugene earnestly.

The next afternoon, when Safina came in to the office, Dr. Ambrose looked at her a little differently. She had a slight smile on her lips and for the first time, looked at Safina from head to toe. Watching the girl go red with embarrassment, her mentor quickly apologised and told her that Eugene had never been interested in anyone before this and she was pleased that it was Safina who had drawn his attention. Up until then, most of Eugene's colleagues had put him down as a perpetual bachelor. Safina was about to explain that she was not encouraging the man in any dreamy way, when Virginia held up a hand and stopped her. "I know you have only agreed to have coffee with him, but please, do consider him more than just a coffee-drinking partner. Eugene is a man of many qualities and I know there are dozens of women dying to be with him. Before you make up your mind about him, know that he cares about you and has felt strongly about you from the moment he laid eyes on you," Virginia said.

Before Eugene had walked into her life, Safina had never felt so wanted or cherished. The sixteen years of age difference between her and the professor did not bother her because so far, the kind of life she had experienced had matured her beyond her twenty-four years. What started as a fifteen-minute coffee break at the Tim Horton's on campus ended up being a two-hour long discussion about indigenous cultures. Eugene could talk ceaselessly on the work he was doing, and Safina was captivated by his eloquence and knowledge. Safina was surprised that Eugene was the only person in the new country whom she could count on as a friend. Besides talking about their work and various topics of interest, the two gingerly started bringing up their past experiences into their discussions. Safina was the first to mention her family and Eugene was amazed at the life and the struggles she had gone through.

CHAPTER 8

It was almost time to head back home and get ready. Safina was going out that evening with Eugene to a recital by a Swedish poet. She was already late and to make matters worse, it had started to rain. Grabbing her jacket, Safina took the elevator to the ground floor and was just in time to catch the bus that would take her a couple of blocks close to home. Normally, she would have walked, but since she was late and it was raining, she decided to bus it. When she finally made it home, water squelching in her boots, Safina could see her mother waiting outside the house with Walter. As it was late on a Friday evening, the house was probably locked, with the other girls out. Samantha hardly ever visited Safina and looking at her standing under the awning, her heart sank. Something serious must have happened for her mother to come out in this weather with Walter and wait for her. "Mom, you are soaked! Why did you have to come out in this pouring rain?" Safina said, as she unlocked the door and stood aside for the visitors to enter. Sitting down in the common living area, Samantha looked at Walter, and after a slight nod from him, started to speak. "Safina, I got a call from Zaheer this evening. He has been called to Islamabad," Samantha said, and taking a deep breath, continued, "Mumtaz Bibi has had a stroke and your father called Zaheer." Hearing Zaheer's name and the fact that he was still in touch with her mother hit a sensitive spot in Safina's heart. "I'm sorry to hear that," Safina whispered, leaning against the kitchen counter for support, too distraught to process the news. Samantha's words were drowning in the hard thumping of her heart. She was saying how much Safina loved the older woman and how she had been like a mother to her for all those years. "Loyalty", "kindness", "biggest support", "such an angel" were all words being said by her mother, but Safina could not catch the full sentences.

The doorbell broke the murmur of her mother's sympathetic, unmusical voice and Walter got up to open it. Eugene had come to take her for the recital. Samantha, taken aback to see a male visitor in Safina's life, looked meaningfully at her husband. Walter on the other hand, seemed pleased and somewhat relieved to know that Safina had some friends. "This is Eugene. My mother, Samantha and her husband, Walter," Safina made the delayed introductions. Taking their cue from Eugene's arrival, Samantha and Walter made an excuse of being late for something and left abruptly.

The heaviness of seeing Samantha and Walter, hearing Zaheer's name, and learning about Mumtaz's condition was bearing down on Safina's nerves. There was a buzzing sound in her ears and darkness was closing in. She was finding it hard to breathe and her legs were buckling. Eugene caught her before she crumpled to the floor and laid her on the sofa. When Safina opened her eyes, she could tell that she had been sick. Eugene was wiping her mouth with a paper towel and looked worried. "Did I just throw up?" she said the moment she opened her eyes.

"Nothing to worry about and nothing your knight in shining armour can't handle," Eugene was saying, without even turning up his nose at the strong, sour milk stench. Safina tried getting up, feeling mortified at passing out and throwing up. "I'm taking you to the hospital so that we can get you checked," he said matter-of-factly. Safina sat up, and told him she was fine and that it must have been the turkey sandwich she had for lunch that upset her stomach.

"I'm sorry about the recital. Why don't you go on ahead and I will just rest," she said to Eugene. However, Eugene was in no mood to go without her, and despite Safina's objections, decided on spending the night on the couch. Safina headed downstairs to the basement to shower and Eugene called for food to be delivered.

"It wasn't the lunch that made you sick, was it?" Eugene asked Safina after he had forced her to drink some soup. "I could tell you were uncomfortable around your mother and her husband, and that they had given you some terrible news." Safina did not like talking about her life or the people in it. Her memories were like precious photographs locked inside an album. It was very rare that the album was opened because when it was, Safina could not stop the rush of emotions that coursed through her. However, it had been a long time since someone had asked how she was doing and tried to look past the composed woman they saw. Eugene was trying to reach inside her soul, and this made her eyes sting. The last time someone had tried to do that, she had ended up giving her heart to him. The hot shower and soup had warmed her insides and she felt better. Maybe it was time again to open the pages of the album and look through the memories that were becoming blurred inside.

Eugene cleared the plates and made coffee for them. Holding the mug of coffee with both hands, Safina stared at the steam rising from it. "I used to think I had the perfect life," she started, "and then it all changed. My mother left us and my father became a stranger to me. My little brother suffered in his own way but I was too miserable and confused to console him. The only person who could understand me was my cousin. I used to think he would do anything for me and believed he would always be a part of my life." Eugene sat away from Safina, listening to her and studying the shifting expressions on her face, which, right now, looked vulnerable in the soft glow from the lamp.

The rain had stopped and Eugene got up to make more coffee. While Safina spoke, he had not said a word but listened intently. He knew she had opened up to him after long deliberation, and he respected that. Talking to him was helping Safina reflect and unburden the weight that she carried inside of her. "Eugene, I've often wondered how true the maxim is, which says that children are shadows of their parents?" Safina asked Eugene, drawing him out of his contemplative state.

"I believe it is partly true and partly not," he replied after a thoughtful pause, looking into her hazel brown eyes. "Scientifically, we carry our parents' genes over which we have no control. Our physical and mental framework is based on that. On another level, we inherit our parents' traits and become a manifestation of their personalities. Of course, circumstances and the environment we grow up in, characterize us to become who we are." Safina pondered his words and questioned how much of a reflection of her mother she was. The woman of her childhood, her charming, fun-loving mother, had gotten lost somewhere during the journey from Pakistan to Canada. Was her mother's life with Khodadad a disguise and the real Samantha transpired when she moved back? Was she, Safina

Khanzada, also living a life in camouflage, or was this the real person who was previously waiting to be unleashed from her life in the village? The thought of being a slave to custom and culture in the village amused Safina. She was more a slave to convention living here. She did what everyone else did. She worked, went to school, paid her bills, worried about survival. Then, what was the difference between the two lives she had?

CHAPTER 9

The rain was coming down in torrents and Samantha could not see through the wind screen. She was trying to manoeuvre the car by instinct rather than by looking at the road. She knew that there was a forest on her left and a river to the right, and all she had to do to prevent crashing into either of those was to keep the car in a straight line. But driving in such conditions, where all you could see was a sheet of white water sloshing down on all sides, was proving insufferable. The car kept skidding on the rain slicked road and each time it slid, Samantha would swerve the steering wheel in the opposite direction. She was trying to remember what Khodadad always said to her, "Keep your focus, filter out all sound and concentrate on what you are doing, remember that you are in control." But try as she would, her car would suddenly veer off and she would hold her breath, waiting to either slam into the trees or fall into the unbridled waters of the river. The rain stopped abruptly and she could see the road ahead clearly. Everything looked washed; the trees were a brilliant green, with glossy leaves dripping water and the river was no longer a tempestuous fury but brilliant glass, languid and undisturbed. Samantha looked in the rear-view mirror and recognized Khodadad's Range Rover behind her, with him sitting in the driver's seat. He was looking straight at her and she could tell he was proud of her. She had done exactly as he had instructed, while giving her riding lessons. She had focused; she had learnt how to control. Just when she felt euphoric to have mastered the trick, Khodadad's face clouded and she could see dread in his eyes. Pulling her gaze from the rear-view, Samantha saw that the peaceful sky ahead was no longer placid and instead, ripped unexpectedly, sending a bolt of lightning aimed straight at the car. The jolt sucked the air out of her lungs and plummeted her car into a spiralled frenzy.

Samantha woke with a start, breathless and gasping. Walter had put down the book he was reading on the couch and looked at her intently. His wife was clutching at the bed clothes and had a panicked look on her face. This was not the first time she had had a nightmare. In the beginning whenever she had the dreams, Walter would wake her and try to calm her down. Now, he knew she would wake up eventually and try to make light of it. It had been nine years since they got married and even today, Samantha always cried out Khodadad's name in her sleep. He never asked what her dreams were about, but he knew with an ache that they continually involved her ex-husband.

"Another bad dream, darling?" Walter asked, closing the book and climbing into bed with her.

"It was nothing, really. Just fighting monsters under the bed," Samantha replied in an unsteady voice, trying to laugh it off. Hearing Zaheer's voice that evening had stirred the dying embers from her past and now, suddenly, the fading coals had come to life. It was almost as if she could hear the wind swishing the tree branches in the village, or taste the ripe peaches from her garden. Mumtaz Bibi, Khodadad, Manju Kaka, Viola, even Adam were people from another life. They belonged to a life she could only visit in her dreams, but sadly, those dreams constantly turned into nightmares. In her dreams, Samantha would be consumed with Khodadad's presence, each fibre of her was acutely aware of his existence. It was almost as if she had been swallowed whole and entered his body and surrounded by it, was protected by him in a bubble-like embrace. Samantha would be consumed with guilt after each nightmare episode. In her dreams, she felt safe and protected by Khodadad and was haunted by a desire to be with him. Waking up and finding Walter as the dull reality she now lived with, she despised herself. She was not aware that each time she had her dreams, she called out to Khodadad with longing, desire, and remorse.

Where her feelings for Khodadad were unchanged, Samantha could not understand her daughter's resentment of her. As a girl, Safina had been so close to her, looked up to her in awe and admiration and when Zaheer had given her the news of her arrival, she thought her heart would burst from happiness. However, her daughter had changed. Her feelings for her had changed beyond repair and their reunion felt cold and unfinished. Samantha longed to tell her daughter so many things. Perhaps if Safina listened to her reasons for leaving them, she would be more understanding, but her daughter's attitude towards her did not encourage any heart to heart discussion to follow. Samantha had caught Safina observing her and Walter scores of times, and each time, her daughter had a look of revulsion on her face. What she did not say verbally, her eyes expressed clearly. It was not difficult to understand that she looked down at them with derision, judged them and was filled with loathing. If her sweet, loving Safina held her in such estimation, Samantha shuddered to imagine what Adam must think of her.

Zaheer put the phone down and walked out of the building to the waiting taxi downstairs. It was a spur of the moment decision to call Samantha and let her know about his mother. He had to talk to someone and he wasn't sure if Samantha or Walter would pick up; it was a relief to hear his aunt's voice on the other end. It had been more than three years since he had been to the village and despite calls from his mother and Khodadad, he had always made some excuse and avoided going there. He did not want to be reminded of where he came from or how his life had taken a different course due to circumstances not in his control. Up until now, people had decided his fate. The feudal butchery that took his family from him and left him and his mother at his uncle's mercy, being away in Islamabad not knowing what a family life was, sleeping in dorms amongst strangers who became closer to you than your blood, and now going back to the place which housed too many memories of a life he thought he could have, with people he thought he could call his own, and be in charge of a life he could possess. He was grateful to Khodadad for making sure he did not lack in anything. His education was paid for in full and he was able to accomplish his dream of working for the Foreign Service without having to worry about expenses. The biggest act of kindness Khodadad had indebted him to was taking his mother under his wing. When there was nowhere for her to go, and she was helpless after her husband and sons had been murdered one after the other right in front of her eyes, Khodadad had come to their rescue.

Everything had gone smoothly up until Khodadad told him not to foster ideas of marrying his daughter. Since the time Samantha used to visit him at boarding school and would bring her daughter with her, he had known he wanted to be a part of them. He wanted to be fussed over and have elaborate birthdays, where lights were strung up on trees; he wanted to watch movies with popcorn during long winter nights, huddled under warm blankets; or take walks in the woods, guessing the names of the stars. He looked at Safina and Adam enjoying all these privileges because they belonged to a complete family unit. Their lives were poles apart, where he stayed away from his mother and shared his days amongst strangers. Whenever Aunt Samantha visited him, all the boys at the hostel were fascinated to see him smothered with hugs and kisses by a pretty white woman, accompanied by her daughter. They envied Zaheer of all the candies and board games and winter jackets his aunt brought him. After such visits, Zaheer would lie awake long after all the boys had gone to sleep and think how exquisite Samantha was. She was the perfect woman; she smelt so nice and always wore beautiful shoes and when she walked, her shiny hair bounced on her shoulders. Safina invariably accompanied her mother on these trips, dressed in cool summer frocks, with her dark brown hair held up in a ponytail and always in awe of her older cousin who seemed to know everything.

What started for Zaheer as a childhood fascination with his uncle's family, developed into a deep longing to be a part of their household. The few weeks he spent in the village with them were his happiest. He finally knew what it felt like to have someone ask what you wanted for breakfast, or have someone play dumb charades in the evening with, or have your mother bring hot pistachio milk with honey before tucking you into bed. Closer to the end of the summer break, Zaheer would start dreading his inevitable return to the monotonous, military-style routine of the school he attended. He wished that after dinner one evening, Uncle Khodadad would suddenly announce that he did not have to go back anymore; that the people who had killed his brothers and father had promised to hold their peace and would not harm him. Why couldn't he also get his education from Viola, like Safina and Adam did? But, he knew the answer to that already. He was a fatherless, landless boy who had to stand up in the world on his own two feet. He had to work hard and fine-tune his competitive spirit to succeed in a heartless world. Zaheer also knew that had Khodadad not been there to guide, encourage, and support him, achieving all that would have been impossible.

When Zaheer made that call to Samantha, there was no one else he could think of to share his fear with. He wanted to tell her how lost he would be if something happened to his mother. When Samantha had left so suddenly, everyone was filled with sympathy for Safina and Adam. He would hear remarks such as, "Poor kids, motherless all of a sudden," or "How will they cope, they are so young?" and wonder why no one felt sorry for him. Wasn't he also suffering? Why didn't anyone see that he had lost someone special and very dear to him? And then, quite callously and with no feeling for his sentiments, after years of fostering his dream of belonging to their family in a permanent way, Uncle Khodadad made it clear to him that he should not think about his daughter as a future wife. Why was it that whichever woman filled a hole in his life was denied to him? And now, his mother—his biological mother—might leave him too. Would he be able to survive that loss? Would he ever recover from a third blow?

When Zaheer reached the hospital in Islamabad, he had expected the worst. He was beginning to believe there was a force bent on taking the people he loved away from him. For Mumtaz, who avoided leaving the village at all costs, being brought to Islamabad meant that his mother was too sick to protest coming to the big city. Previously, she had made all sorts of excuses not to accompany Khodadad and his family on their visits, and when all else failed, Mumtaz would put up a fight to be left alone where she belonged. As a boy, Zaheer had wished his mother would visit him at his hostel, but with time, he gave up, knowing she could be as stubborn as a mule when she wanted, and would never come. He found Khodadad sitting on a prayer rug on the floor in the hospital prayer room, his head bent. Zaheer could tell he was crying. He took off his shoes, entered the quiet room, and sat next to his uncle, putting an arm over his shoulders. "Zaheer, I tried to tell her many times to come to Islamabad and see a specialist. She wouldn't listen. You know how she can be. I thought I had lost her when she had the stroke this morning," Khodadad spoke between broken sobs. Zaheer had never seen his uncle cry, and his heart sank to see him reduced to tears. Mumtaz had been experiencing sharp pains in her chest since almost a month and on the village doctor's recommendation,

Khodadad had contacted medical specialists and set up appointments for her in Islamabad. However, no amount of cajoling, persistent reminders, or threats had worked on the woman who had out rightly declared that if she was going to die, it was going to be on her own soil, near the graves of her loved ones who were waiting for her in another world. When Manju Kaka went to Mumtaz's room that morning to give her tea in bed, he found her lying prostrate on the carpet. Within minutes, she was laid back on the back seat of the Range Rover, with Khodadad cradling her head in his lap, and the driver took them at breakneck speed to Islamabad's military hospital. A team of doctors was already waiting to take her to the emergency and after a quick exam, Khodadad was told she had to be rushed into surgery. That was when Khodadad had called Zaheer and asked him to drop everything and come to Pakistan. The four hour long cardiac surgery had gone well, but Mumtaz was in the ICU and in critical condition.

"You can see her now, but please try not to excite her. We want to be careful and will keep her here for another few days," the doctor said to the two men, who had spent the whole night and a good part of the next day waiting to be let inside the ICU. Mumtaz had her eyes closed, and for a moment, Zaheer thought the frown on her forehead was not because she was in pain but at the annoyance at being taken out of the village. Khodadad lifted her hand and touched it to both his eyes and kissed it before putting it down. Mumtaz squeezed his hand slightly, indicating she was aware of him standing next to her. Zaheer, who stood at the foot of the bed, reached under the blanket and placed his hands on his mother's feet, unable to say anything. He had been told that Allah had put "jannah" or paradise, under a mother's feet and right now, he wondered how good a son he had been to deserve such a prize. For the past few years, he had avoided the woman lying in front of him, holding her partly responsible for letting Safina slip out of his life. Had she insisted and put her foot down, she might have swayed Khodadad. But his mother never made the effort, and he always wondered why.

Mumtaz stirred and opened her eyes, and after surveying the room she found herself in, she let her eyes rest on her son. "Zaheer, you came all the way for me. I thought I would leave this world without seeing you for the last time," she said in a feeble voice, so contrasting to the loud, commanding tone she always spoke in. Zaheer could not move and he did not trust his voice to say anything. He simply held onto his mother's feet a little harder and kept his head down.

Khodadad spoke for the first time, "Bibi, you are going to be fine, the doctor said you have a strong heart. Now, you need to get well so that we can go back home and you can make halva for me."

Mumtaz turned her head slightly to look at her cousin, and in a stronger voice, addressed Khodadad, "What happened to me? I remember feeling very tired, then there was a tightness in my chest, and then everything went black. I thought I was dying and felt happy to be going to my maker." Both men exchanged troubled looks, and Zaheer came to his mother's side and broke down for the first time after his father's murder. Too weak to console her son, Mumtaz felt helpless and closed her eyes to push back the pain she felt in her heart, which was not a result of the surgery she had had.

Two weeks later, Mumtaz was finally given a clean bill of health and left for the village with Khodadad and Zaheer. The doctor advised she come to the hospital every four months for a check-up, which Mumtaz dismissed with a wave of her hand. "I am telling you, I will be perfectly all right the moment I leave your hospital. This place has no trees, no fresh air, nothing! When I look out the window, all I see are lifeless concrete buildings. Come to my village and you will see what you are missing. I wake up to the sun coming up from behind the mountains," Mumtaz said to the young doctor who, along with the rest of the hospital staff, were now used to having her give a talking-to to everyone in sight, while going into raptures describing her village. It was a relief to see the old woman back in form and so thrilled to be heading home.

CHAPTER 10

The weather was always beautiful in the village during the summer. Where most of the plains throughout the country experienced scorching, oppressive heat, the air up on the mountains and in the valleys was a balmy, cool breeze. It was the time when flowers would be in full bloom and tree branches would be heavy with fruit. The caretaker of the family orchard would send home crates of the sweetest peaches, and the blackest plums bursting with juice; there would be baskets of soft, ripe apricots and crisp pears nestled carefully in soft hay to prevent bruising, all grown and harvested exclusively for the Khodadad family. The Range Rover turned the last bend in the road leading to the house and Mumtaz asked for the car to be stopped. "Ah, I can smell the peaches from the orchard. Please let me walk home by myself the rest of the way, I want to feel the earth under my feet," she said as she got out of the car after taking off her sandals, then crossed the road barefoot to get to the rusty gate that led to the orchard.

Khodadad put a hand on Zaheer's arm and refrained him from joining his mother. "She will be fine, God willing. Let her be by herself for a while," he said. Khodadad understood that Mumtaz wanted to visit her husband's and her two sons' graves, which were at the far end of the orchard, and would want to spend some time there alone. She had made Khodadad promise to place her next to her husband when the time came. Khodadad shuddered to think how close he had come to fulfilling that promise.

Each person who reached the house had mixed emotions about returning home. Babar, who had stayed back to take care of the business, met them at the gate. On seeing Zaheer, his first reaction was of surprise and then of a detached aloofness. Manju Kaka rushed to Mumtaz and started to cry, trying to say something which was lost in his toothless moans. The walk had tired Mumtaz but she was ecstatic to be home. She looked around the immaculate garden as if she was seeing it for the first time. There was a riot of colour and overwhelming fragrance wherever one looked. Were the flowers already in bloom when she left just a couple of weeks ago? she wondered.

The return to his childhood summer haven was anything but joyous. Zaheer did not want to be reminded of the happy days he had spent here. Where Mumtaz noticed the splendour of colours, everything appeared monochromatic and unappealing to Zaheer. He could not even pretend to be cheerful, and he walked through the main doors of the house as if he were entering a burial chamber. To him, the house appeared to be shrouded in mourning. Lying in his old room at night, he was reminded of the night he had helped Safina escape. He often wondered if he had done the right thing. His motives for helping her leave were anything but selfish. Reuniting Samantha with her daughter was Zaheer's way of repaying his aunt for all the kindness and love she had showed him as a boy. There were times he used to wonder if she was the only person who truly cared for him. His other reason for doing what he did was Safina's distress. He knew she would end up in a loveless marriage, when she would rather be with her mother who would never force her into anything. Mother and daughter needed to be together and he had just been an instrument in bringing it about. But this was not what was worrying him. The thought that he had brought about the reunion behind his uncle's and mother's backs was what bothered him. Had Khodadad not rushed his mother to the hospital in time, he would have no mother today. He owed his mother's life to the man.

Khodadad's generosity in taking him and his mother in when there was no one else willing to do so was fresh in Zaheer's mind. He remembered the early morning when he was told to quickly pack up his things and wait in the principal's office. Mr. Farmaan, who at the best of times looked as if he was about to explode, looked ashen when he came and sat behind the desk in his office. "Zaheer, someone is coming to take you home. There has been a tragedy and you need to be in your village," he said uncomfortably, and with sympathy in his voice. At that moment, Zaheer was not sure what had happened, but on his last trip home, he remembered his father telling Uncle Khodadad that it was not safe for his family to stay there, but Mumtaz refused to leave without him. Uncle Khodadad had suggested that at least Zaheer should continue with his school in Islamabad as it was the safest place for him. He was confused when the driver, Dilawar Bhai, who came to get him, took a different route to reach Khodadad's house. They left the jeep on an unpaved road and made their way across a wobbly rope bridge. The bridge swayed mercilessly and Zaheer had a hard time trying not to throw up. Holding onto the lines was an ordeal; there was a strong breeze and the swinging motion made it necessary to cling to the ropes. After getting off the bridge, they had to walk along a path parallel to the river, which took them to the woods behind the big house. Entering the house from the back door made everything seem different. Previously, he had rarely visited here without his parents, and whenever they came, there was always someone to welcome them and make them comfortable. Today, he was let in through the kitchen door and taken to a back room. The cook, Kaka Manju, then a middle-aged man and much more energetic, told him to have the food laid out on the table, and instructed him not to leave the room at any cost. He was to sleep, and was told that his mother would be with him soon. Kaka Manju locked the room on his way out. Zaheer remembered waking up to the sound of the room being unlocked. He must have slept for a long time because it was dark outside. The door opened to let his mother and uncle Khodadad's father, whom he called Agha ji, in. He recalled rushing to his mother to hug her and who looked like she had been crying; he wanted to hold her close and tell her he would make whatever was making her sad all right. Agha ji sat down, and taking his hand in his, spoke to him, "Zaheer, you are not a boy anymore. You must listen to what I have to say. The people from the eastern villages raided your house. There was a long-standing land dispute between them and your father. There was an argument during a meeting between the elders in which your baba and Qasim and Ibrar lost their lives last night. Look at me, Zaheer. I promise you, we are going to find the people who did this and take our revenge," he said looking in his eyes, but the rest of his words were lost to Zaheer because all he could understand was that his father and brothers were killed.

He did not remember Khodadad entering the room, but noticed him when he spoke. "Zaheer, you have to be strong. You will stay here for a few days and then go back to your school and work hard so that one day, you can be bigger than the people who did this to your family," he said.

Zaheer stayed in the small room with his mother for the next few days. Kaka Manju would bring them their meals and mother and son would console each other. Most of the time, his mother cried and prayed with her eyes closed, at other times, she would tell Zaheer that he had to stay away from the people who did this and go back to school.

And Zaheer had done just that. He had channelled his grief in excelling at school. He worked harder than anyone else and kept reminding himself that he had to overcome his loss by achieving distinction in both his courses and in sports. Khodadad was his biggest source of encouragement and along with his school expenses, would finance his after-school programs, taking a keen interest in everything Zaheer did. Where he might have lacked the harmony of family life, Zaheer's days were filled with school work and his evenings with martial arts training, riding, or fencing. Furthermore, Khodadad arranged for a tutor from the Alliance Francaise to give Zaheer private French lessons and Zaheer would look forward to the summers when he would practice his language skills with Viola, making the Frenchwoman proud with the progress he made each year. The favours Khodadad had bestowed on him were countless, and they continued long after he had finished school and started his career as a junior diplomat. Zaheer had shown an interest in taking up global studies, and before long, his uncle, true to his generosity, had sent him to Paris for a year to study at the Sorbonne. Later, Zaheer received a scholarship to do his Masters from the University of Berlin, and as a reward for getting a scholarship, Khodadad gifted him with a five-week paid trip across Europe. And now, his uncle had saved his mother's life. Zaheer turned in bed, unable to put out of his mind that in trying to reciprocate the love given to him by Samantha and Safina, he had in fact, deceived his saviour.

Eugene waited for Safina to finish her work and sat chatting with a faculty member outside the office. It was Safina's twenty-fourth birthday and he was taking her and Virginia out for dinner. Since it was her final semester before she got her graduate degree, Safina was pushing herself to bring her dissertation to a close. Observing the blueprints of her treatise one day, Eugene had marvelled at the amount of time, research, and dedication that had gone into producing it. She had been working ceaselessly lately, and had to be forced to make time to go out tonight. Eugene was relieved to see the ladies finally emerge from the office; he was getting bored listening to the doddering old professor of classics talk about Homer's *Odyssey* as a prelude to modern-day politics. And besides, they were late for dinner. "Reservations are for eight-thirty. Let's hope we don't get stuck in traffic and make it on time," he said, starting his Mercedes. They reached Toronto's Commercial District and went to Drake One-Fifty for dinner. Eugene had ordered a sumptuous meal of their rotisserie bird in Tennessee hot sauce, with grilled baby carrots and courgettes, snow crab and the baked black cod. At the end of their meal, the maître d'hôtel surprised Safina when the band started playing happy birthday, and all the patrons joined in. Later, they went to the Tsujiri Tea House for dessert. It was late when they left the tea house, holding waffle ice-cream cones, which the restaurant was famous for, and walked the few blocks to where Eugene had parked his car. It had been a perfect evening and Safina was light-headed at being spoilt with her friends' attention. Birthdays had been such a fuss when she was growing up, and it was after many years that she celebrated one with so much interest. They were passing by a coffee shop when Safina stopped moving forward abruptly. Coming out of the shop was Zaheer, with a woman leaning on his arm. The woman, a stunning brunette in high heels and clearly a little drunk, was whispering something in Zaheer's ear. Eugene and Virginia stopped, wondering what was holding Safina up. They looked back at her and noticed she looked suddenly very pale as she focused on the couple emerging from the coffee shop. Eugene called out to Safina and upon hearing her name, Zaheer stopped mid-way from replying to the woman and turned to look at her. An eerie stillness descended onto the group and for Safina, the world seemed to be shrinking. Disengaging himself from his date, Zaheer came forward and looked at the woman of his dreams. "Hello Safina. I was not expecting to find you here. Happy birthday."

When Safina didn't respond, Eugene came to her rescue and introduced himself. "You two must be very close for you to know its Safina's birthday today. Hello, I'm Eugene and this is Virginia," he said extending his hand.

By this time, Safina had overcome her initial shock and recovering, introduced Zaheer to her friends. "We have known each other since we were kids. I was just very surprised to see him after so many years," she explained laughingly to everyone, trying to hide her embarrassment. The brunette, who seemed slightly ignored and very uninterested with the proceedings, excused herself and left in a taxi, which Zaheer engaged for her. On Eugene's suggestion that they all sit down for some coffee and let the birthday celebrations continue, the party walked down to the nearest Tim Horton's and settled in awkward silence around a table in a corner. Zaheer had recovered from this unexpected surprise, and being the diplomat he was, started regaling the group with his adventures in Africa and Europe. He had been working in Canada on a project since a few weeks and was out celebrating the successful close of a complex assignment.

During all this time, Safina stayed very quiet. Eugene and Virginia knew Safina well enough to recognize that the pair shared some history together, which was making her uncomfortable. Zaheer's forced show of casualness and dry humour, and his avoidance of looking directly at Safina was their cue to leave the two alone. "Eugene, I think its best we take off. These two are seeing each other after a long time and might have some catching up to do," Virginia suggested to their host, "Zaheer, I trust you will make sure Safina reaches home safely and at a decent hour," she added. Safina was not at all happy about her friends leaving her and protested that Zaheer must have work to do and she should be heading out as well.

"I will be a true gentleman and make sure the lady gets home safe. I would like to gossip with my cousin for a bit," Zaheer ignored Safina's objection and answered Virginia.

After a few minutes of stillness where both were contemplating how to break the silence, Safina spoke. "How is Bibi now? I heard she was very sick."

Zaheer looked at Safina for the first time since they came into the restaurant. She looked older, more mature and even more beautiful than he remembered. Her hair was shorter now and the glow from the overhead light caught copper tones in her dark brown hair. There was a kind of Grecian exquisiteness to her features; her widow's peak appeared more

MEerifying

prominent with her dark hair pushed back from her forehead into a knot at the nape of her neck. She wore no makeup yet her skin glowed with a radiance giving her an innocent, unsullied look. Her smooth, heart shaped face looked so vulnerable, almost as if she would crumple and break down any moment. It would be so easy to hold her face in his hands and lose himself in those eyes, Zaheer thought. He will need to tread with care. A wrong word and he knew those hazel eyes, which right now looked so reproachful would tear up. "She gave us all a scare. You know how she is, she doesn't believe in taking medication of any kind. I think the stroke was just waiting to happen. Uncle Khodadad took her to the hospital in time for the surgery," he replied. "Tell me, how you are doing and what is going on in your life."

Safina told him about the work she was doing and how lucky she was to have found a mentor in Virginia. She wanted to continue doing research in history and concentrate in tribal dynamics of the Ottoman period and how they shaped modern day Turkey. Safina knew she had to ask Zaheer why he did not reply to her calls or responded to her innumerable letters. There were many unanswered questions in her mind and she did not know where to start. Sensing her uncertainty, Zaheer brought up the matter himself. "I know you must be angry at me for not trying to reach out to you." Zaheer paused, noting the pained look in Safina's eyes before continuing. "I did not want to give you false hopes, Safina. You have been and always will be very dear to me. When Uncle Khodadad made it clear there would be no possibility of a future for us together, I moved on. I had to move on. As an old friend, I suggest you should let go of the past and do the same." Safina knew Zaheer's words had put finality on anything that they had previously. He was always so sensible and level-headed; he could see things in a practical and detached sort of way—something she could never do. Safina may have deceived her father by leaving secretly, but she was still his daughter, and as such, she had his pride. Taking a deep breath and looking straight into Zaheer's eyes, she got up from the table smiling. Her eyes were dry and her chin was up. Suddenly, she did not look vulnerable anymore. Zaheer knew she was signalling an end to their discussion and he suggested they call a taxi so he could drop her home.

"I'm not a little girl anymore who needs someone to help her cross the bridge, Zaheer. I can make it home by myself. Thank you, Zaheer and goodbye," saying this, Safina wrapped her coat closer to her body and walked out of the cozy warmth of the restaurant and into the gusty October night of the street outside.

CHAPTER 11

It was after 1 a.m. when the taxi turned into Safina's street. What an overwhelming day it had been, she mused. A roller coaster ride of emotions; the rush of adrenalin to complete her work for the day, the pleasure of being indulged and cared for by close friends and finally, the wretchedness of heartbreak and wounded pride. It had been a pitiful end to a day which was going so well until she saw Zaheer coming out of the coffee shop, a strange woman clinging to his arm and whispering in his ear. Getting out of the taxi, Safina noticed a familiar black Mercedes parked at some distance. "What? Are you stalking me, Eugene? It's past one in the morning!" Safina exclaimed, laughing. Eugene had gotten out of his car and was briskly walking towards her with a sheepish grin on his face. She had never felt so happy to see someone as she did right now, and she held him in a tight hug. This was the first time Safina had ever held Eugene and he felt a surge of exhilaration at this unexpected display of emotion.

"I wanted to make sure you came home safe; you had suddenly gone so quiet and thoughtful," he replied. He did not want to ask why Zaheer did not come to drop her off or that he could tell that she needed a friend after the chance reunion he witnessed just a couple hours ago.

Safina invited Eugene in for coffee; she was in the mood for company and it was the weekend, so they could afford to stay up late. Safina thought it was funny that whenever she needed to be with someone after an emotional turmoil, Eugene just happened to be there. Right now, she was more than grateful for his presence.

As they settled down on the living room couches with hot coffee, Eugene sat observing Safina. "So, this was the cousin who helped you change your life. I can see that you were not prepared to meet him like this," he started, to which Safina shrugged her shoulders and didn't say anything. "I don't want to probe, but Safina, it is obvious you were hurt and disappointed tonight. Look, I think you already had the answers to the questions that came to mind when you saw your childhood friend. After hearing them from him, and recognizing where you both stand will make it easier for you to let go of the ghosts from your past," he said to Safina, who was thoughtfully staring into her cup of coffee. Eugene was an observant man and it was easy for him to perceive from the charged air at the table that Safina and Zaheer either had to come together defying all obstacles, or let go of memories of each other and move on in their lives. Eugene continued and said that Zaheer had or was trying to move on. He had shrugged off whatever held him back and Safina needed to do the same. When Safina continued to stay silent, Eugene went on. "As far as that woman you saw with him, you have to understand Zaheer is a diplomat. He is young and refined and good looking, to say the least; there will always be women around him. I wish you don't let your mind dwell on that." Safina thought she detected the slightest trace of a pleading tone in Eugene's voice. The man truly cared about her and her feelings. He did not attempt to make Zaheer the bad guy or put him down. Instead, he tactfully tried to make her see the circumstances from Zaheer's standpoint. It would have been so instinctive for Eugene to have talked critically of her cousin but instead, he had tried to lessen Safina's hurt by making light of it.

Listening to Eugene made Safina feel better. He had tried to show her things from a different perspective. Seeing that Safina was considerably less gloomy and smiling again, Eugene yawned widely and decided to leave. "I only came because I couldn't let a pretty girl go to bed feeling so miserable on her birthday," and saying that, he left Safina.

CHAPTER 12

Safina reached a hand out to turn off the alarm. She had set it for 6 a.m. the night before to wake up early and get a head start on working at fine tuning her dissertation. Surprisingly, last night she had not lain in bed going over the details of the evening. Instead, after the therapeutic conversation with Eugene, she had felt light and somewhat relieved, almost as if a weight had been lifted off her. It made sense why Zaheer had tried to detach himself from her, and she was content to let the past be. Safina thought to give herself another hour before getting up and turning around, fell asleep instantly.

Safina woke to the sound of somebody pounding on the door. It couldn't be a dream; somebody really was knocking, or rather, trying to break the door down. Throwing her housecoat over her pyjamas, Safina quickly went upstairs from the basement. The rest of the girls were either away for the weekend or were sleeping off late drinking parties to notice the noise.

When she opened the door, Safina found a patrol car parked in the driveway and two policemen standing outside. "Good morning. We would like to see Miss Safina Khanzada?" the tall Nordic-looking one said, towering above her. Safina's heart sank; she could not recall violating any rules to be dragged out of bed by the police on an early Saturday morning. And surely the men asking for her were not here to wish her a belated happy birthday.

"Hi. Yes, my name is Safina," she replied. The policemen asked Safina to change her clothes and come with them to the police station. They wouldn't give her any reasons why.

When she reached the station, Safina found Virginia sitting on one of the hard metal chairs, and one could easily tell she had also been dragged out of bed. Seeing Safina enter the precinct, Virginia got up and rushed to her, holding her in a tight embrace. The older woman was trembling uncontrollably. "Safina, how could this happen! I find it so unbelievable!" sobbed Virginia, clinging onto her shoulder. Safina pulled herself away forcibly, unable to comprehend what was happening and asked Virginia to explain what the matter was.

The inspector sat down with the women. He needed a statement. Eugene Russo was met with an accident last night, or at two-thirty in the morning, to be exact. His car had gone over the Fulham Bridge; it did not seem like foul play but rather, a hit and run. They were keeping an eye out for any witnesses. The police could not understand how it could have happened. The road was clear at that time, there was no rain, and the victim had no traces of alcohol. Since Safina and Virginia had been the last people to see Dr. Russo, the police wanted to know if they knew anything that could help them understand the cause of the accident. They wanted to know if the victim was going through some mental breakdown or had been suicidal.

Safina explained to the police how she was surprised to see Eugene at her door when she came back from the Tim Horton's, and that they had chatted for about an hour before he left at around two-fifteen in the morning. If anything, Eugene had been cheerful throughout the evening and a perfect guest. Safina added that they had met with an old friend of hers as well but Eugene and Virginia left shortly after they met in the street by chance. Virginia corroborated her story and added that Eugene was a very good driver and never drank alcohol, especially when he was going to be behind the wheel. The women were allowed to leave after giving their statements, with a promise to call if anything came to mind.

Leaving the building, the women walked to a tiny Italian restaurant to share each other's grief over the unexpected loss of their dear friend. They sat in an indiscreet corner and held each other's hands across the table. The thought of Eugene's death had shocked them beyond words and they clung to each other for support. Safina recalled how Eugene's face had glowed when she had held him just a few hours ago. She knew he cared deeply for her, and was perhaps even in love with her, but did not want to push her to reciprocate his feelings. He wanted her to let go of her emotional baggage and be free of the guilt which she carried like a millstone around her neck.

For a woman who hardly ever displayed feeling, Virginia was white as a sheet and still trembling. The hands that Safina held were cold and rigid. She had known Eugene far longer than Safina and their friendship went a long way. "Eugene has always been a part of my life," Virginia finally said when she had calmed down a bit. "We went to the same school; my baby brother and he were best friends, and then we moved apart when work or university took us in different directions. But no matter where we were, we always knew what was happening in the other's lives." Virginia took a deep breath and paused for a moment before continuing. "When Keith lost his life in the Gulf War, I thought life had come to an end. I was still in university at the time and had to take a year off. Eugene, who was himself suffering inside, came to rescue me. He quit school and moved to Ithaca to be with me and slowly nursed me back to life. Safina, he taught me so many lessons in life about giving and sacrifice that I can't even keep count of," Virginia said, as a fresh wave of tears fell down her face, spilling onto the red and white chequered table cloth. Hearing Virginia talk about Eugene and his generosity made Safina realize that he was one of the few who gave of themselves completely to others. He had strived to make her pick up and move on, and gave freely of his time, asking nothing in return. This was the second time in her life that Safina lost someone who gave meaning to her existence. She was not sure if she could get over the loss and fill the void it left in her.

It was time to do something for someone other than herself, thought Safina. She could not let Virginia suffer all alone in her house in a secluded Toronto suburb, and decided to stay with her and do what Eugene would have done. It felt strange to think about Eugene, trying to do what he would have done and knowing he was the reason for her trying to care for Virginia. It had been almost eight hours since the women had been jolted out of their sleep, and it was time to head home. "Virginia, I will be coming to stay with you for a few days. I think we could both use each other's company. Let me just pick up some of my stuff from my place, and then we can head out to your home," said Safina. The older woman was too distraught to object and besides, they both needed each other more than anything else.

Adam looked at his watch for the second time. He had been waiting for the man to show up for about thirty minutes, and Adam wasn't a man who liked to be kept waiting. When the detective came out of the building, Adam signalled for him to get in the car with him. "I hope you were able to do what I asked," Adam said, putting the car into drive and pulling out of the parking lot. He hardly drove anymore, but whenever he came abroad, he enjoyed driving the sports cars he loved so much. His trips to North America and Europe were becoming more frequent lately as Khodadad had delegated most of his responsibility on his son's shoulders, and Adam had taken the initiative and expanded their gem export and timber business to other countries. Babar accompanied Adam on most of his trips, but this time, Adam left him behind on purpose. There were things he had to take care of which Babar did not need to know about. The detective knew better than to beat around the bush and came straight to the point.

"I made sure no one saw me. It was late at night and no one was around," he said. Hearing that, Adam handed him the packet of cash and dropped his passenger off at the next intersection, driving off at high speed in a state of satisfaction.

Adam weaved through the downtown traffic and reached the low rent student housing area. He parked the Mercedes-Benz AMG SL across from the park overlooking Safina's house. Safina and the woman, Adam looked at the file in front of him and read the name scribbled on it—Dr. Virginia Ambrose—came out of the house, with Safina holding a small suitcase and a knapsack. They got into the car that was parked in the driveway and headed east. The file had enough details in it for Adam to know where they were headed.

The silver Mercedes unobtrusively made its way into the exclusive neighbourhood. The streets were lined with red maples and ancient oak trees, giving the area a homely, lived-in look. Virginia's house was at the far end of the survey and overlooked Lake Ontario in the distance. The lights in the house were turned on and after a while, the lights in the upper floor also lit up in two rooms, indicating the women had settled in for the night. It had been a long day for all of them, he thought with a grimace. There was not much he could do now, and it seemed pointless to waste a beautiful night lying in wait. Adam revved up the engine, taking pleasure in the powerful sound and headed west.

CHAPTER 13

"**S**o, you could not do what you initially set out to do and that is making you feel as if you lost, is that right?" the petite doctor looked at Zaheer, amused at his uneasiness. The man sitting in front of her had been coming to her for the past few months and was a complex man to read. Immaculately dressed and irresistibly good-looking, he had the air of a man who had always got what he wanted. It was a source of amazement for Zaheer to realize that his charm was ineffective in drawing the doctor out of her professional detachment. Secondly, for a man who had always taken his achievements for granted, he was unable to come to terms with his inability to see his plans fall into place. "Did you think that randomly finding you on the street with a gorgeous woman would be enough for her to start having feelings for you again? Did you believe your love was so potent that she would want to be with you after so many years of you deliberately ignoring her?" the psychologist questioned him. Zaheer, who was hardly ever lost for words, was finding it difficult to come up with an answer that would convince both him and Dr. Marion. "This is the same woman who defied her father, the society she grew up in and against all odds, made it to Canada—albeit with your help, of course—and is now on her way to achieving a graduate degree, all on her own, right?" The doctor's piercing black eyes bored into Zaheer's head. It was obvious he had underestimated Safina. When he had planned on accidentally bumping into her, he had expected a more animated encounter with his boyhood passion. However, Safina had taken him by surprise and responded with dispassionate disdain and reproach. She had not even shown the slightest bit of resentment at finding him with the woman he had engaged for this purpose. Things were not going as he had expected. This was a feeling he was not used to experiencing, and it bothered him.

At the end of his twice a month session, Zaheer got up to leave. "I'm guessing you did not give Safina the impression that you are still in love with her. If you did, you would be ruining her chance at any happiness she may have, as well as yours," Dr. Marion said as looked at her patient and wondered how he was able to dupe everyone with his show of self-assurance and charisma. Inside Zaheer Farhan Khattak was a man who was unsure about his value in the eyes of people he cared for. But, there were ghosts he had inherited from his ancestors which would not let him be.

Safina quietly closed the door to the bedroom. Virginia had finally fallen asleep after tossing and turning in bed for the past hour or so. The two women had kept each other company for the weekend. Safina was due to go back to her house the next day, but wasn't at all sure if she could leave her friend in the state she was in. Since the day they had been called to the police station, Virginia was unable to get over the blow of losing Eugene. Safina had spent the past two nights trying to console her through bouts of weeping, verging on hysteria. On the first night, Virginia had pulled out old photo albums and had shown Safina pictures of Keith and Eugene as boys. There were photographs of their high school graduation and of summer vacations at the beach, where the sunburnt faces of the boys reminded Safina of the kids from the village. There were so many memories locked inside those albums, and both women pored over them the whole night, sometimes crying and sometimes laughing. Tonight, Virginia had a fever and Safina worried that her grief was taking its toll on her health. Entering her room, she left her door ajar to be able to hear Virginia if she called her in the night. "I have to be strong for both of us," Safina said out loud to convince herself. She tried not to think about Eugene, but it was not easy. He had become such an integral part of her life and his untimely death had left Safina feeling shattered and alone.

Safina sat down to look at her notes for her thesis. She had to block out all thoughts to take charge of the task at hand. There was still a lot of work to be done and Safina worked through the night, falling asleep in the middle of editing her document. Waking up with a start at the sound of Virginia crying out in her sleep, Safina rushed to the next room to soothe her friend. Virginia was sweating profusely and talking incoherently in her sleep. The bedclothes were on the floor and judging from the contorted expression on her face, it was apparent she was going through a bad dream. "Wake up Virginia! It's just a dream. Wake up, please!" Safina gently shook Virginia's shoulder.

The woman woke up with a start and looked at Safina with a disoriented look on her face. "They couldn't pull Keith out from under the rubble! They took too long to save my baby! Oh, Safina, he was in so much pain!" wailed the woman. How was she to ease Virginia's pain? Safina wondered. She was reminded of a similar time of horror very long ago when, on her birthday, her father had been brought into the house, bleeding from bullet wounds. Her mother had howled and doubled up in pain to see her husband like that. Bibi, who was just as distressed to see her cousin haemorrhaging on the marble tiles had kept her cool, and taken charge calming Samantha down and assisting Dr. Yakov with the surgery.

Safina thought it was time to give of herself completely to her mentor. She realized up until then she had only lived for herself; dealing with the absence of her mother, learning to live with the bitter knowledge that Zaheer and her were never meant to be together, and putting her work before anything else. She would also live with the regret of letting down her father and Mumtaz Bibi and of not reciprocating Eugene's sentiments. Perhaps doing something for another person would fill the emptiness that followed her like a shadow wherever she went.

Coming downstairs in the morning, Safina found Virginia at the kitchen counter squeezing juice out of pink grapefruits. She had something cooking on the stove and the table was laid. "What are you up to, Virginia? You should be in bed!" Safina exclaimed. Virginia's face looked drawn and pale. There were dark circles around her eyes and she seemed to have aged at least five years within the past two days.

"I've been a very negligent host. You are just as much in mourning as I am and I've been behaving as if Eugene was only my friend," Virginia said looking up. "Thank you for being here for me. It really means a lot. Now, sit down and let me spoil you a little," she added with a weak smile.

Virginia had had time to think and had decided to take a few months off from work. She said she needed time to herself and would go on a vacation, perhaps on a cruise somewhere to get her mind off things. She was going to be looking into booking her tickets as soon as she could get away.

Safina sat pondering what Virginia had said and thought this was perhaps the best option she had if she was to bounce back to life. Looking at her friend with a grin on her face, Safina surprised the older woman. "When you book your tickets, book for two," she said. Virginia, who was not prepared for Safina to leave her education at the point she was at, thought she misheard.

"Are you suggesting coming along with me? But what about school?" she asked. It took a while for Safina to convince Virginia that she was not changing her mind, whether Virginia agreed to the idea or not. Once she did, both women burst into laughter at the prospect of getting away from everything to lose themselves in a stress-free and changed environment.

It had been a peaceful flight and Adam woke with a start when the cute flight attendant woke him to buckle his seat belt. He had hardly slept since the past two weeks and had been knocked out for most of the duration of the flight. It felt good to be coming back. He hated being away from Pakistan for too long. He wondered sometimes if he could just delegate his work abroad to Babar, but he knew that was not possible. Babar was not ready yet. When Adam had returned from England after completing his degree in political science almost four years ago, he had taken upon himself to relieve Babar of some of the tasks he had taken up to assist Khodadad. Adam had forced Babar to complete his education privately and even made him stay in Lahore to study under a tutor known to help students pass exams through crash courses. Babar had finally completed his bachelor's degree and had returned to the village, resuming the life he had before. Where previously he had accompanied Khodadad on his trips, he now stuck around with Adam.

Right now, Babar had come to pick up Adam from the airport. The two had a few days of work in Islamabad and were heading back to the village after that. "Are my dad and Bibi alright?" Adam asked his childhood friend the moment he sat in the car.

"Yes they are well. Agha ji and I went out hunting for three days, but had to return early because he got the fever again," Babar informed Adam. Lately, his father had not been keeping too well and this was worrying

Adam. He would come down with a high-grade fever every few days, which would leave him too weak to even get out of bed. "Bibi has been asking him to see a specialist in Islamabad, and even volunteered to come with him," added Babar with a smile, "but he said he would wait until you got back." Khodadad, who had now opted to live a semi-retired life, relied on his son not only to take care of his business but also everything that concerned the people in the house. Most of Khodadad's time was spent either in the library or in the *dera*, where he settled the affairs of the locals of the village and surrounding area. He now went with the moniker Agha ji, like his father many years ago, denoting age, wisdom and respect amongst the people in the village. His father's health worried Adam. The days Khodadad was too sick to leave his room, Adam would stay home, personally catering to each of his needs. At such times, even Mumtaz would give up and let the son have his way. Adam would work from home, with his workers coming to the library to take instructions and Babar managing the affairs outside.

For all his show of hardiness, when it came to his father, Adam would fret and worry like a mother of an infant. He hated to see his father laid up, and would stay up nights if his father needed him. "You need to get yourself a wife so that you don't have to worry about me all the time, Adam," Khodadad said to Adam one night as he sat in his father's room reading, while his father slept through a fever. "You should have your own family to take care of." The fact was, Adam's love and care for him had more than made up for the hurt Samantha and Safina had given him. The son's devotion to his father was known throughout the village, and parents set him as an example for their children of what a good son should be. It was not uncommon to hear someone remark on Adam's absence from business because of his father.

Upon hearing about his father's illness, Adam decided to postpone his meeting with the trade minister. There was always time to come back for the export permits that needed to be signed and registered at the ministry. Babar was not at all surprised when Adam told the driver to head the car to the village instead of their home at the base of the Margalla Hills in Islamabad. It was close to one in the morning when the Lexus SUV pulled into the driveway, and even though Adam had been travelling for more than thirty hours, he headed straight to his father's room. Khodadad was fast asleep when he stole into his room and stood looking at his father in the soft glow from the night lamp. Sensing someone standing by the bed, Khodadad stirred and opened his eyes. "Adam! When did you get home? I wasn't expecting you until Thursday," exclaimed Khodadad, trying to sit up in bed. Adam did not want to tell him he was worried about his health and instead made up an excuse that the meeting with the minister had been postponed. "But it took you months to set up that up. How could the minister just move it forward? This is very unprincipled! I will mention this to the Home Secretary," Khodadad replied, sounding furious.

Adam sat down on the bed, and taking his father's hand in his, kissed it. "Baba, please don't do that. The truth is, I was missing home and wanted to be here. I will reschedule for next week, don't worry," he told his father. Khodadad understood his son had returned on his account and his heart filled with a wave of love and tenderness for him. This was not the first time he knew Adam had dropped everything to be with him.

Khodadad was feeling well enough the next day to go and sit under the gazebo in the rose garden. The old gardener had died to be replaced with his son, who was a younger version of his father. He had the same slouch from years of bending over plants and hedges and worked with the same leisurely speed his father did. It was a beautiful October morning and Khodadad was glad to be outside. Khodadad was reminded of the time Safina used to sit for hours on the same seats working on a sketch. She would work quietly and Khodadad would watch her silently from the window of the library. His daughter reminded him so much of her mother. She had the same light brown eyes, which showed specks of gold in the sunlight. Safina had inherited her mother's elegance in the way she walked or the way her face would light up when she saw something that pleased her. Adam, on the other hand, was a replica of him, Khodadad thought with some joy. And even though the siblings were different in some ways, they both had had their share of the sorrow of losing their mother at a young age, bringing them closer than was apparent. Where Safina had closed herself to the world outside, Adam had gone headlong and taken life by the horns to deal with his pain.

Manju Kaka, who was as old as the mountains surrounding the village, brought Khodadad his breakfast of oat porridge with dried apricots and honey, both from the Khodadad orchard, on a mosaic tray that Adam had brought from his last trip to Barcelona. While putting the tray down, he noticed that Khodadad was slumped to one side and breathing heavily. He dropped the tray with a clatter, sending porridge and blue and white pieces of ceramic all over the gazebo floor. Upon hearing the noise, the gardener rushed to where they were and saw Kaka Manju pale as a sheet, and Khodadad slumped in an awkward position. The gardener ran to the kitchen door, screaming for all to hear that Agha ji had fainted. Mumtaz Bibi's screams could be heard all the way to the annexe across from the kitchen and upon hearing them, Babar was the first to sprint to the garden. Adam, whose room was at the back of the house, heard the commotion after a few minutes and rushed out through the breakfast room window to find the whole house gathered around the gazebo, with Babar carrying his father in his arms towards the kitchen entrance of the house.

Without wasting any time, Khodadad was put in the back of one of the Range Rovers, with Babar at the wheel. Adam sat cradling his father's head in his lap, while the jeep made its way to Islamabad at break neck speed. Another jeep followed behind with Mumtaz and Manju Kaka, who found it impossible to stay back.

The drive to Islamabad was proving difficult as suddenly, the balmy weather of an October morning turned into torrential rain. Several years ago, Khodadad had pushed the civil government for the construction of a metal road from Islamabad to the northern areas and because of that, it was possible to cover the distance in three hours instead of five. However, the rain was making the roads slippery and several times, the four-wheel drive teetered close to the edge of the mountain, taking them down to the plains.

CHAPTER 14

Dr. Amir Pervaiz called Adam into his office. He was the medical specialist at Shifa Hospital in Islamabad and was the son of one of Khodadad's friend, who was from a neighbouring village. "Agha Ji's reports are showing weakness of the immune system, and that's probably the cause of the recurrent fever. We will need to conduct some more tests to rule out anything else," the doctor informed Adam. "You can go and see Agha Ji now. He is waiting for you."

Adam entered his father's room. A nurse was writing something on a chart and looked up and smiled at him before leaving the room. There was a heart monitor and an I.V. attached to Khodadad, and his eyes were closed. Adam went up to his father and lifted his hand to his lips. The older man opened his eyes and gave a weak smile. "I am being such a nuisance. You are still in your jet lag and I know you will not leave my side until I'm out hunting again. What kind of a father am I to put you through so much hassle?" Khodadad said to his son.

"Baba, please don't talk so much. You know I would rather be near you than anywhere else," he replied, tears coming to his eyes. "Don't ever question what kind of a father you are." Khodadad squeezed his son's hand and closed his eyes to go back to sleep.

Adam had sent Mumtaz and Kaka Manju to the Margalla house. They had spent the whole day at the hospital sitting in the lobby, praying for Khodadad and now looked washed out. Adam also sent Babar home, saying he would come for a shower and nap in the morning. The doctors had sedated Khodadad and he slept through most of the night. A nurse came in every half hour to check up on him. There was a sofa in the hospital's private room and Adam made himself comfortable on it with his feet up on another seat. Adam woke to the sound of his father mumbling in his sleep. The nurse was standing next to him checking his pulse and motioned for Adam to be quiet. Khodadad was having another bout of high grade fever and was delirious. It was difficult to understand what he was saying but one could make out the words "Safina" and "sorry" in his feverish mutterings. Adam felt a lump in his throat. His father hardly ever mentioned his sister's name and for him to call out to her in his sleep, meant the pain of her leaving them was still fresh in his heart. The nurse added some medication to the I.V. bag and left the room, saying she would return shortly. A few minutes later, Khodadad appeared to have calmed down. His breathing was normal and his body did not burn anymore. Adam left the room to get some air and met the nurse at the door. "I think his fever has gone down now," he told the nurse, "I hope it doesn't come back again." The nurse asked Adam to rest as he looked just as bad as his father. Adam returned to the room after a short stroll in the hospital lawn and found Khodadad sleeping peacefully.

Another nurse woke Adam gently in the morning, saying that the doctor would be making his rounds soon. Khodadad was awake and sitting up in bed and was troubled to find his son curled up uncomfortably on the sofa. "I won't stay here another day if you continue fussing about me like this. You are going home right this minute and getting some rest," ordered Khodadad, his voice firm and final. Just then, the doctor walked in and seconded Khodadad's order, saying that Dr. Pervaiz wouldn't be coming in until after noon, so it was best that Adam did as his father suggested. Unable to refute his father, Adam reluctantly left for the house to send Babar in his place.

The hot shower and breakfast had chased away all tiredness and sleep from Adam. Instead of going to bed for a nap, he walked through the house, remembering the days he had spent there as a kid when his life had some semblance of normality. He vaguely remembered the colourful parties his parents used to hold there and how different the house looked then. Flowers used to be placed on every available table and there would be music and laughter in the house. And although the caretaker family kept everything clean and aired, the house had taken on the look of a barren, colourless tomb. The furniture in most of the rooms was covered in white sheets and some of the rooms, such as his mother's suite, were locked. "I want all the rooms to be opened immediately," Adam ordered the couple who looked after the house. "Everything needs to be dusted and cleaned, and the windows opened to let the air in."

The house had been cleaned and the locked rooms had been unlocked. Adam walked into his father's study. As a child, he had been forbidden to enter the room, which used to overwhelm him at the time. The windows, which overlooked the Margalla Hills had been opened to let in the air. Everything looked the same as he remembered. Adam sat behind his father's antique desk and ran a hand over the intricate African carving. The table, which was a work of art in the fragrant Thuya wood had been a gift to his grandfather from a Moroccan ambassador. Adam opened the top drawer of the table and his eyes fell on a leather binder with "KWK" embossed in gold on it. Hesitating for a moment, Adam pulled out the folder and placed it on the desk.

The folder was his father's journal, Adam realized, with dated entries made in an untidy hand. The journal started when his mother, Samantha, was pregnant with Safina and reading it, Adam could hear the joy in his father's writing. His love for his wife and his devotion to his family in the village were all apparent in the words that followed one after the other. There was the year that he was born. The entry read: "Adam Wali Khanzada entered the world today. I feel my joy is complete. I thank Allah for His blessings." Another entry read, "Taking Saman and Safina to the village for the first time. Allah, make things easy for me. You have taken all my family from me. Help me with the responsibility you have placed on my shoulders." Several years ahead, the writing in the journal was even messier. It was the year Safina had left the country. A long entry read, "I wish I had listened to my daughter and not forced her into getting married. I should have let her continue her studies in some university abroad like Adam, instead of being tied down to someone." Further down, it read, "Safina had expressed to me her love for Zaheer. I wish I could have made Zaheer a part of the family. But how could I? I couldn't let my daughter marry someone whose father and brothers had suffered from mental illness? How could I do that to my daughter?" The words jumped at Adam. No one had ever mentioned that his older cousin's family had a history of mental illness. And all the years he had known him, Zaheer had given no indication of being ill in any way whatsoever.

Mumtaz stood by the open door of the study, looking at Adam. She had been standing there for a long time, noting the changing expressions of surprise, sorrow and regret on Adam's face. This room was out of bounds for everyone, under explicit orders from Khodadad. How could the servants open it? she wondered angrily. Adam looked up from reading the journal and was startled to see his aunt's massive frame in the doorway. "Bibi, I was just looking around for some papers. I should now be leaving to see Baba," he said, getting up from the chair.

"You might want to put your father's private things back where they belong. I don't think he would appreciate you snooping in his desk," she replied with a frown on her face.

CHAPTER 15

"**I** don't think we have very good news to share with you, Mr. Khanzada," one of the doctors in the room said to Adam. "The reports are here and after consulting with each other, we have arrived at some conclusions," the doctor continued. Babar had stalled the doctors from speaking with Khodadad, requesting they wait for his son to be there. Rushing to the hospital after Babar's call to get to the hospital, Adam mentally prepared himself for the worst. Reading his father's journal just hours ago had made him realize how broken and hurt his father really was. All these years he had put up a brave front to spare his family and tribe from seeing his suffering. Now, when he sat facing the team of four doctors, he knew there was bad news coming his way.

Dr. Pervaiz spoke for the first time. "Adam, Agha Ji has Leukaemia, or more specifically, Non-Hodgkin's Lymphoma," the doctor said, pausing to take a deep breath. "This type of cancer attacks your body's defence system and can be very debilitating." Adam knew his father was sick but he was not prepared to hear what the doctor just told him. He felt tired suddenly, almost lifeless, and wanted to leave the room. Observing him, the four doctors exchanged concerned looks and one of them, an oncologist by the name of Dr. Usman—who was visiting Pakistan from the States—spoke for the first time. "Mr. Khanzada, judging from the reports, it appears that your father's cancer is still in its early stages and we have a good chance to fight it," he said. "We will be doing further tests and I will also consult with my colleagues at the Anderson Cancer Centre in Houston and see what they recommend," he added.

When Adam entered the hospital room, he found the nurse from the previous night chatting with his father. Even in his sickness, and in a hospital bed wearing the crude gown, his father looked handsome; there was an aura of refinement and authority that surrounded him, thought Adam. The nurse blushed when she saw Adam and left the two men together. "Salaams Baba. Were you flirting with the nurse?" he asked his father jokingly. Khodadad seemed to be better and was in good spirits. He smiled at Adam cheerfully, his blue eyes crinkling.

"I was just telling the pretty girl she should get married. I offered to find her a good boy from our village. She has been taking care of me and she drops in now and then to keep me company." Adam was grateful that his father was lively but was not sure how to break the news about his illness to him. Khodadad looked at his son and asked him to sit by his bed. "Adam, don't worry about me. I've known that I'm not well since a while now. I will feel worse if I know that it's making my son sad," Khodadad said. "You are Khodadad's son; don't forget this. You will have to be very strong. A lot of people will depend on you for their lives, their happiness, and their livelihood. If you are not tough and resilient, you will let them all down. Don't let that happen." Just when Khodadad ended his request, the team of doctors walked in.

After brief introductions detailing their areas of expertise, the doctors let Dr. Usman give the news to Khodadad. He was told about his cancer and its implications. The chances of his recovery were positive, but he would need further comprehensive assessment of his condition. Khodadad listened without saying anything and his face showed no changes. Dr. Pervaiz asked Khodadad if he had any questions to which he replied, "When do we start with the testing? I have to be back in the village for a polo match with my friends next month." The taut atmosphere of the hospital room felt less rigid and everyone relaxed to see how well Khodadad had taken the news. Adam felt a lump form in his throat. He would do everything in his power to help his father get well. The man sitting up in bed was, after all, all that he had.

It had been more than two weeks since Eugene's funeral. He had been a popular professor among both students and colleagues. News of his death appeared on the evening news as well, and there were eulogies written in various newspapers praising his work and lamenting what a big loss his death was to the world of anthropology. Virginia's name also appeared several times, mentioning the close ties both professors had. Virginia had been quiet since the accident and seemed to go further into her shell after the funeral. Safina knew she had to take her friend away before she had some sort of a mental breakdown.

The tickets were lying on the table in the foyer in Virginia's house. Safina had collected them after leaving from the university. When Virginia returned home late one night after a meeting with the faculty members regarding delegating her duties while she would be away, she let out a sigh of relief to see the yellow and green brochure with the tickets waiting at home. "You don't know how difficult it was to make Dr. Dietrich understand that I was fine and was only taking a holiday, which was long due. For a man with a Ph. D in English, it sometimes gets very difficult to make him understand simple sentences. He is nosey at the best of times and tonight, he was downright annoying," Virginia said, sounding exasperated. Safina listened with a smile on her lips, glad that Virginia was showing an emotion other than the gloom and despair she carried everywhere. They were to leave in three days and tomorrow, Safina was going to clean out her locker at the university. Despite all that had been happening lately, she felt light-headed with excitement at the prospect of getting away for six months.

Virginia was adamant on paying for the trip, saying she needed Safina's company and would not hear otherwise. The women were flying business class on Turkish Airlines and heading to Istanbul. They had booked a suite with two rooms at Swissotel The Bosphorus close to the Dolmabahce Palace. Virginia insisted they have separate rooms so that they could have some privacy to carry on with their research and stay close to each other. Both women finished their pending work and spent the last day before their trip shopping for their holiday. Virginia knew that Safina was barely making ends meet with the part-time research work she did for her, and her teaching assistant job at the university. Therefore, she took them to the less expensive shopping areas. As they stocked up on casual clothes, shoes and toiletries, the women felt like teenagers, showing each other the clothes they tried on and looking for discounts, and they let their minds empty of all dark thoughts—a refreshing change for them.

The women settled into the comfortable luxury of business class, amazed they were able to put life on hold and make time for themselves. Virginia ordered a glass of white wine and settled herself with a book, while Safina, who was tired from packing up her house the night before and moving her belongings to Virginia's house, snuggled deeper into her seat by the window and fell asleep instantly.

The tap on Virginia's shoulder startled her. As she turned around, she felt her heart skip a beat to see him so soon. The man motioned for her to come to the rear of the cabin. Virginia looked nervously at her sleeping friend before getting up to go. "Let's take these empty seats for a while. Hope everything is going according to plan,'" the man spoke to Virginia, sitting down four rows behind from where the women sat. "I will be in touch if I need to through my contact in Istanbul," he continued, while Virginia kept looking above the head rests to see if Safina had woken up. She turned to look at the man sitting beside her and was struck by his stark features. There was a ruthless look about him and Virginia wondered if she was doing the right thing by indulging in the conversation. "If you need to get in touch, just leave a message at the front desk of the hotel," he said. Virginia listened, unable to trust her voice to say anything. The air craft suddenly dipped and the "Fasten Seat Belt" sign overhead lit up. Virginia's heart rate was already on the rise due to anxiety, and she froze when she saw the flight attendant coming down the aisle, checking up on passengers to buckle up in case of turbulence. Looking at Virginia, the man smiled, and his features softened somewhat to reveal even, white teeth. "For a professor who gets paid to intimidate and speak in front of students, you are a woman of few words. No need to be so nervous. We won't be seeing each other after this, or at least not until a long time, I'm hoping." Hearing him talk so smugly infuriated Virginia and she got up without a word, and made her way to her seat before the flight attendant reached Safina.

Safina stirred from her sleep, her face looking flushed and rested. Virginia tapped the menu card in front of her, indicating she should pick what she wanted to eat. The air craft had an in-house kitchen, which served freshly prepared meals in the air for their business class patrons. There was a huge variety to choose from and both women had fun deciding on their meals. Safina realized that this was the first time in many years she had felt so relaxed; there were no people to please, no curfews to observe, and no deadlines to meet. It was pure bliss, she thought, smiling inwardly.

The flight would land at the Ataturk International Airport in about twenty minutes, so the women decided to freshen up. Safina was waiting by the galley when a man came out of the lavatory and suddenly turned around when he saw Safina. He had moved so quickly, that Safina was unable to see his face, but she felt a strange feeling of familiarity and fear creep up her spine. Later, Safina looked around for the man, but could not see him anywhere. Shrugging off the feeling of unease, she made her way to her seat and settled in for the plane to make its descent.

It was a beautiful day in Istanbul and the women found it a pleasant change to feel the warmth of the sun after the chilly weather they had left in Canada. The hotel looked massive and elegant and was located just a short walk from the Dolmabahce Palace and Taksim Square. Their suite overlooked the Bosphorus and gave a magnificent view of the clear blue waters. Safina and Virginia took a round of their accommodations and marvelled at the beauty of the rooms. "Virginia, we could have easily checked into a less luxurious place, you know? I feel embarrassed about the amount this must be costing you," Safina said, looking guiltily at her friend. Virginia did not reply and instead turned a deep red. "I really would like to pay you back for this extravagance someday," Safina continued. Virginia looked at Safina and answered that they both deserved to be spoilt and that it was a treat for her to have her as a companion.

"You can return the favour by giving me company and finishing up your work in your spare time," she answered. The women then decided to change and go out for dinner, discovering the town in the early evening.

They spent the next few days enjoying the sights and soaking in the culture. Turkey was a beautiful country with a rich history and friendly people. The locals were always helpful when they asked for directions or suggestions for food and fun. "I think I will be as big as a house when it is time to go back," Virginia said, biting into her second serving of lamb shawarma, which they had ordered from a road side cafe in Pera. Her companion looked at her and smiled, not doubting what she said. The fact was, in Canada, Virginia hardly took any interest in her diet. She worked around the clock, eating mainly from the university cafeteria or when she had to go out with friends. Eugene had often berated her for her unhealthy eating habits and would bring in nourishing packed meals from various restaurants to feed both her and Safina. Since they had arrived four days prior, Virginia insisted on savouring everything from the local cuisine. They dined at expensive restaurants, ate from roadside stalls and even at the beach where fresh caught fish was grilled right before their eyes and was served with vegetables and fragrant rice. Each morning, when they left the hotel, Virginia made a point to speak with the concierge to find out about places to visit and new things to eat. Safina found the cuisine close to the food that was indigenous to her own roots. Many of the grilled meats which were cooked slowly over charcoal, tasted just like they did in the village.

Safina came down the elevator one morning wondering what adventure Virginia was planning for the day when instead of finding her friend at the desk getting ideas from the concierge, she found her near the entrance talking to a bellhop. "Safina, meet Dogan, my newest Turkish friend. He is a local of Istanbul and he strongly suggests we check out the Burc Beach," Virginia said excitedly. Safina was amazed at the adventurous girl that her friend had transformed into, and reminded her that it was close to November, and too cold for the beach. "Oh, but you have to listen to this. This beach has so much to offer. We can go for sea catamarans or canoeing or even wind surfing, what do you say?" she continued excitedly. Safina knew she would not be able to convince Virginia otherwise, and went back to their suite to get their beach sandals and light sweaters. Dogan had also informed them that each evening, the beach, which was owned by the University of Bogazici, held concerts where the students performed to the sound of the waves crashing in the night.

The beach was a beautiful stretch of lovely white sand, offering all the activities that Dogan had mentioned and more. There was a charming little restaurant and bar and a game of volley ball was in progress when the women reached there around noon. Virginia, whose latent exploratory spirit had surfaced with rapidity during the last few days, elected to try out wind surfing as soon as she had changed into her white bikini, which sported tiny red maple leafs all over. Safina, who preferred to stay in a T-shirt and capris, lay down under a beach umbrella to watch the volley ball game.

Safina must have dozed off watching the game, but became aware of someone pausing near her sleeping figure before moving away. Opening her eyes, she saw the receding shape of a familiar figure. It was the same man she saw coming out of the lavatory on the plane. Although she could not see his face to recall where she had seen him before, she knew it had to be him. Who was this person and why was he hesitant to even look at her? she wondered, her pulse suddenly rising. Safina got up to catch up to the man but before she could reach him, he disappeared into the crowd by the restaurant. "It must be my nerves playing up on me," she tried to convince herself, but a niggling worry kept returning to her.

The volleyball match had ended and Safina could make out Virginia coming back as she chatted with a life guard, with a wide grin on her face. She had never looked so laid-back and happy before, Safina thought. "You don't know what you missed! This was the most exhilarating experience I have ever had in my life," said the older woman, sitting down with a plonk on the sand near her, her short bob in disarray. Safina smiled indulgently at her friend and suggested they both get something to eat.

The restaurant was busy at this hour and the women had to wait to find seats. When they finally sat down on ornate rattan chairs, Safina ordered the Iskender Kebab and Virginia a dish of Manti, which was a kind of Turkish ravioli. The elderly couple sitting at the table next to them were having lamb Shish kebabs and Karinyarik, which was stuffed eggplant, and Virginia longingly eyed their meal while waiting for theirs to be served. The food was delicious and Safina had a hard time convincing Virginia not to opt for seconds. Just as they were finishing off their flaky Baklava with sweet apple tea, the old man, probably in his late seventies, dropped his plate, sending kebabs and eggplant all over the floor. His wife let out a scream, while the man slumped to one side, holding his chest with one hand and the table with the other. There was commotion around the place they sat and a couple of young boys in shorts quickly left their table to lay the man flat on the floor. They spoke in Turkish, which Virginia understood perfectly, and were asking the man's wife if her husband had a heart condition. Just then, a tall, burly man parted the on-looking crowd, announcing *"Ben bir doktorum, kenara cekil"* and bent down to check on the old man. It was obvious that the person was having a heart attack and the man bending down deftly started to pump the old man's chest.

"Somebody, please call an ambulance, this man is having a heart attack!" he shouted above the crowd. Soon enough, two paramedics arrived and took the old man away in an ambulance. An odd silence descended on the previously noisy crowd, and Safina and Virginia decided to head back to their hotel.

CHAPTER 16

When Zaheer received the call from his mother about Khodadad's illness, he had arrived in Germany just three days ago to take over his new assignment. He had spent the whole day in office assisting in closing an important construction deal between Pakistan and Germany, and was now heading to a cafe in Berlin's Kurfurstendamm to meet an old friend for dinner. Just before he got into the taxi, Renata, the assistant who was assigned to him, rushed to tell him his mother was on the phone, insisting to talk to him. Going back inside the red brick building and making his way to his office on the third floor, Zaheer picked up the phone, only to discover the line had been disconnected. He waited by the phone, knowing his mother would call again. Sure enough, after about fifteen minutes, he heard his mother on the other end of the line, and evidently agitated. Hearing what she had to say amid tears and wails of grief in both English and Darri, Zaheer's hands went clammy and he felt as if a cold, metal vice held his heart in a tight grip. He never imagined a man like Khodadad, who seemed so much larger than life, could succumb to something as vile as cancer.

Zaheer gave rapid instructions to Renata to contact the friend he was to meet and cancel his dinner. He also asked her to book a flight to Islamabad. The plane took off from the Schoenfeld Airport within a few hours after he received his mother's distressing phone call. Throughout the eight and a half hours of the flight, Zaheer's mind played scenes from his childhood where his uncle made every effort to give him and his mother a life of comfort and ease. Zaheer's thankfulness for his uncle was immense but he also could not help but feel a pang of loss and inadequacy when he reminded himself that it was the same uncle who had wrenched Safina out of his life; a pain he could never reconcile with.

The Boeing circled the symmetrically laid out and verdant city of Islamabad and made a smooth landing at the Benazir International Airport. Zaheer took a taxi directly to the Margalla Hills house and surprised his mother, who was finishing her afternoon prayers. Looking at her son, Mumtaz broke down in tears and clung to him, weeping. "Zaheer, I can't let anything happen to Khodadad. He has been more than a brother to me. I don't know what to do!" she sobbed. Zaheer could feel his mother's body shuddering with each word she spoke and it pained him deeply to think how much he had neglected the people he loved.

Adam met Zaheer in the hospital lobby. Both men hugged each other in the traditional frontier way of greeting and held each other's hands in a tight clasp. "How is he doing?" Zaheer asked his younger cousin. Khodadad had been taken into the surgery to get a biopsy done. His reports from the procedure would determine what treatment the doctors would start and how strong his body was to be able to withstand it.

It had been four days since Khodadad had collapsed in the village, and even though he tried to appear in good spirits and cheerful, his reports said otherwise. The doctors had been hopeful that his cancer was at an early stage; however, further tests revealed that it might prove more resilient to the medication they intended to give him. Khodadad had his eyes closed when Zaheer and Adam walked into his room. The medication he had been given had made him drowsy. Zaheer looked at his uncle for a long time, unable to believe he had withered so much since the last time he saw him. It was only a few months ago that they had celebrated his birthday and he had looked so well—full of life and spirit. The man lying on the bed had aged considerably, his former robust complexion now an ashen white. The hands resting on the blanket with an IV tube attached to one of them looked frail. These were the same hands that had patted his head countless times and taught him how to handle a gun and hold the reins of a horse. Adam could sense the emotions his cousin was experiencing and motioned for him to come out with him. Leaning against the door outside, Adam looked at Zaheer deep in the eyes. The lack of sleep and the anxiety he had undergone in past few hours had left Zaheer with dark circles under his otherwise clear eyes. "We both have to be strong for Baba. The thing that pains him the most is his family worrying and fussing about him. For the same reason, I try to keep Bibi at home most of the time because she cannot help controlling her emotions each time she sees him." Zaheer understood perfectly. For a man whose pride had never let him show his pain even when his wife and daughter left him, any form of sympathy or kindness would injure his self-esteem. He just prayed that Khodadad's toughness and determination would see him through this ordeal, and he would be back at the helm of the family, keeping it together and strong.

News of Khodadad's illness had reached the village. The hospital would be thronged with people coming to see him each day. However, the doctors had advised against visitors and most of the tribal people would return to the village without seeing Agha Ji after being told by Adam that the best way they could help him was by praying for him. Many people would stay back for Adam to solve issues relating to their land or families. Such cases could have been dealt with by Babar, but since Babar was out of the country away on business, the whole responsibility fell on Adam's shoulders.

"Adam, I have decided to take a long leave of absence to be here with Agha ji. If you need to be in the village or go out of the country, rest assured, I will be here with him," Zaheer told Adam after dinner the next night at the house in Islamabad. Mumtaz had the cook prepare the boys' favourite stuffed lamb with basmati rice, and tried to keep herself occupied with household chores to keep her mind off Khodadad. She now listened to their after-dinner conversation, unable to decide if she should share what was on her mind. Adam refused Zaheer's offer to stay back saying there was no need but if in case he needed him, he would let him know. Babar was trained enough to handle the business affairs independently and whenever he needed support, Adam guided him. Adam would delegate most of his duties to him so he could stay with his father.

Mumtaz spoke after long deliberation. The glow from the chandelier was making her ruddy cheeks shine. "I have been thinking for a long time about what I'm about to say and I want you both to listen carefully. I think we should tell Safina about her father. She needs to know," Mumtaz said staring at her folded hands on the table. For a long time, no one spoke. Both Zaheer and Adam had their own reasons for not replying immediately. Zaheer could not share with them that he had met with

Safina just days ago. A meeting he had planned and which ended badly. Adam could not bring himself to say he had followed his sister to her friend's home in Toronto. Seeing her after so many years had convinced him that his sister had moved on, and did not look back or miss the people she had left behind. Were he to approach her, she might refuse him, not wanting to come back. Like his mother, Adam felt his sister had shrugged off the life she had lived in Pakistan like an old piece of garment.

"What would Safina's coming here serve, mom?" Zaheer asked Mumtaz. "Has Uncle Khodadad forgiven her? Do you think he would forgive us if we were to do this without his knowledge?"

Mumtaz could not understand the mindset of the men sitting in front of her. She was astonished to see they both nursed their own pain and worry about Khodadad. Why did they not understand that Safina loved her father just as much? How could they be so selfish and overlook her feelings in this matter? She was surprised to see they only thought about their own feelings, forgetting how Safina would feel if something were to happen to her father. However, Adam could not be convinced. He refused to agree to inform his sister saying that, like their mother, she had chosen the life she was living. She had made their father suffer grief and shame, and had compromised his dignity when she decided to disappear one day. Adam believed, if she had some remorse, that his sister would have attempted to contact them, apologised, or shown some regret for her actions.

Zaheer stayed quiet through Adam's outburst, wondering what they would think if they only knew the details of how his sister left the country, or what role he had played in making that possible. In Khodadad's absence, Adam was responsible for all the decision-making within the family, and the matter of not informing Safina was closed with finality. Mumtaz left the two men to themselves and went out of the room with a sad, empty heart.

CHAPTER 17

Safina sat in her room going through her notes. Two weeks of non-stop fun and adventure had worn the women out, and they both decided to take a couple days off to catch up on their work. Virginia looked considerably better and was enjoying herself, and Safina was thankful she did not slide back into depression. This had been a much-needed break for them both. They had spent the previous day at the hotel spa, spoiling themselves with massages and facials, and had come out looking and feeling rejuvenated. "I could do this every week, if you ask me," Virginia spoke to her companion.

The women were relaxing on spa chairs after their facials with mud masks covering their faces and slices of cucumbers on their eyelids, while two girls gave them pedicures. Safina felt too lethargic to reply after the Hamam, where her body had been scrubbed and exfoliated and later massaged with heavy, fragrant oils. She could only murmur an "ummm hmmm," in response, concentrating on the blissful feeling of having her feet kneaded with hands that knew how to make her even more drowsy.

They spent the next day locked in their rooms, working on their respective tasks. Safina's research focused on the Ottoman Dynasty and its ascendancy to world dominance, which spanned six centuries to be replaced by the Turkish Republic in 1922. Her interest in the subject was further augmented by the fact that Virginia, who had a Doctorate in the subject, had channelled her interest to concentrate on a topic area which related directly to her own roots. Safina was particularly fascinated by the tribal dynamics which had led to the founding of the empire. The progression of small Turkic tribes forming alliances against the Mongols and Crusaders to establish a dynasty, which staggered the world with its might and splendour for centuries, reminded Safina of the tribal conflicts in her village, which her father was able to quell and unite. Poring over her books and notes for hours had exhausted Safina, and she decided to check on Virginia and ask if they should have their supper. When she got no reply after knocking, Safina gingerly opened the door to Virginia's room only to find her friend fast asleep with her head on her desk and her notes lying untouched on the table. It was obvious Virginia was in no mood to get back to anything serious, and her body continued to relax and unwind after years of working ceaselessly. Closing the door quietly behind her, Safina decided to go out for a stroll and pick up something to eat on the way back for them.

Grabbing her jacket and purse, she headed out of the hotel and walked briskly towards the shoreline. At this hour, the Bosporus was dotted with lights shining from ships in the distance. It was a beautiful sight to see and Safina sat down on a wooden bench to watch the anchored ships bobbing languidly in the dark waters. She sat there for a long time, not realizing how late it was getting. Trying to dispel the lethargy that was engulfing her, Safina got up reluctantly to head back to the hotel, which was more than two miles away. Taken by the beauty of the calm waters and the lights reflecting on them, she hadn't realized how far she had wandered off. There were fewer people about and very little traffic moved on the road. She inwardly cursed herself for wasting so much time and quickened her pace before the food sellers packed up their wares and left for the night. Just when she turned the corner, which would take her to the street her hotel was located on, a group of three young, poorly-dressed men started following her. At first, Safina thought they happened to be going in the same direction as her, but after a few minutes, she realized they were tailing her. She started to walk at a brisk pace, hoping to lose them but that seemed unlikely. Alarmed, Safina started to run, her heart rate rising and fear settling into the pit of her stomach. Sensing she had caught onto them, one of the boys sprinted very close to Safina and while passing, elbowed her in her ribs and sending her to one side. Unable to resist the surprise impact, Safina lost her balance and fell flat on the pavement, with her arms askew, and hit her head on the concrete. Another one of the boys tried to yank her cross-body purse off her, but Safina was too dazed to know what was happening. Abruptly, all three boys left, leaving their victim sprawled and hurt.

Safina passed out just when a pair of strong arms lifted her off the street. She was aware of people talking rapidly in Turkish before she opened her eyes. Her head hurt and judging from the sharp pain, she seemed to have knocked her shoulder on the pavement. "*Iyi misin?*" asked a man looking straight into her eyes. "*Iyi misin? Acitir mi?*" he repeated. Safina tried to place the face—she had seen it somewhere—but she felt too woozy and trying to jog her memory proved very draining, so she just gave up.

When she opened her eyes for the second time, Virginia was peering at her, her face taut with apprehension and her eyes like two large saucers. She was in the hotel lobby and Dogan was holding a glass of water to her lips, while a small crowd of people looked at her semi-recumbent position on the floral sofa. Safina tried getting up but the man, who seemed very familiar, made her lie down again. "You just had a concussion. Please don't get up," he said.

Virginia spoke for the first time, her voice edged with worry, "What on earth were you thinking walking the streets of Istanbul so late in the night? You were lucky you didn't get killed!" she chided. Safina remembered now. The man who had spoken to her in Turkish earlier and who now stood like a column next to her was the same person who had come to the aid of the old man having a heart attack in the restaurant. She recalled he was a doctor and had given first aid to the man, while waiting for the paramedics to arrive. "If it wasn't for Dr. Yildirim here, you would probably have been mugged or worse, knifed in the ribs!" Virginia continued with her tirade, her cheeks red and her chest heaving.

Safina could only offer a weak, sheepish smile in response and looking at the man said, "Are you always at the right place at the right time or was this another coincidence?" The man, or Dr. Yildirim, towered above everyone else. He looked more like a football player than a doctor, with his broad shoulders and muscular arms.

Dr. Yildirim and Dogan helped Safina back to her room and lay her on the bed. Dr. Yildirim, or Engin, suggested she come to the hospital tomorrow to get a complete check-up to rule out any broken bones she might have. He also sent Dogan down to his car to bring his medical bag upstairs. While Dogan was gone, the doctor gave Safina a shot for the pain in her shoulder and a mild tranquilizer. "I want you to come to the hospital tomorrow and we will give you a thorough check up," he said to Safina, while closing his bag. Virginia had regained some of her composure and joked that they would let their knight in shining armour continue being their saviour and would be at the hospital the next morning.

"Virginia, please stop fussing over me!" Safina said to her friend the next day. "I am absolutely fine. Trust me. There's no need to go to the hospital. Look here, I can walk around and do everything perfectly well, and nothing is hurting anymore," she pleaded. The fact was, Virginia was worried sick about her friend. She felt guilty for falling asleep and not going out with Safina the night before. Now, she was having a difficult time convincing her to go to the hospital to rule out the possibility of a broken bone or any other complication. However, Safina wanted to just lie in bed and watch television. She refused to leave the room. Giving up, Virginia decided to stay indoors as well and give Safina company.

The phone rang around midday and answering it, Virginia mouthed "it's him!" to Safina. "No, she seems perfectly fine, I don't think there's any need to worry," she was saying into the telephone, "Yes, we decided not to go out today and enjoy ourselves at the hotel," she continued. Putting the phone down, Virginia looked at Safina with raised eyebrows and a smile on her lips. "That was Dr. Yildirim on the phone. He was asking why you didn't show up at the hospital today," she said. Safina rolled her eyes, annoyed at having the subject of refusing to go to the hospital brought up again and turned up the volume on the television, trying to be engrossed in the movie she was watching. Virginia decided to drop the subject and went to her own room to catch up on an article she was writing about Suleiman the Magnificent and his foreign policies in the sixteenth century.

Hours later, she realized just how long she had been working. No wonder her eyes were starting to hurt. There was a knock on the door and Virginia thought Safina must have called for room service but when she opened it, she was surprised to see Dr. Yildirim standing there.

"Hello. I thought I'd drop by after work to check up on my patient," Engin said, his huge frame looming in the doorway. Letting him into the sitting room, Virginia warned him that Safina had been in a bad mood all day, probably from feeling sore and not being able to do much in terms of her work or going out. Also, she wasn't eating, thereby making herself grumpier. Engin smiled, revealing dimpled cheeks and crinkly merry eyes, which transformed his otherwise forbidding appearance into that of an impish boy. Virginia noted he had a pleasant, open air about him, so unlike the detached, professional person he came across initially. "Just as I thought," he said, "I figured Safina must have put up a fight not to come to the hospital."

At that moment, Safina walked into the sitting room and hearing the last part of his sentence, replied, "As you can see, Dr. Yildirim, I'm perfectly fine. Do all Turkish doctors make house calls for their patients at their hotels? Or are you part of the health police?" she said sarcastically. Engin's smile broadened and he got up from his seat. He explained he was heading home after work and decided to check up on them, and since Safina looked quite recovered from her fall, and since she had not eaten all day, he was taking both ladies out to dinner. Safina and Virginia were not expecting this. Clearly, doctors in Istanbul were either very committed to their work, or Dr. Yildirim was an exception and went the extra mile for his patients. Before Safina could protest and refuse, Virginia accepted the invitation and asked that they be excused for a moment to change into warmer clothes.

"How could you agree to let him manipulate us into going out with him?" Safina whispered to Virginia the moment they closed the door to Safina's room.

"Safina, you have had your way all day today. Now, can you stop acting like a spoiled kid and change out of your PJ's so that we can go out? I'm starving as it is," Virginia replied, reaching into Safina's closet to pull out some clothes for her.

It was a beautiful evening and Safina took a deep breath, inhaling in the fresh sea air. It felt good to be out after staying inside all day. While they waited for the valet to bring his car, Engin told them about the place he was taking them to. He said they would be dining at the Nusr-Et, owned by the world-famous chef, Nusret Gokce, nicknamed Salt Bae. Safina, who had been least interested in food just a half hour ago, beamed with excitement the moment she entered the exotic restaurant. There was a warm, languorous ambience to the place and low Turkish music played in the background. Both women felt a surge of excitement when they saw open fire pits next to each table with a chef preparing the meal in front of the customers.

The maître d' seated them near the west side of the steak house, which overlooked the sea and gave a view of the whole restaurant. The women left the selection of the food to Engin, who appeared to take his cuisine very seriously. They ordered the beef carpaccio for starters with a goat cheese salad. For their main course, Engin insisted they try the Asado beef ribs, the filet mignon steak and the roasted neck of lamb. A chef came shortly and started preparing the meals at their table, cutting up choice pieces of meats in front of their eyes. The famous Salt Bae came to their table just as the cooked meat was about to be served and deftly carving it, he performed his signature salt sprinkling act and placed the platters on the table with a dramatic flourish. "People don't just come here for the performance. The food is actually very delicious," Engin said to his guests, who seemed fascinated with the elaborate preparation and presentation of their meal.

The meal was by far the best the women had had since their arrival. And even though Safina had protested to going out to eat, she showed a healthy appetite and finished all the food on her plate. Engin suggested they go to a coffee house for dessert but the women declined. Instead, they elected to walk around the streets of Pera for a while before Engin dropped them off at their hotel.

"You don't have to come upstairs to drop us, you know," Virginia said to Engin when they reached their hotel. Engin's face showed the tiniest bit of disappointment but he agreed, saying he had to be at work early in the morning. While going up in the elevator to their rooms, Virginia looked at her friend and noticed the soft glow on her face. The grouchy Safina of the morning had turned into a sweet, pliant young woman. The older woman saw that Engin's attention and generosity had mellowed her. She could also see that Engin was not going to give up and that they would be seeing a lot more of him.

Mumtaz was sure she had instructed that the box be placed in her car, but after checking her luggage, she could not find the blue and white cardboard box. After she caught Adam rummaging through Khodadad's desk that day, she had decided to take his journal and a few other things back with her to the village. She would lock up Khodadad's things in the library where no one could touch them. But now, the box was nowhere to be seen. She would have to check which car the driver had placed it in, coming back from Islamabad.

The few days everyone had anticipated they would need to be in Islamabad for Khodadad's treatment had stretched to four weeks of endless tests and re-evaluation of his condition. Dr. Usman had returned to the States and would be coming back in two months, and would then determine where Khodadad was to be treated. Despite Khodadad's insistence that she return to the village, Mumtaz had stayed in Islamabad to be close to him and Adam. Now, all three had come back to their house to wait for Dr. Usman's return to Pakistan.

Manju Kaka, who had been sent off earlier to prepare the house, greeted the family at the entrance. He had been instructed to not let anyone know of Khodadad's arrival, to avoid visitors dropping in to ask about his health. "We will give him a few days to settle and then have some of his friends come visit him," Adam had said. Watching him get out of the jeep, the gardener noted how much weight his master had lost and the gritty hand he raised in a backhand salute of welcome shook slightly. Khodadad gave a sigh of relief as he entered his room; it was good to be back home.

It was late at night when Adam closed his bedroom door behind him. After making sure his father was comfortable and giving detailed instructions to the household staff regarding Khodadad's diet and care, he had left with Babar to a neighbouring village to settle a dispute over an irrigation channel. Ignoring the pile of mail stacked neatly on his desk, he reached under his bed and pulled out the box he had switched from Bibi's car to his jeep before they left Islamabad.

The leather-bound journal sat opened on his desk. He had pored through random entries spanning the time from when his sister left until his return from England—that was where the journal ended, or at least there were no more entries after that. Reading the bold, scrawny writing had felt as though he was delving into his father's mind. Where Khodadad appeared to the world as a stoic, magnanimous tribal lord, proud of his ancestry, his thoughts in the journal revealed him to be a man of deep passion, benevolence and finesse. There were aspects of his father's life that Adam was not aware of. For instance, he did not know that Khodadad funded two orphanages for children who had lost parents in the Taliban wars or that he donated heavily to an institute in Switzerland, which conducted research on genetics and mental disorders. "I am hoping for the day they tell me he is fine and shows no signs of carrying his father's sickness," wrote Khodadad. The entry was made some time after Safina's departure. Adam supposed this was in regards to the mental disorder he had read about concerning Zaheer's family. The journal also revealed to Adam his father's love for poetry. As far as he could remember, he had never seen his father show any aptitude for music or art, even though he went to great pains to have his children trained in both. The quotes from Persian poets, which appeared randomly throughout his writing, illustrated his appreciation for the finer and deeper things in life. Reading further, Adam came across an entry which spoke about how profoundly his father felt for Zaheer's loss of his family. Khodadad wrote he would make sure his nephew never came short of anything and that he would protect both him and his mother. He had bequeathed his orchards in Islamabad to Zaheer as well as some land in the village. Adam closed the journal. He would have to come back to reading it later. The call for morning prayers resounded in the valley and Adam rolled out his prayer mat and facing the Kaaba, offered up his prayers.

There was a knock on his door. Looking at the clock, he realized he had slept in. Kaka Manju entered with a cup of coffee and the message that he was expected at a meeting with the village elders in an hour. Adam showered and dressed in a crisp white *shalwar qameez* suit and Peshawari sandals, replete with a waist coat and turban. His short beard needed trimming, he noted as he looked in the dressing room mirror. As a precaution, in case Bibi came into his room in his absence, he locked the box with his father's personal items in his wardrobe.

Adam was told his father was relaxing out in the garden with Bibi. He put on his gun belt, which hung in the entrance closet, and walked out to join them. Sitting outside in the late morning sun with his dogs at his feet, one could not tell that Khodadad had spent the past few weeks in the hospital. After wearing the hospital gowns for so long, his father looked elegant in his starched clothes. He was leaning back on a recliner under a garden umbrella wearing dark aviator Ray Bans. Babar and Mumtaz sat close to him and upon seeing Adam come out of the house, Babar got up and collected his own gun belt, which was hanging from the back of his chair. It was obvious he was looking forward to joining Adam for the meeting with the elders. Adam bent down to kiss his father on the cheek, inhaling in his favourite Givenchy Gentleman, before climbing into the jeep with Babar and heading out.

"What is the update on your trip abroad?" Adam asked Babar the moment they hit the road. "I hope everything went smoothly?" he added. Babar gave him a quick rundown of his tour, filling in details about the roadblocks he ran into and how he handled them.

The meeting with the elders was taking place in a village an hour's drive to the east. Reaching their destination, the men were surprised that very few of the local people came to welcome them, as had been the custom in the past. The son of the village school master came to receive them and they walked together to the "dera", or sitting area, of the village head. After about half an hour of waiting, five or six of the elders from the surrounding areas came and greeted them. There was frostiness to their otherwise warm, demonstrative welcome, which Adam could not understand.

After a round of hot 'kehwa' with 'asheela', fried rice cakes with sesame, the leader of the Hota tribe, Sherbat Murad, a man in his sixties and a childhood friend of Khodadad's, spoke first. "Adam, we are pleased to see you. We heard what happened to Khodadad and pray he recovers from his sickness," the man paused and looked around the men, who were sitting on low seats in a semi-circle. "The reason for requesting this meeting is that we feel, with your father being ill, it is important we hold an election to decide who will be the next chief," the man finished the sentence with some difficulty. "We are all sad that he is not well and pray for his recovery, but you know the rule of the land. The rule says that a tribal chief, aside from being fair and honest, must be present to hold the people together. Agha Ji has been gone for a long time and we don't know when he will return. In the meantime, we need someone who can take charge of things and be part of our lives," the spokesman for the group ended his speech.

Adam was furious. His father had only been gone a month and was still alive and capable of making all decisions, yet the other tribal contenders had moved in like a pack of hyenas. They assumed Khodadad would not survive and had started planning for a replacement. For the briefest moment, Charles Darwin's maxim of 'Survival of the fittest' crossed his mind. One of the lessons his father had taught him was to never let your anger show, especially in a tribal discord of this sort. "You must learn to curb your emotions and do not assume people are going to be sympathetic if you show your weakness," his father had said to him time and again. "When there's a majority of people against you, agree to what they are saying instead of getting into an argument. Let them cool down and make them believe you agree to what they want. Wait a while and let them think they have persuaded you. Then, present them with another option which they can't refuse."

Adam asked Sherbat Murad who it was they had in mind to replace Khodadad with. The faces turned towards the leader whose village they were at, who up until now had remained quiet. "We believe Gul Hassan will be able to lead us as the next tribal chief," another man spoke to which the assembly started nodding their heads in agreement, murmuring quietly. Adam said he agreed to what they said, however, keeping their traditions in mind, they would need to hold elections to reach an agreement. Another round of nodding and whispering started taking place. They agreed that the twentieth of the next month would be a suitable date to hold the elections.

The men sat long after Adam and Babar had left, marvelling at how effortlessly they had convinced Adam to give up the seat his father had fought for many years ago. There were some who sheepishly suggested that Adam would have made a fine alternative to Khodadad as the new chief. He had the same virtuous and capable qualities, which they looked for in a leader. The fact that he possessed an education from abroad and followed his traditions to the letter made him an excellent candidate for replacement. However, the suggestion was quickly thwarted by Gul Hassan and his supporters. These people, quite frankly, were intimidated by Adam's ability, like his father, to balance the leisurely, tranquil measured pace of the village with the fast tempo of the outside world. It was true that Khodadad had achieved the impossible in the years he had worked as the tribal chief. He had involved the federal government to take interest in the northern territories, giving them sanctions to dig through the mountains and channel waterways to the plains. In return, the government had invested in the construction of bridges and roads linking the village to the southern and eastern parts of the country. The construction of a hospital was underway and local children were given the opportunity to compete in board exams to pursue further education. Khodadad had made local businesses accessible to the rest of the country, thereby improving trade and increasing prosperity. These were not small achievements and only a person like Khodadad, a man with a vision and important contacts in Islamabad, could have accomplished.

The contender, Gul Hassan, was a stalwart man in his late fifties who had been one of the people who had vehemently opposed Zaheer's father as tribal lord due to the fact that in the past, his ancestors had shown signs of mental disorders. Some said it was spirits that possessed the family, while others believed they had been cursed by God. As a result, there had been violent conflicts ending in Zaheer's family being butchered and his father's lands being taken away. With time, Khodadad had managed to placate the people and bring some order in the area, educating them that such an illness did not always get passed down to the next generation. During the past few years, Gul Hassan had remained subdued, not wanting to create any disruption amongst the locals. However, with the news of Agha Ji's waning health, he saw his chance to realize his dream of becoming tribal chief once more. He had worked hard to convince his companions that it was time for a change, and that they needed a more robust leader in command.

CHAPTER 18

Adam sat with Babar in the backseat of the jeep while the driver drove through the unpaved road, which was to take them to the lumberyard. He was livid at Gul Hassan's audacity. The man seemed to have forgotten the many favours his father had bestowed on him. His only son, who had gone to Italy two years ago on a trip with his friends from his university in Islamabad, had died in a boat accident. It was Khodadad who had contacted the Italian Consulate to release his body and have it transported to Pakistan. The man had fallen crying at his father's feet, begging him to help him, saying he could not bear for his only heir to be buried in foreign soil. Khodadad had gone to great lengths to have the body brought to Pakistan as the Italian police would not release the corpse. Gul Hassan's son, who had been driving the boat, had been intoxicated and was the cause of another girl's death who was riding with him. In addition, Khodadad had once saved Gul Hassan a lot of money and stress by lending him workers from his mining business when his own men had thrown down their tools due to some altercation with their supervisor. How the man could overlook these acts of kindness his father had done for him was beyond his comprehension.

The men reached the lumberyard and Adam took a tour of the premises. He was pleased to note that in his absence, the work continued as before. Lumber and its transportation was one of the businesses which brought revenue to the Khanzada family. The river which flowed to the east of the lumberyard and made its way around the village, going behind the Khanzada house, made its descent to the plains providing a cheap and quick means of transport to the three lumberyards of the village.

Khodadad's yard controlled the transportation of the wood. The wood was cut up and made into even planks, which reached the wood treatment factories in the south. "Babar, I want you to oversee that the river is diverted to the eastern channels. No wood coming from Gul Hassan's yard will go down this river," Adam instructed his assistant. Gul Hassan will get his first shock in the morning when he will see there is very little water in the river to transport the wood stacking in his yard. He will have to hire expensive trucks to send his wood south before it gets ruined sitting outside in the low temperatures, rendering it useless for trade. There will be no more cheap transportation for him, Adam thought.

Reaching home, Adam found his father resting in his room. "How did the meeting go?" asked Khodadad. "I hope there were no serious issues you had to deal with?" Adam did not want his father to know how the locals were closing in to take over the leadership and how it was possible for another series of skirmishes to set off, marking the end of peaceful life in the village.

"Oh it was the usual. Just some routine matters I had to take care of. Everyone sends you their best wishes," he said. Khodadad closed his eyes and thought of the responsibility that rested solely on his son's shoulders now. Adam would have to be very strong, he thought, very strong and wise. Tribal culture could be harsh and he had a rough road ahead of him.

Adam sent for Babar to join him for a ride the next morning. The men took their jeep until they arrived at the family orchard, then got off and made their way on foot to the other end of the fields. Khodadad kept his horses in stables which were built away from the house but not so far that one could not access them easily. Their riding boots made squelching sounds in the earth as it had rained the previous night and the fields were muddy. Reaching the stables, both men got on their horses and took off on a trot to the east, where the river ran close to the lumberyard. Adam had been quiet since they started and Babar knew him well to understand there was something important on his mind. On days when Adam had something important to discuss and didn't want his father to know, he took off on his horse in search of isolation. On reaching the grove which hid the river, Adam stopped his horse. The previous day's events had made him uneasy and he needed time to think what steps to take in order to keep the family's dominion of the lands intact. "Tell me about the men who were at the meeting yesterday. What are they like and how close are they to Gul Hassan?" Adam asked Babar. Babar, who spent most of his time in the village, dealing with the commoners, traders, and the tribal elders, knew a lot more about them and their families than most people.

Babar gave Adam the information he needed. While most of the people gathered at the meeting were loyal to Khodadad and preferred the continuation of the Khanzada leadership, many of them were intimidated by Gul Hassan, who had a reputation for being a troublemaker. He coerced the locals to give in to his demands and often threatened and used violence. His only son had died two years ago, but he had two brothers and a bunch of goons who did his dirty work. Sherbat Murad, according to Babar, was the most loyal to Khodadad but was helpless in doing anything with so many elders joining Gul Hassan's side.

"And how influential is Sherbat Murad?"Adam asked his friend. Babar paused before answering. Sherbat Murad was a gentle person by nature who believed in peaceful negotiation rather than using brute force. He owned lands towards the west of the area and was an educated man who had gone to college in Peshawer. Because of his education, most people respected him and came to him for advice. His friendship with Khodadad was also seen as a bonus. He had declined taking active part in the tribal affairs since last year due to a personal set back. Sherbat Murad had seven children and last year, his youngest and his favourite daughter's husband lost his life when his car veered off the mountain. The girl had been married only a few weeks. The bride, widowed at a young age, had been labelled as cursed by the villagers and this was a source of great sorrow for the old father. Because of this reason, Sherbat Murad seldom left home, and became somewhat of a recluse. In the past, he had proven his loyalty to Khodadad by his support in electing him as the tribal chief. Moreover, he and his sons had stood up to fight alongside his grandfather when Zaheer's father and brothers were ambushed many years ago. In the skirmish, he lost his second born, Sabzali Murad.

Adam pondered the information and turned his horse around, starting off at a gallop towards home. He knew what steps he had to take.

Reaching home, Adam showered and spread his prayer mat. He sat on it for a long time, praying that the decision he was about to make proved auspicious for everyone concerned. Maintaining his father's respect and hegemony over the land took precedence over every thought and action he took, but at the same time, he did not want to ruin anyone's life. Adam raised his hands in prayer and asked for guidance and forgiveness.

Khodadad was sitting in his favourite chair in the library by the fire. Mumtaz sat close to him and was busy knitting something. Adam entered the room and sat across from the pair. "Bibi, since when did knitting become your newly found pastime?" he joked with his aunt. Then, unexpectedly, he realized that the woman sitting with his father had dedicated her whole life to their family. He hadn't noticed before that Bibi had started wearing reading glasses or that her hair was more grey than dark brown. The long braid which used to sway on her hips with each step she took was no longer thick and bulky; rather, her hair had thinned with age and wisps of grey escaped the tightly coiled plait framing her face. There were deep wrinkles around her mouth and her hands looked worn and hard.

Bibi was looking at him over her glasses. "Adam, you are staring at me as if you're seeing me for the first time. What is on your mind? And as for the new hobby, I took it up because it helps the arthritis in my hands. I only know how to knit socks and I make them for the kids at the orphanage," she said. Adam smiled. No matter how old she gets, Bibi would always have an earful for everyone, he thought fondly.

Adam brought up the topic which he wanted to discuss with the two people who mattered to him most. He told them of his wish to marry Sherbat Murad's youngest daughter as soon as possible. Mumtaz and Khodadad exchanged looks of astonishment and alarm. Mumtaz broke the silence by asking if the urgency was due to some transgression or misconduct towards the girl on his part; whether he had wronged Sherbat Murad or his family in some way. Adam let out a chuckle, his eyes crinkling in amusement. "Bibi, do you think you raised me into a man who would do anything to compromise a girl's honour? I would have to remind myself of the hiding I would get from you before even thinking about doing something as stupid as that," he said, finding hilarity in the conclusions his aunt was jumping to.

His father spoke, looking deep into his son's eyes. "Adam is this the girl who lost her husband last year?" he asked, and after receiving a nod in the affirmative, continued, "I went to the funeral. It was a sad affair.

Sherbat Murad could never recover from the grief," he said and continued, "the girl's name is Gulrukh, I believe. She is a very nice girl and her brothers dote on her." He looked at Mumtaz who had stayed quiet through the account. She looked a bit uneasy. Rumours of her being unlucky and cursed had reached her ears, and although she did not give heed to gossip, she feared Adam would have to face backlash later in his life. Any misfortune or illness in their family would be linked to the girl's presumed bad luck. Sensing her train of thought, Khodadad gave the answer to her apprehensions. "I believe Gulrukh would make a wonderful wife. She comes from a respectable background and anyone thinking her past is going to have any effect on her future as the daughter of this house can keep their opinion to themselves."

It was decided that Mumtaz and Khodadad were to go to Sherbat Murad's village to ask for his youngest daughter's hand in marriage for their son in five days; exactly two weeks before the elections were to be held for the new tribal lord.

CHAPTER 19

"**D**id you see this?" exclaimed Gul Hassan, throwing the gold embossed card across the carpet. His wife stopped her rummaging in her closet, and looked at her husband, recognizing the anger in his voice too well to say anything. "And why are you going through your wedding outfits? What is so special about this marriage?" he glared at his wife, who was now cowering near the door of the closet. Gul Hassan gave her a look of disgust and left their bedroom, slamming the door behind him. When Shirin was sure her husband had left, and would not return to the room, she moved towards the foot of the bed and bent down to pick up the wedding invitation. Shirin was a mild woman, who had lived with a brutal man for forty-two years. She had been blessed with six children who been unable to fight tuberculosis and died in infancy. Her last child, who cheated fate and survived, was a boy and was the apple of his parents' eyes. As with most children born after a lot of hardship, Qasim grew up with all the luxuries his parents could afford and more. He only had to look at something and his father would move mountains to grant it to him. All the attention and privileges lavished on him had turned Qasim into a spoilt, arrogant and conceited young man. More than a year ago, he had called his father from college in Peshawer and had said he wanted to see the world. He had told him he was planning a trip with his friends to visit Europe, and Gul Hassan had not hesitated for a moment, and had arranged for his son to go on his coming of age journey to broaden his horizons and discover the world. Shirin had meekly suggested to her husband that perhaps their son should first complete his undergrad degree, which he was failing to pass since the past two years. The reason why he had not been expelled from college already was because his father would give the institute fat donations each year. These donations in return added a new sports block or medical centre or chemistry lab to the college. The new buildings had plaques at their entrances with "Gul Hassan" emblazoned on them. Nobody in their right mind would ever think to expel the son of the college's most generous benefactor. Shirin's objection was discarded like most of her objections and instead, she was brusquely told to mind the kitchen and household staff as was her duty, rather than involve herself in matters which were of no concern to her.

When news of Qasim's accident and death reached the village, Gul Hassan had been sitting on the veranda at his home, watching his younger brother whip a young boy who had been caught stealing apples from their orchard. Upon reading the telegram, Gul Hassan had gotten up from his chair, snatched the whip from his brother's hand and had started flogging his assistant who had brought the ominous telegram from the village post office. He lashed at the man with such ferociousness, that he had to be pulled back by people, fearful he might end up taking the tired messenger's life.

After the funeral, people said that Gul Hassan had been punished for his ruthless nature and that God was chastising him for his evil deeds. They predicted there would be a transformation in the man's nature and he would now turn to God with hopes to expiate his sins. However, the villagers were proven wrong when Gul Hassan became even more sadistic and thrashed out at anyone that crossed his path. Shirin suffered the most of his harsh temperament and often had bruises or a cut lip to prove it.

Picking up the card, she ran her hand over the raised gold lettering, caressing the words and thinking of her own boy and the dreams she had of seeing him in his wedding clothes. Being a God fearing and kind hearted woman, Shirin chided herself for feeling the slightest bit of envy at Khodadad's son's marriage. She pushed back her own sorrow and forced herself to feel happy for the family. Shirin had then pulled open the door to her closet which held her shiny, wedding outfits—outfits reserved for happy occasions, thinking she would do justice to her husband's importance in the village and clothe herself in her best. Gul Hassan had startled her when he stormed into their bedroom and made her feel guilty for even thinking they would attend the wedding.

News of the imminent wedding spread throughout the village like wild fire. There were several speculations regarding the subject. There were those who believed Khodadad was nearing his last days and wanted to see his son married and have children of his own before he left the world. Some thought that Mumtaz Bibi was getting too old to run the house and was pushing to bring a daughter-in-law to assist her in her chores and give her company. Those who liked to object to everything claimed that bringing a cursed girl into the family would be their downfall; one just had to wait and watch how quickly the Khanzada's would be engulfed in misery and sorrow the moment the bride crossed their threshold.

The wedding was scheduled to take place in six weeks, fifteen days after the elections. All village elders, their families and their extended families had been invited to the event. Large marquees had been set up several days prior to the wedding to feed the poor. The Khanzada house had been given a fresh coat of paint and decorators and wedding planners had arrived from Karachi and Islamabad to take care of all the arrangements. A special pen had been erected to house hundreds of lambs and goats, and Khodadad's poultry farms in Murree delivered chickens each day for the big iron cauldrons and spits that prepared the fare. The annexe and all extra rooms in the house were being utilized to house guests coming from out of town. There were many who would make day trips from Islamabad and Peshawer and Lahore for the wedding and leave after the ceremony and reception was over.

Despite her aching knees, Mumtaz had made a weeklong trip with Babar to Islamabad and Lahore to purchase clothes and jewellery and cosmetics for the bride. Khodadad had asked her to spare no expense and Mumtaz had happily splurged on buying the choicest items in the markets. Strings of pearls and gold bangles, diamond-studded bracelets and countless rings and earrings filled the safe in the Margalla Hills house. Khodadad's business partner in Dubai sent cases of the best perfumes, handbags, cosmetics and shoes. The several formal ensembles for the bride were being prepared by the best designers of Lahore, and Mumtaz would go through each completed outfit, checking for errors. This was going to be a wedding fit for a king, she thought fondly.

The atmosphere in Sherbat Murad's house was festive and cheerful. Sherbat, who had previously given up on life, came alive with the thought of seeing his favourite child given a second chance at happiness. Where he had shunned company and closed his ears to the rumours in the village tagging his daughter as ill-fated, he now went to the village meetings with his head held high and could be often seen having his '*kehwa*' at the local tea house or playing chess with the headmaster under the walnut trees.

The change in Sherbat Murad's disposition did not go unnoticed by the villagers. People were pleased that the man who had once been part of all their grief and happiness was finally finding his own bliss in his daughter's upcoming nuptials. The man once again involved himself in their affairs and gave sound advice when asked. When people were hesitant to approach Khodadad directly, they had often asked Sherbat to intercede on their behalf on account of his friendship with the tribal chief. The wedding would fuse the two families into one entity. It was a match like no other, they thought. Where people had previously taken for granted and had been coerced to accept that Gul Hassan would be the new leader, they now questioned the assumption. Village elders met in each other's' houses after their evening meals to discuss the elections and weigh the pros and cons of having a brute of a man lead them, or continue with the same family and pass leadership onto his son. Everyone saw that Adam possessed all the qualities of his father, and where his father had deviated from tradition and had married a white woman, Adam proved his devotion to his roots by choosing a girl from his village. They could see a brighter, freer future with the younger Khanzada. The elders left the meetings, stroking their beards and nodding their heads, satisfied they had come to a mutual decision and not made a blunder by blindly entrusting their lives to Gul Hassan.

Khodadad insisted on accompanying Adam and Babar to the Eastern Hill, an area reserved for important events pertaining to tribal affairs. Despite his decreased weight, Khodadad looked striking in his starched white *shalwar* suit with a turban and embroidered waistcoat. The leather gun belt across his body was dotted with brass studs. For the occasion, Adam had a new pair of Peshawari sandals sent from Peshawar's Kochi Bazaar, which had delicate silver needle work covering its soft kid leather.

Mumtaz had stood at the entrance door while the men left, admiring her cousin and silently praying for him to always be part of their lives.

The moment the jeep turned the bend which began the ascent to the hill, throngs of people started cheering the approaching men. Babar had to slow the vehicle because there were many who clung to the windows of the jeep, trying to peer in to have a look at their tribal chief. Khodadad rolled down his window and briefly shook hands with whoever tried to grab him. It was almost impossible to get off the jeep with the swarm of well-wishers around them. Father and son were escorted to the main area reserved for the elections and seated on a *charpoy*, or low string cot. Right away, two young boys holding trays of steaming hot milky tea and dried nuts and sweets appeared and started to serve the guests. Sherbat Murad came and sat next to Khodadad after holding him in a tight, lingering hug. He could feel his friend's bones, where once he had admired the tall, muscular frame. The atmosphere changed from excited buzzing to hushed murmurs when Gul Hassan's entourage of four vehicles came to a halt at the entrance of the grounds. Gul Hassan was accompanied by his three brothers and several tall, ferocious-looking men sporting luxuriant beards and moustaches. The man arrived in his usual display of pomp and arrogance. He approached the area which seated the elders in a ring of charpoys with a swagger, and barely looked at Khodadad as he sat down at the farthest end from him.

The selection for the new tribal leader began and Fathe Khan, the village imam, started the proceedings with recitation from the Quran. Before the village head master could introduce the candidates, Khodadad asked to say a few words. After greeting everyone, he explained that he was not well and would therefore not be one of the contenders. In his place, his son, Adam Khanzada, would be standing for the elections. Loud applause and clapping followed his words and the head master suggested they commence with the task at hand. A carved wooden box was passed around to all the elders to cast their votes.

The announcement of Adam as the unanimously elected tribal chief did not sit well with Gul Hassan, but that was to be expected by everyone present. When Adam got up to say a short speech of thanks to his supporters, Gul Hassan stood up and shrugging his clothes as a sign of displeasure, turned to leave in a huff. The crowd parted immediately to make room and people refrained to look at him, afraid he might strike anyone who dared to observe his defeat. His brothers and supporters left with their vehicles speeding mercilessly, raising a cloud of dust in their wake. The crowd put up a series of loud jeering and name calling the moment the group turned the bend.

Adam's victory was punctuated with a succession of beating drums and guns fired in the air. There was an atmosphere of festivity and delight. The elections ended with a large feast of kabali pulao, dum pukht, mutton karahi and sheep slow-roasted on open charcoal pits.

"This is a big responsibility on your shoulders, son," Khodadad said on the way back to their house. "You will be accountable for a lot of people. Do not disappoint them and always hold high your traditions and family's honour." Adam listened quietly. There was something else on his mind. Babar had informed him that morning that he had heard from Dr. Pervaiz. They would have to head to Islamabad at the earliest to finalize the dates to commence treatment. He wondered if he should postpone the wedding. His father always came first.

CHAPTER 20

Virginia tried on the new jacket she had bought at the Istinye Park Shopping Centre earlier that day. She had definitely put on weight, she thought, as she looked at herself in the full-length mirror. She had bought the dark green jacket as it was a longer cut and gave her a slimmer look. Safina poked her head into her room and let out a short whistle by way of appreciating her friend. "You look stunning, madam!" she said, "but we need to hurry up. Engin will be here any minute." Dr. Yildirim was taking them out again that evening. The women were now used to spending most of their evenings with him; he refused to take no for an answer. Just two days ago, on his day off, he had given them a day tour to a village that specialized in making different cheeses, and tonight, he wanted to take them to Akdeniz Hatay Sofrazi located in the Pera district. He had raved so much about their pilaf and chicken cooked in a mound of salt, that refusing a chance to savour their food was out of the question.

Coming out of the restaurant after yet another enjoyable meal and company, the group decided to walk the streets of Pera before heading back to their hotel. They had found a friend in Engin who was living in Istanbul by himself. His family had moved to Berlin when he was just a boy. After his father's death five years ago, he had waited to complete his specialization in orthopaedics before fulfilling a dream his father had always had. Engin and his older brother had grown up on stories of the glories of the Ottoman Empire. When he was a child, his father would spend time with his two sons while his wife, who was a nurse, worked night shifts at the hospital. Onur Yildirim was a professor of mathematics at the University of Berlin and had a love for Turkish history. He firmly believed in the importance of instilling the love of their traditions in his sons. Each night, when his wife left after giving them dinner, Onur would sit down with the boys and tell them stories about their glorious heritage. The children would listen spellbound and would often request narratives of their favourite characters to be retold. Onur had a yellowed genealogical document which traced the Yildirim family's roots all the way to the Kayi tribe, which was the tribe of the father of the founder of the Ottoman Empire. Osman the First founded the ottoman dynasty after his father Ertugrul Gazi brought the Mongols and Crusaders to heel, following years of relocating their camps and a lot of bloodshed. Onur had named his first born Ertugrul to honour his ancestor. It had always been Onur's dream to return to Turkey and trace back his roots to the Kayi tribe, and now, Engin had resolved to fulfil his father's wish. He had already made a road trip following the route the Kayi's took, setting up camps and relocating from Anatolia all the way to Sogut. He had visited the battle sites of the confrontations the Turks experienced with the Mongols and Crusaders.

Engin spent hours talking with Virginia on the subject and it fascinated him to see the amount of knowledge she possessed. Engin was due to return to Germany by the end of the year and before that, he intended to complete his father's wish of connecting his roots to his ancestral tribe. Coming back to his studio apartment, he remembered he had to call his mother. She had the day off and would be at his brother's house, spending time with his family. Farah Yildirim picked up the phone on the second ring. "I can always tell when it's you who is calling," she said in her sweet voice, "I've been waiting by the phone, while Ertugrul took the kids out for skating," she said. Engin listened to his mother's voice. She kept herself busy with her work and various charities she volunteered at. Farah was a petite woman, who along with her husband, had worked hard after immigrating to Germany more than twenty-five years ago. When they had first moved to the new country, the young couple had decided they would not fall into the category of their contemporaries who chose to open shawarma joints or set up Turkish food stalls to get their feet firmly in the ground. Instead, they had both upgraded their degrees after years of going to university during the day and worked odd jobs at night. Their two sons valued the sacrifices they had made to achieve their goals and felt blessed to have them as parents. Farah always asked her younger son if he had found a nice Turkish girl for himself and tonight was no exception. She had expected the same answer she always got where her son shrugged her off saying it was too soon for him to settle down and that he had a lot of things to do before he did that. However, she was not prepared for the answer her son gave her tonight. "I may have found someone who I would like to spend the rest of my life with, *annem*," Engin said.

Farah paused for a moment before replying, "Are you serious or are you just leading me on? she asked.

"*Annem*, I have found a girl who is both talented and fun to be with. She has a sense of humour, which I know Baba would have loved, and she is very down to earth." Farah listened without interrupting and felt thankful that her son was talking about a woman instead of his work and his quest to trace back his roots to the Kayi tribe. Engin wanted his mother to visit Turkey on her next long weekend and meet his new friends. Tomorrow, he intended to speak to Safina about how he felt and perhaps, if she reciprocated his feelings, he would propose to her before he left for Germany.

Khodadad would not hear of postponing the wedding when Adam told him that it was important for him to be in Islamabad on Dr. Pervaiz's orders. "I have told you both time and again that Dr. Pervaiz can wait another few weeks. And if he can't, then I can find myself another doctor," saying that, he stormed out of the breakfast room, leaving both Adam and Mumtaz staring after him. Mumtaz was infuriated that her cousin was being so stubborn. She couldn't understand that a man who was so particular about everyone's health was being so careless about his own. She also knew that when Khodadad made up his mind about something, there was no way of changing it.

Adam stood by the window overlooking the rose garden his mother had planted with so much care and planning years ago. The bushes had grown to become time-hardened plants, which had withstood the changing seasons and two gardeners. More rose bushes had been added to the initial lot. There were over fifty different varieties and more colours than could be counted. Adam was not particularly fond of the garden; it was a depressing reminder to him that something as beautiful and fragrant as a full-bloomed rose had the potential of hurting you with its nasty thorns. He couldn't help comparing his mother to a rose, who had hurt his father knowingly. She had hurt her children and Bibi, and changed the course of their lives only to suit herself. Sighing, he turned from the window and looked at his aunt. Mumtaz was dabbing at the tears running down her ruddy cheeks with a tissue. He knew how much she adored his father and the thought of losing him made her miserable. "Bibi, lets carry on with the wedding. Changing plans is only going to make Baba angry. I will talk to his doctor and explain the circumstances," he said by way of placating his aunt.

Mumtaz sat on the sofa in the drawing room with Khodadad, with boxes of the clothes from the designers stacked all over the carpet. Babar had just returned that afternoon with the rest of the shopping and had everything put into the large room to be inspected before being hung up in the new bride's closets. Walking into the drawing room, Adam was amused to see the two looking like excited kids in a candy store. A maid was lifting the lids off the boxes one by one and pulling out the silks and chiffons from mounds of pink tissue. The room looked more like a boutique than a formal sitting area for guests. Khodadad was holding up an emerald and diamond necklace. The light from the chandelier glinted on the exquisite gems and created dancing patterns on the curtains behind him. "Adam, did you see the size of this emerald?" Khodadad said without letting his gaze leave the string he was holding. "It was mined from the Bursar quarry by your grandfather. He had kept it saved for the first daughter of the family." Khodadad's father had four sons, Khodadad being the youngest. The desire for a daughter had died with the patriarch when he had been killed along with his three older sons. Ideally, the emerald and several other gems of rare size and beauty would have been passed on to Safina; however, Khodadad and Mumtaz had decided to use the choicest of the stones for the new bride. Mumtaz paused in her scrutiny of a light blue organza suit of loose pants and fitted shirt with intricate silver embroidery worked into the weave. As happy as she was for the upcoming wedding, she kept thinking of Safina. Had she been here, she would have supervised all the wedding preparations for her brother, and perhaps would have been married herself by now. Mumtaz wondered if the girl ever missed her and her life in Pakistan. Khodadad had pushed her away by his indifference to his feelings and now suffered the most to have lost his daughter. Of course, he never spoke about it, but Mumtaz knew he sometimes went into

Safina's old room and sat at her desk, going through her sketchbooks or standing by her open closet inhaling her scent. Her cousin could be such a complex man when it came to his relationships with the people closest to him. She just prayed that Adam never disappointed him. It would make things so much easier if father and daughter could patch things up between them—life could be as it was before.

A few days before the wedding, Sherbat Murad had sent his two older sons to deliver the bride's trousseau. Being the only daughter, her mother had collected beautiful things to adorn her daughter's house. However, when Gulrukh had sadly become a widow, all her belongings, which her in-laws had returned to her parents' house, had been given away by Sherbat Murad. He wanted no reminder of the wedding that had taken place only to be replaced with sorrow in such a short time. With the sudden change of events after Mumtaz and Khodadad's propitious proposal for their daughter's hand, the Murad family had sprung into action and sent their two sons to Islamabad and Karachi to get beautiful jewellery and clothes for Gulrukh. Now, the brothers sat in the Khodadad's family's drawing room, while workers unloaded suitcases and carved wooden boxes from their two cars. Mumtaz sat with the boys and made small talk. "You know, that there is no need for all this. We have already had several outfits made for the new bride. She will have everything she needs right here," she said to the brothers while they stared at the carpet with their gaze lowered, partly out of respect and partly intimidated by the matriarch.

Khodadad sat in the library, with a folder open in front of him. The man that sat across his desk was the solicitor for the family. His late father had been a close friend of Khodadad's father and had executed all his legal dealings. It had been a few years since Khodadad had visited their office in Islamabad. Faheem Siddiqui now visited Khodadad in the village and settled his affairs on a two-day trip. Right now, he sat looking at his client, not letting the concern for his health show in his eyes. When it came to business, Khodadad was very professional, and any reference to his illness would displease him.

"Are you sure this is what you want to do? As your solicitor, I would like you to think about this a little more," the man said to Khodadad. The truth was, Siddiqui was concerned that Khodadad was rushing his decision to change his will. When Samantha had left many years ago,

Khodadad had gone to Islamabad and had drawn up his will. He had instructed the firm to send a hefty amount to his wife and severed off all ties with her. He had also given orders to return any mail sent by her returned to the sender, unopened. The sheet of paper that Siddiqui held in front of him now clearly did not make sense. "I don't understand your reasons to reconnect with your ex-wife after all these years. We know that she has remarried, so you are not obligated to do this for her," Siddiqui said, raising his bushy eyebrows over his half-mooned spectacles, furrows creasing his pasty forehead. Khodadad got up from his chair and slowly walked towards the window behind the desk and stood looking at the peak of the Bursar Mountain in the distance, the mountain that housed the quarries for the rarest emeralds in the world that were sold all over Europe. He did not speak for a while and stood motionless with his hands clasped behind his back. Siddiqui, a man whose pallid, chubby face belied his shrewdness tried to calculate what was going through his client's mind. Surely he was not having a change of heart for Samantha? Why put her as joint beneficiary with his daughter in his will? he wondered.

"When I first made the will, I was sure I would live for a long time, Faheem. Cancer changes a lot in a person. If I am not around, I want someone to look out for my daughter. And her mother is the best option," Khodadad replied without turning.

"But you have Adam who would do anything for you, even if it meant reconnecting with his sister. Why don't we let him be responsible for her?" Siddiqui asked.

Khodadad turned, facing the lawyer and replied, "Because he is as proud as his father. He has felt hurt and betrayed just as I have, and will never feel for her what Samantha might feel for her daughter," Khodadad said with finality.

Siddiqui left the next day with directives to leave the Canadian shares in stocks under Samantha and Safina's name. In the event of Samantha's death, Safina would be the sole owner of the shares. Khodadad had also bequeathed his uncut emerald and ruby collection to his daughter, to be given to her on her marriage. A trust fund was also set up under Safina's name, which was only to be given to her on Khodadad's death. He had left most of his property to Adam, including the orchard business in the village as it had been in the family for four generations, as well as the timber business and the emerald, copper and ruby quarries. Several acres of land and the orchards in Islamabad had been left to Zaheer, as well as an apartment and some stocks. In addition, Khodadad had left some land and jewels for Mumtaz and set up a trust fund in her name.

CHAPTER 21

The women packed their small cases quickly, stuffing as many essentials as they could think of in such short time. Safina looked under the bed for her running shoes, and not finding them, let out an exasperated screech. "Calm down, Safina! You're frightening me. Look under the sofa, I remember you taking them off there last night," Virginia said by way of trying to help her friend. Engin had called just twenty minutes ago, excited to have found a breakthrough in his search for his Kayi tribe roots. He wanted both women to share in his happiness and asked them to come with him for three days. They were meeting him at the station in half an hour to catch a train to Bursa and would then take a taxi from there to Sogut. Safina had wanted to refuse and stay back and do some editing on her paper but looking at Virginia's eyes light up, she couldn't say no.

Safina zipped up her parka against the blustering wind, and after picking up her bag, she helped Virginia with hers. They now had to look for Engin near the coffee shop at the station. Sure enough, Safina spotted the red jacket from far and could see him walking towards them, his face beaming. The three sat in the cafeteria warming their hands around hot coffee mugs and munching on bagels. "Next time, could you please give us some margin time, Engin? I had barely gotten out of bed and before I knew it, I was sitting in the back seat of a taxi with Virginia urging the driver to hurry. You all know I'm not a morning person," Safina said with eyes half-closed, the coffee still not taking effect of waking her completely.

"Believe me, I had no choice. I got the invitation just this morning and knew we had to hurry to make it to Sogut if we want to meet this person. I'm honoured that he has agreed to see me!" said Engin. In his search for his Kayi Tribe roots, Engin had located the last of his ancestors, a patriarch by the name of Cemil Suleiman, who settled in the town of Sogut. Mr. Suleiman was the leader of the last remnants of the tribe and was more of a recluse. After weeks of correspondence with his manager, Engin was told that Mr. Suleiman had agreed to host him and his two female guests at his house in the mountains.

The train was not very crowded and the trio managed to stretch their legs and make up for their lost sleep through most of their journey. When they got off at the station at Bursa, to their surprise, a man was waiting for Engin to take them to Sogut. "Dr. Yildirim, Suleiman Bey sends his greetings. I am here to take you to the house directly," the man with longish hair and kohl rimmed eyes said to them, then turned to open the trunk of his Mercedes to store their luggage. Safina and Virginia exchanged an uncomfortable look, but it was evident Engin was in no mood to accept any pessimism at this point. The journey was pleasant enough. Their driver, Cengiz, was the man who Engin had spoken to earlier on telephone and was Suleiman Bey's manager. The black eyes and long hair belied an entertaining companion full of amusing stories about how Suleiman Bey rescued him from a bunch of pirates when he was only a boy, and his adventures with the Bey all over the world. They learnt from Cengiz that Suleiman Bey hardly left his house now, and mostly preferred to visit his vineyards and lands.

The car started to ascend a narrow path lined with sycamore and pistachio trees. As they reached the top of the mountain, they were taken aback by the beauty of the surroundings. It seemed as if time had left the terrain untouched and was moving at a slow pace. There were fields with horse drawn ploughs, as well as a few barns, and low tables sat under the shade of trees from which old timers watched the slow traffic go by, and women looked out from windows or hung laundry out to dry. The scenery was in sharp contrast to the fast-paced and progressive life they had been living in Istanbul for the past few months. The car turned a bend and going up a little further, came to stop at a massive stone structure surrounded by wild maple and sycamore trees. Two German Shepherds came up to the car excitedly and abruptly stopped their barking the moment they spotted Cengiz. "Welcome to the Kayi House," Cengiz said to the travellers, and showed them inside.

They had been given two rooms near the back of the house to freshen up before they met with Suleiman Bey in about an hour. Safina decided to quickly shower and change while Virginia curled up on the sofa overlooking the breathtaking landscape. Coming out of the shower, Safina found her friend fast asleep, one leg curled under her on the sofa and the other dangling on the beautiful silk carpet on the floor. Quickly drying her hair, Safina decided to dress up in anticipation of her meeting with the elusive Suleiman Bey. She put on a beautiful light pink cashmere sweater over dark blue slacks and a pair of new loafers she had just bought. Selecting a large peach from a ceramic bowl on the table, she sat down on another sofa, waiting for Virginia to wake up. Her friend stirred after a few minutes, clearly refreshed after her nap and eyeing the peach, she could feel her stomach grumbling with hunger. "I can see that you're all dressed up and ready. We should see what Engin is up to. I hope we can have some lunch soon," she said, jumping up and heading off to freshen up.

They met Engin in the drawing room sitting and chatting with Cengiz. Suleiman Bey had still not shown up. "I hope you found the room comfortable. We will be having lunch soon," Cengiz said to the women. Virginia and Safina exchanged glances, both wondering if they were going to dine without meeting Suleiman Bey. Engin would be very disappointed if he had to wait another day to meet his ancestor. An elderly maid in a starched black uniform came in and announced lunch, and the company left for the adjoining dining room. Engin and Safina sat on one side, while Cengiz and Virginia sat opposite them. The head seat remained vacant. When everyone was seated, the door opened and Suleiman Bey walked in wearing a long dark coat that reached below his knees. Safina had been talking to Engin and did not notice him enter. When she turned and looked at him, for a moment, she forgot where she was or what she was doing among the people sitting around her. On cue, everyone got up but she just kept staring at the man who looked so much like her father. Virginia could sense something was wrong and looked at Safina, hoping she would snap out of whatever she was thinking and get up to greet their host. Suleiman Bey was a tall, imposing man with clear blue eyes that could see right through you. Age had softened his features but it was evident he must have been a very good looking man once. His thick, silver hair was combed back and he looked at everyone graciously, finally letting his eyes rest on Safina. Regaining composure, Safina had managed to get up but was unable to look away from the man who stood so close to her. She wanted to touch his face or hold his hand but instead, stared at him woodenly, not trusting her voice. Their host smiled at her, and gestured for everyone to sit down.

Engin and Virginia thoroughly enjoyed their meal of grilled lamb with apricots and figs and yoghurt with soft, warm bread, but Safina could hardly taste anything. She was feeling a sense of loss and gloom sitting at the table, unable to follow the conversation between Suleiman Bey and Engin. Instead, she stole glances at the face of the man sitting so elegantly to her left, or his hand when it came to rest on the table. He had the same tapered long fingers with square nails as Khodadad's and the fine blonde hair on his hand glistened in the sunlight that came in through the window. She could tell that their host could not be much older than her father and perhaps, seeing his resemblance to him had triggered some sort of regret in her. She was struggling to keep her features blank but her heart was pounding and she wanted to get away. Looking at Suleiman Bey she was filled with a longing to be back in her village, among her people, and close to her father. She was at the wrong place at the wrong time and was thankful when lunch ended and everyone got up to sit outside under the sycamore trees.

The group easily conversed in Turkish except for Safina and inwardly, she was thankful for this. It gave her a chance to sit back and observe the patriarch without being too obvious. Virginia took her aside before they sat down and asked in a whisper if she was all right. Safina gave her a smile in response, letting her know all was well. Engin and Suleiman Bey chatted in both Turkish and English and Virginia intervened whenever the topic involved anything about the Ottoman Empire. Engin was clearly energized after tracing his connection to the Kayi tribe. He had shown the faded genealogical map to Suleiman Bey and was jubilant to hear that his great, great grandfather had been known in the area as Korkusuz Adam, which translated to fearless man due to his daring contributions in the later wars between the Russians and the Ottomans.

Safina could not help but draw similarities between their host and her father. All these years, she had tried to block the fact from her mind that she had left her home, while breaking so many hearts in the process. She had been consumed with a longing to reunite with her mother, and meeting her had not been what she had expected. Instead, the disappointment and at times revulsion she felt at the stranger that had birthed her surprised her. Her inability to accept change and accept that circumstances have the capacity to alter people had come as a shock. Her mother had become the person she was because of the struggles she must have had to face coming back to Canada. Likewise, Safina herself had transformed from an introverted, sheltered girl to the driven, motivated woman she was now. She was more focused on what she wanted in life and went with a certainty towards her goal. She was still a shy person but could surprise everyone with her self-assurance when the occasion demanded. Now, looking at Suleiman Bey, she saw a man tied to the earth by his love for the land, a man who valued his roots and his ancestral heritage as his most prized possessions. A man such as him would never forgive deception and secrecy in a person, especially if the person was as close to him as his own child. How could she ever expect her father to forgive her when all she had done was wounded his pride and deceived him?

Cengiz volunteered to show them around the small town. Suleiman Bey excused himself and went inside, promising to see them at dinner time. The group preferred to walk and made their way towards the lively marketplace of Sogut. There were quite a few people around in the narrow streets of the colourful town. A group of children walked by carrying their books in satchels coming back from school. There were small coffee houses called kahve evi, where people sat idly observing the world or chatted with each other. Most women had their heads covered and were dressed in long skirts which reached their ankles and were so unlike the women they had seen in Istanbul. The town also had a tiny shop which sold souvenirs and local handicrafts, most of which were carved with the Kayi tribe's emblem on a blue background. Engin bought several mementos to take back with him, feeling a sense of pride in his connection to the tribe. Walking back to the house, the women decided to rest until dinner, while Cengiz and Engin went off in the car to visit the graves of the founders of the Ottoman Empire.

Safina felt restless and could not bring herself to fall asleep. Virginia had kicked off her shoes the moment they had entered the room and dived onto the bed after setting the alarm on her watch for one hour. Within seconds, she was asleep. Safina heard the midday call for prayers from a mosque and listening, couldn't help the tears that flowed freely down her cheeks. It had been so long since she had prayed, and coming to Sogut had somehow stirred up emotions which she had felt would be best left undisturbed. After doing the ritual cleansing with water before praying, Safina wrapped a scarf around her head and went off in the direction where the sound for the prayers came from.

It was easy to locate the mosque as several people were walking towards it with their heads covered and rosary beads in their hands. Safina joined a group of old women and walked to the separate entrance for women. The area reserved for women was not very crowded and Safina found a corner where she could pray without anyone noticing the tears that refused to stop coming down her face.

Safina felt a tap on her shoulder and opening her eyes, saw a pair of beautiful green eyes peering at her. A girl of around fifteen years of age was holding a wad of tissues for her to use. She took the tissues thankfully from the girl's hands, and wiped her face carefully, trying to clean her eyes that must have has smudged mascara by now. The girl, probably a farm worker— judging from her coarse outfit and rough hands—sat down next to her and held Safina's hand. The gesture was so unexpected, that it brought a fresh wave of sadness and longing to be with her family. They both sat like this for a while, not saying a word. It seemed as if the girl could sense the sorrow in her heart and offered a part of her soul to console Safina.

When the girls left the mosque, Safina did not know how to thank her acquaintance. She hugged her by way of expressing her gratitude, then quickly walked towards the house they were staying at. She had lost all track of time adrift in her reverie at the mosque and did not want Virginia to get worried and start looking around for her.

When she returned, Virginia was already up. "Where have you been roaming around? Oh, my Lord! What happened to you? Have you been crying?" Virginia exclaimed, shocked to see Safina's puffy eyes and pale face. Safina explained that she had gone to the mosque and prayed after many years, and the experience had left her overwhelmed. It took a while for Virginia to believe what she said but in the end, she took her explanation as the truth and let the topic drop. They had an interesting outdoors dinner with Suleiman Bey to look forward to.

For the two days they were there, Suleiman Bey had been a courteous and gracious host. There was always Cengiz to keep everyone entertained if Bey was not around. Safina had kept to herself most of the time and tried as much as possible to visit the mosque during the time of prayers, and her new friend, Hilal, who was the mosque's Imam's daughter, would often come and sit by her. The day they were to leave, Suleiman Bey had sent beautiful gifts for everyone with the maid. Engin had been presented with an antique dagger, which belonged to the Kayis, and a book in Turkish about the ancestors of the tribe. For Virginia and Safina he sent beautiful Turkish headgear embedded with semi-precious gemstones, which local women wore on formal occasions.

Safina hurried to the mosque for the evening prayers the night before they left. Cengiz was driving them all the way to Istanbul early in the morning. Just as she stepped out of the house, Safina could feel someone behind her and turned back to see Suleiman Bey walking briskly to catch up with her. Safina slowed her pace, certain that the older man wanted to be with her alone. "I have seen you going for your salat and thought I would join you this evening," Suleiman Bey said in broken English. "Perhaps you could wait for me outside the mosque when you are done your prayers," he added.

After her prayers and after she said goodbye to Hilal, Safina waited outside the mosque. It was dusk and most traffic on the road had ceased. There were a few people who were headed home after work or after their prayers but otherwise, the street was deserted. Safina leaned against the brick wall with tiny inlaid blue tiles, sad that they were leaving the next day. Sogut had made her realize a lot of things and she knew she had to reach out to her father before it was too late. Suleiman Bey had been out of the mosque since a few minutes and stood observing Safina. He could tell the girl had a burden weighing down on her young heart. "What makes you so sad, my daughter?" his words broke into Safina's thoughts. Her pent-up emotions, which she could not share with her companions, and the closeness and concern of her host at a time when she felt vulnerable and unsure were too much to put up with and unexpectedly, Safina burst into tears. Suleiman Bey pulled her into his strong arms and cradled her head on his chest and let her sob. The world seemed to pause in its revolutions. Safina could smell her father in the woody cologne the older man wore. The years of living away from him and lost memories seemed to be replaced with an overwhelming sense of love and forgiveness in the warm embrace. There was no awkwardness in being held by him; only understanding and acceptance. No words were needed to explain and none were asked. The pair stood like that for several minutes. Finally, Safina looked up into the eyes that reminded her so much of Khodadad and thanked him. Suleiman Bey lightly kissed her forehead, while cradling her face in both hands and ran his thumbs across her eyes to wipe her tears. "Do what you have to do to find peace in your heart, my daughter," he said, looking deep into her eyes. Suleiman Bey's simple phrase lifted a dead weight from Safina's heart. She smiled at the man, feeling a ray of sunshine warming her, and they started off slowly towards the house in silent companionship.

CHAPTER 22

Khodadad would not hear of lying in bed. He had been coughing uncontrollably the previous night and Adam had stayed in his room. A male nurse had been sent by Dr. Pervaiz in the last three days to administer intravenous medications to keep him well enough to move about. Now, Mumtaz was having a heated dispute with him. She wanted him to stay in bed but he refused to listen, saying it was his son's wedding and he had to personally see to the final preparations for the evening. Zaheer, who had arrived just that morning, was appalled to see how weak his uncle had become, and looked exasperatedly at him and his mother arguing. Adam had been admonished to his room to rest before the guests arrived later in the day. He looked just as worn out as his father, with all that he had been going through recently. Giving up, Mumtaz stormed out of Khodadad's room, snapping her fingers at the startled nurse to get busy and not let his ward out of his sight.

Adam had tried futilely to nap but got up suddenly and went outside. It had been not been easy to put away fleeting memories of his mother. He had been a mere four year old when she had abandoned him, Adam thought bitterly. Whenever he would see Aunty Rabia visit Babar or when he would watch children with their mothers, he would wonder if his mother had ever felt protective towards him. It hurt to think his mother did not love her children enough to stay with them and nurture them as did the mothers he saw around him. It was best to obliterate any recollection of her. Thinking of her would only emphasize that he had been deserted by her.

Trying to forget Safina was not that simple. His heart refused to believe his sister did not love her father and him and their life in the mountains. Two years after his sister's disappearance he had secretly tried to trace her whereabouts. He had understood from the conversations between his father and Bibi that she had reunited with their mother. The private investigator he had hired did not take long to give him a detailed account of what his sister was doing in her life. It was some consolation to him to know she did not live with his mother and her husband but was doing something meaningful with her life. There were times he wanted to just show up at the small house she rented a room at or even just pass by her while she walked across campus, but he could not gather the nerve to do so. It pained him to see how she struggled or how friendless and alone she seemed, but his pride and anger would not let him reach out to her.

Everything changed when his father was diagnosed with cancer. It brought Adam to realize how devastated he would be if something were to happen to him and how unable he would be to cope with the loss alone. He reluctantly took Babar into confidence and let him know about what the investigator briefed him about Safina every few months. "If you do not want to face your sister, how do you expect me to watch over her? Do you think she would like that her brother has kept tabs on her and is now sending his childhood friend with an olive branch?" Babar asked incredulously, his hands clammy just thinking of Safina's reaction to seeing him. Adam took a deep breath and outlined the plan he had in mind. He explained that to keep an eye on Safina, all Babar had to do was to involve Virginia. She had to be made aware of the conservative background Safina came from and the conditions under which she had moved to Canada. Virginia had to be convinced that Safina's wellbeing was the ultimate reason to keep Babar's involvement secret. Showing the picture he pulled up on his phone, Adam told Babar about Eugene and how he was trying to make inroads into his sister's heart. "I cannot let him become something permanent in Safina's life. Make sure that never happens," he said meaningfully to Babar.

Adam walked across the lawn and headed towards the annexe. Babar was standing by the mirror putting on his turban. "Did you speak to the woman?" Adam came to the point. "Did you tell her it was time to go back?" Babar turned around and motioned for Adam to sit.

"I met her at the hotel last night. They had been away for three days. She thinks Safina is upset about something but she won't tell her. She also said Safina had been praying at the mosque, something she has never seen her do before," Babar said.

"Did you mention anything about Baba?" Adam asked, to which Babar answered in the negative.

Babar paused for a moment and then continued, "Dr. Ambrose thinks Safina misses home and has seen her crying a lot lately." Adam listened to the last statement and went quiet. His sister had been on his mind since his father had been diagnosed with his illness. But there was nothing he could do without letting his father know. He did not want to upset him in any way and he knew how inflexible he was when it came to his feelings. Adam let out a sigh and got up. There were other pressing matters for him to deal with right now—checking up on his father being the foremost.

The wedding ceremonies had been divided over three days. The first day was the henna ritual, where the bride's family celebrated at their own house, applying henna paste on the prospective bride's hands. There would be a lot of merry-making, with all the bride's friends teasing her and taking turns to rub unguents, herbs, and fragrant oils on her body to ensure it was soft and glowing the next day. The evening would end with a feast and singing of traditional wedding songs. The next day would hold the main event, called the baraat, where the groom and his family would go to the bride's house for the religious ceremony, which would be conducted by the "qazi" and the pair would be bound in wedlock, and the bride would then leave with the groom for his house. The final day was the valima, hosted by the groom by way of thanks for a blissful union.

It was the day of the "baraat" and two diplomats who had been long friends of Khodadad's when he had been in Europe had arrived and settled in the annexe to freshen up before the evening festivities began. Relatives coming from afar were given rooms in the house and some were staying at different homes in the village. A small entourage, consisting of close friends and relatives, left the house with Mumtaz and Adam sitting in one car, with Khodadad to go to the bride's house for the nikkah ceremony. Zaheer and Babar had already left for the bride's house minutes earlier to announce the groom's arrival. Khodadad had been coughing continuously and Adam and Mumtaz had requested Sherbat Murad to keep the evening as short as possible.

The groom's family was welcomed with splendour. Colourful lights adorned the road leading from the village outskirts to the house, and just when the car turned the bend, which would take them to Sherbat Murad's residence, Babar and Zaheer—along with several young men from their village—could be seen dancing to the sound of traditional music beaten on drums, heralding Adam's arrival. Sherbat Murad clasped Khodadad in a tight embrace and led the party to the marquee which was set up for the occasion. The nikkah ceremony was conducted in solemnity and was followed by a lot of congratulatory handshakes and pats on the back for the groom. Despite the strain on his body due to exertion, Khodadad sat straight on the sofa, graciously accepting people's well wishes and looked proudly at his son. Sherbat Murad could see the effort his friend was making to enjoy the festivities, and hurried to have the food served. He did not want the day to end with Khodadad collapsing on the day of his daughter's wedding. "Baba, we will be leaving soon. Why don't you let me take you indoors to lie down for a while and let Bibi take care of you?" Adam said slowly into his father's ear. He was alarmed to see sweat beading his father's forehead despite the cold weather. Khodadad looked up at his son, who was dressed in a simple cream coloured shalwar suit with a black waistcoat. For a moment, he looked into the blue eyes and was reminded of himself. He wished his daughter was there tonight. Khodadad nodded and let his son lead him to the main house, with Sherbat Murad making way for them through the crowd of people. The ring on Adam's hand that clasped his father's elbow glinted in the bright lights. It was a stunning specimen of beaten silver embedded with a rare turquoise and surrounded by tiny sapphires which had belonged to his grandfather. Khodadad touched his son and ran his hand on the ring, feeling a strange warmth from the stone, which had been in the family for generations. He felt assured his son would carry forward the family's values and name with dignity.

The bride sat in the back of the Mercedes with Mumtaz Bibi, clad in an exquisite red silk suit embedded with tiny pearls surrounded with fine gold needlework. Her bent head was covered with her dupatta and she let Bibi hold her soft hand in hers throughout the journey, letting the tenderness in those careworn hands dispel the fluttering in her heart. She did not want to be reminded of her first marriage from not so very long ago. Rather, she wanted more than anything to strongly bind the two families together and bring her parents happiness, which had become a rarity for them. The car turned into the Khodadad residence but Gulrukh was too nervous to notice her surroundings. She let Bibi help her out of the car and another maid quickly came forward to hold up her heavy clothes and help her into the house. On entering the house, Khodadad, who was supported by Adam on one side and Zaheer on the other, came forward and opened a small velvet-lined box, which Mumtaz handed him. Nestled within the silky box was a ring matching that which Adam wore. It was a small turquoise surrounded by minute sapphires mounted on a platinum band. Taking Gulrukh's hand in his, he placed the ring on his daughter-in-law's finger and after kissing her on the forehead, left for his room.

Adam left his sleeping wife to go and check on his father. Pulling a curtain to one side, he could see the sun's languid rays trying to peep over the Bursar's summit. Khodadad was asleep and the nurse abruptly stood up from his seat by the bed when Adam entered. Adam motioned for him to keep sitting and went and stood by the bed. His father's breathing was even but he seemed paler than before. Adam wanted the valima to be over and done with so he could take his father to Islamabad without delay.

The day went by in a whir with Adam, Zaheer and Babar getting a string of instructions delivered in true military style by Mumtaz. A snap of her fingers or a cold glare was enough to send the rest of the staff scurrying off to take care of different tasks assigned to them. Musicians who had been brought from Peshawar tuned their stringed instruments and practiced tunes from folk music, and smoke curled up from the back of the house where a large area had been cleared for all the food preparation. Adam prayed his father would calm down and stop inspecting each aspect of the festivities. Even now, he could see him walking with the aid of a walking stick and talking to Zaheer about something to do with the seating arrangement. It was a segregated event with a screen dividing the men's and women's sections. The head table was set up for the bride and groom and their families at the end of the screen so both the men and women could see. Gulrukh's dark green eyes were rimmed with kohl and looked stark against her pale complexion. She wore a light pink chiffon shalwar suit with very small rubies embedded in its heavy gold embroidery, while Adam wore a black sherwani, or long coat, which came down to his knees and a silk turban on his head. The pair looked magnificent together and those who had reservations about Gulrukh earlier, promptly changed opinions to state that the couple were made for each other. The bride and groom's families sat at the head table, with Khodadad sitting at one end and Sherbat Murad at the other. Kaka Manju hovered within range of Mumtaz's vision to pass down orders from her to the waiters on duty. Khodadad had left no expenses spared and the guests were served with the most lavish spread.

Khodadad stared at the white gloved hand extending a dish of smoked pheasant on his left. The brass handles of the dish appeared to move and get blurry. He was having a hard time focusing and could not bring his hand to signal for the waiter to stop adding to his plate. Kaka Manju, who was observing the waiters with a hawk's eye, could tell the waiter serving Khodadad looked confused. Kaka made it just in time to warn Mumtaz as Adam caught his father before he collapsed on the carpet. A minor commotion erupted amongst the guests. They could see their host had buckled suddenly and were curious to see what would happen next. Necks craned forward and some crowded the group trying to revive Khodadad. Mumtaz Bibi, who always knew what to do in a panic, asked the startled musicians to start playing something with a quicker tempo. She urged the guests to enjoy their meal and graciously thanked those that opted to leave.

Babar had the Range Rover ready, and the nurse and Mumtaz climbed into it with Khodadad at the back. Zaheer and Adam took another jeep and sped out of the driveway before anyone else could see what was going on. Gulrukh saw her father staring at the departing vehicles and felt sorry for him. She knew what he must be thinking. She also knew there was no point worrying about what people thought of her and her imminent bad luck, and gathering her heavy clothes about her, she decided to take one of her brothers and join her new family in Islamabad.

Kaka Manju looked at the deserted lawn littered with tables, chairs and flowers. The musicians were packing up their instruments, while several of the servants walked about aimlessly. Sherbat Murad had seen off the last of the guests and apologised on Adam's behalf, then left for Islamabad with his daughter and his oldest son.

CHAPTER 23

"**B**ut this is so sudden!" exclaimed Engin into the mouthpiece upon hearing from Safina that they were planning to return to Canada in ten days. Virginia had gone out to collect her order of mosaic plates, which was to arrive from the Hanli Pazar, and Safina had decided to stay back to clear the desk in her room. They had collected so many things over the past three months that some of their belongings would have to be shipped to Canada. Safina felt a sudden sadness creep over her after putting the phone down. Perhaps she had tried too hard to read into the way Engin often looked at her or how he showed concern for her well-being. She had hoped their friendship would lead to something more permanent. After Zaheer, she had believed that there would be no one to creep into her heart the way he had. However, with Engin, she had looked deeper into his casual remarks and his light-hearted and relaxed attitude. Virginia's sudden announcement the night before about heading back had put Safina in a despondent mood. The thought of returning to a tiny, cold room in the basement and the colourless routine did not appeal to her.

Farah had just finished work for the day when she got the pager to pick up the telephone line. Upon picking up the handset, she could tell from her son's casual hello that something was not right. "Engin, stop beating around the bush and tell me what's bothering you, son" she said. Engin knew better than to deny what she said. His mother knew him better than anyone.

Taking a deep breath, Engin told his mother about how much he feared losing the woman he thought he would spend his life with. "I haven't even told her how I feel about her and I don't know if she even feels like that about me," he said. Farah could hear the sadness in her son's voice, which he tried to cover with offhand remarks. She knew what she had to do, and after placing the phone down, went straight to the MO's office to ask for a week-long leave. Heading home, she packed a small case and called a taxi to head to the airport.

It was always easy to spot Engin in a crowd. His six foot, four-inch frame stood out close to the exit. When he saw his mother come out of the arrivals door, Engin leapt forward to sweep Farah off the floor and held her in a tight hug. *"Annem,* you came so quickly!" he said, inhaling in the older woman's strawberry shampoo.

"Let's not waste any time. I would like to meet my future daughter in law," replied Farah with a smile.

Safina and Virginia walked the short distance from the hotel to the restaurant Engin had invited them to. He had sounded quite mysterious on the phone and said there was someone he wanted them to meet. Engin was already waiting outside the doors to the Mikla Restaurant located on top of the Marmara Hotel. His face lit up the moment he saw them. "Who is this person we are to meet today? You sounded so secretive, Engin. It is so unlike you!" Virginia exclaimed, hugging their friend.

Engin paused before replying. "I want you to meet a very special woman. She is the one person that truly understands me and loves me unconditionally," he said and started to head inside the restaurant. The women looked at each other, clearly taken by surprise. Safina tried not to let her emotions show, but she could feel a lump starting to lodge in her throat. She wished she could leave and run away somewhere but doing so would end up in a lot of embarrassment for all of them. It was obvious Engin was committed to someone else and it was better to put on a smile and get a grip on her feelings. The women followed their host inside and got their second surprise when a delicate, salt and pepper-colour haired woman got up from the table and extended both her arms to take Safina and Virginia in a joint embrace. Safina stepped back and could not help compare the mother of her childhood to Farah. Like Samantha, Farah was petite, with clear skin and deep eyes. She was dressed in a simple black dress that reached down to her knees and wore a single string of pearls. She seemed to exude elegance and refinement. Her hair was cut in a short bob and was tucked behind her ears. She spoke English haltingly in a soft voice. "This is my mother, Farah Yildirim, who has flown in from Germany to meet my Canadian friends," Engin beamed, happy to see appreciation and approval in his mother's eyes, and warmth in Virginia's and Safina's.

Their host had booked a table at the restaurant's rooftop hotel with a breathtaking view of the Bosporus. They all agreed to let Engin select the menu as he seemed to know exactly what everyone would enjoy and as always, the entrees that were served were excellent. The cozy atmosphere combined with low Turkish music and delicious food had lifted Safina's waning spirits, and she felt lightheaded with the knowledge that the woman Engin doted on was none other than his mother. Unlike her son, Farah was a quiet woman who listened to their talk with interest, her head tilted slightly to one side and with a smile on her lips. Engin would translate into Turkish for his mother whenever the English got too confusing for her.

Close to the end of their meal, Engin appeared to have gone suddenly quiet. They left the restaurant and walked down the bank of the Bosporus. Farah said she felt a bit tired after her long day of work and travel and wanted to sit on the bench by the edge of the water, and asked Virginia to keep her company. Engin and Safina walked on ahead. Safina looked at the lights from the ships speckling the water and felt an overwhelming gloom overcome her. The time she had spent in Turkey had been filled with scores of memories and most of them included Engin. The thought that their time together was ending saddened her. "There is something I have to tell to you, Safina," Engin's voice broke into her thoughts.

"Engin, since when do you need permission to speak? You are probably the most talkative doctor..." Safina cut her light banter short when she saw the seriousness in Engin's eyes. She understood without words what Engin wanted to say to her. The eyes that always twinkled with laughter were sombre for once, and Engin's voice sounded nervous "Safina, for a man who loves to talk, I will not say too much right now. I would be honoured if you could be my wife because I cannot think of a life of happiness without you in it." Safina could only smile in answer and moved closer to put her head against his chest. The arms that were clasped firmly around her held the promise of love and security and a blissful life ahead.

Virginia and Farah looked at the pair walking towards them and after seeing their faces, knew they had found each other. Virginia let out a hoop of joy and jumped up to hold Safina in a tight hug. Farah kept sitting on the bench and Engin bent down and held his mother. "I was hoping you would ask her and be done with. It took you a while, didn't it?" Virginia said to Engin, as she wiped a tear from her eye. Safina was astonished to learn that Engin had confided in Virginia some time ago about how he felt but was not sure if his feelings would be reciprocated. Safina now understood why Farah kept looking at her so much and smiling throughout dinner, and she understood why Engin seemed jittery. The lights in the distance seemed to dance on the water and she did not step back when Engin moved close to her and took both her hands in his.

The overhead lights went off and Adam got up to stretch his legs. He gently moved Gulrukh's hand from his arm and looked at his bride. She was a rare specimen and he felt lucky to have found her. When Dr. Pervaiz told him it was best his father leave for the States as soon as possible, and that Dr. Usman had already arranged for him to receive the best treatment at the hospital he worked at, Gulrukh had not hesitated for a second and told Sherbat Murad to send someone without delay to get her passport from their house in the village. She was going to accompany her husband for her father-in-law's treatment. On hearing this, Mumtaz had smiled inwardly knowing that another headstrong woman like herself had come into the family and she would do all of them proud. Within two days, Khodadad was on a plane to Houston, accompanied by his son and daughter-in-law.

Adam returned to his seat with a glass of orange juice. He touched the cold glass to Gulrukh's cheek and waking up, she smiled at him. There was no false coyness in her, nor did she put on nervous airs typical of new brides. She was practical and bold and these were virtues which Adam admired in a woman. "You have been sleeping for such a long time. Baba was wondering if I had drugged you to bring along with us," Adam said, handing her the glass. Gulrukh drank the juice thirstily. Her dark hair escaped her head scarf, framing her face in disarray.

"One can't help but fall asleep on these wide seats. I knew first class was supposed to be comfy but this is almost like you're sleeping in your own bed," she said getting up. "I will go check up on Baba and if he's awake, I will give him company."

Khodadad had the first two seats of the first class cabin to himself and was sitting up and watching a comedy. "Come sit next to me," he motioned for Gulrukh to take the empty seat beside him. "The three stooges have always been Bibi's favourite and I can see why," he said laughing. "Larry looks exactly like Manju Kaka when he was young." Gulrukh sat down and took her father-in-law's hand in hers.

"It's good to see you're up and enjoying your flight. Let's get you something to eat now," she said, to which Khodadad made a face as he had no appetite and had hardly eaten anything the past few days. Gulrukh selected a peach from the fruit basket the flight attendant placed near them and sectioned it into thin slices. "These are such bland peaches. I can hardly taste them. Have you ever tried the fruit from our orchard? Safina used to have her own special trees there. Her favourite was the cherry tree, which had the most succulent fruit you could ever dream of," Khodadad spoke to Gulrukh, not realizing how easily he had mentioned his daughter's name to her. He went on to reminisce about Safina's childhood and about her sketches and how fluent she was in French. It was obvious he missed her terribly but did not bring her up in front of his son. Gulrukh listened with fascination because growing up, Khodadad's two children had been more of a mystery to the rest of the children in the village. Apart from catching glimpses of them while they travelled to the plains or went riding, no one had really seen Adam or Safina. The kids had a white mother and that set them apart. However, Adam often accompanied his father when he got older, and had grown up to be a steadfast tribal. Gulrukh remembered fragments of a conversation her parents had had where her father was telling his mother that Khodadad had married without his father's consent. When conflict broke out amongst the tribes, his father had asked Khodadad to move to the village but unfortunately, before he could make the move, his family was killed and Khodadad's wife never got to meet them. Very few people had met the white woman, who had been very beautiful but preferred to visit Islamabad instead of the people in the village. In the end, she had disgraced the family by leaving her husband, and the same was said of her daughter who joined her later.

Adam came up to the front of the aircraft, and Khodadad suddenly ceased talking about Safina. Instead, he changed the subject to Zaheer's marriage and asked Adam if his cousin had found anyone he liked. The group continued chatting about a mixture of topics but avoided the one uppermost on everyone's mind, namely, the clinical ordeal Khodadad would be facing upon his arrival to the States. Khodadad was taking pains to keep up a cheerful front for all of them, and especially for the new addition to the family. He wanted Gulrukh to remember him as a pleasant, jovial person rather than a lethargic, boring man fixated on his health. He wanted his grandchildren to know how pleasing his company had been, rather than Gulrukh telling them she had spent her few days with their grandfather on his death bed, holding his hand or giving him his medications.

The overhead lights to fasten their seat belts went on and Adam moved to the back of the cabin to his seat. Gulrukh stayed back with Khodadad and he resumed talking about his children's growing years. She noticed he avoided all mention of his wife but spoke fondly of both his children. He talked about Adam's aversion to wearing western clothing and how much he had protested going to England for his education, or how as a child, Safina would befriend every hurt animal she would find and how she had once almost fallen into the river while trying to sketch. Khodadad tried to give Gulrukh an image of Safina with the stories he told; perhaps he hoped one day the brother and sister would reconcile, and as Adam's wife, Gulrukh did not find her a total stranger. Soon, it would be time to land and Gulrukh knew she would not be able to share another intimate moment with her father-in-law for a long time. She had grown up with an impression of cold reserve and authority about the former tribal chief but was pleasantly discovering another side to him, a side which was warm and companionable and one she would be sorry to lose.

The aircraft made a smooth landing at the George Bush International Airport and an ambulance with paramedics was already waiting on the tarmac to take Khodadad directly to the Anderson Cancer Centre. The rest of the family followed in a limousine. Babar had arranged for a condo, as well as a house keeper in a building very close to the hospital so visiting Khodadad would be easier. Khodadad was already with Dr. Usman when Adam reached the hospital after dropping off Gulrukh at the condo. There were two other doctors there and they all seemed to be engrossed in deep discussion. Upon seeing Adam enter, Dr. Usman looked up from the folder he was reading and discussed the procedure they were going to administer to Khodadad to stabilize his breathlessness. They would start with chemotherapy the following day. The travelling had tired Khodadad and he was settled soon into a private room with a view of a park with a fountain. When his father had fallen asleep, Adam left to walk back the short distance to the condo. The next day was going to be a long one, and he wanted both him and Gulrukh to be rested beforehand.

CHAPTER 24

Safina looked in the mirror and for a moment, was reminded of her mother. There was something about her eyes today that made her look like her. Perhaps it was the eye shadow that Virginia had insisted she wear or maybe she looked more womanly and fragile in the white gown Farah had picked for her. Had she been in Pakistan, she would have been dressed in the deep red Kashmir silk Bibi had been saving for this day. In fact, everything about this wedding seemed unreal. Suleiman Bey would be giving her away instead of her father, Virginia had unexpectedly taken on the role of a mother rather than a mentor, and instead of wearing her family's heavy jewels, she wore a simple rope of pearls circling her throat. Safina looked at the solitaire that Engin had given her. It was an elegant ring, which he had surprised her with just moments after she had agreed to marry him. In principle, it was a day to be joyful, yet Safina could not help feel the burden of the years since she had left her family sit like a weight in her heart. There was so little about her that Engin knew. Perhaps he would hate her for abandoning her father and brother or even be surprised at how she had turned away in repugnance from her mother when she was reunited with her in Canada after years of being apart. She was aware of how close Engin was to his brother and how much he adored his mother, but he did not know how much his future wife had hurt her own family. The weight in her heart spread its ugly claws around her throat and she saw her face contort into a repulsive grimace. The woman reflected in the mirror was not the kind and compassionate person Engin thought he was marrying. Rather, it was a selfish woman who had sacrificed nothing for anyone but only lived for herself. The door opened and Virginia breezed in holding up a hat box in one hand and a bouquet of light pink hyacinths in another and the spell broke. Safina's misgivings and guilt dissipated and were replaced with the excitement Virginia exuded.

Suleiman Bey had graciously offered his home for the wedding and suggested the official ceremony take place at the village mosque. Engin had been thrilled with the invitation, but going back to Sogut had brought back memories of her own village for Safina. Virginia could tell Safina was feeling emotional, after all, a wedding was a big day for any woman, but she sensed that Safina was missing her own family. The phone call Virginia received only three days ago had disturbed her immensely and she was tempted to share it with Safina. She had been told that Safina's father was going to be in Houston for treatment as his condition had worsened. Somehow, Virginia kept the news from her as she felt it might prevent the wedding from taking place. In addition, telling Safina would mean she would know about her secret encounters with Babar. Suddenly, she felt nervous. Virginia knew Safina was a private person and did not like talking about her family or her past. She feared Safina would be upset were she to know that Babar had been in contact with her.

A car pulled into the porch and heavy steps could be heard making their way up the wooden staircase. There was a knock on the door and the maid entered, moving aside to let Suleiman Bey through. He had come to take the bride to the mosque.

Engin's brother and his family had also come for the wedding and were already waiting in the mosque with him and Farah. For the occasion, the groom had opted to wear the traditional Kayi garb of loose pants with shirt and cummerbund and for effect, he had the wrought dagger Suleiman Bey had gifted him tucked into the waistband. He also wore a headgear of sorts, unlike the ones worn in her village, Safina noticed with mild amusement. Engin had undeniably taken pains to look like a classic Turkish of the Kayis. Hilal met them at the mosque's entrance and brought everyone to where her father, the imam, sat. Several people from the village were also present, partly out of curiosity to see who the special guests were that Suleiman Bey was hosting at his house and partly because they wanted some entertainment to add zest to their day.

The imam started the proceedings with verses from the Quran and performed the nikkah, binding the couple in holy marriage. He made a short speech in which he outlined the duties of both the spouses towards each other and the importance of honesty and patience for a marriage to succeed. He quoted from several religious examples of what a perfect marriage should be and gave blessings to the new couple. After his sermon, Hilal went around passing Turkish delight and candied almonds wrapped in pink tissue to all present in the big hall, and everyone broke into joyously congratulating the new couple. For a woman seldom given to emotion, Virginia shamelessly dabbed at her eyes, her makeup running down her face. She almost felt like the mother of the bride, giving her away. Farah was quiet for her own reasons. Her husband would have been so proud of his son getting married and that too in Sogut, the seat of the Kayi tribe. She wished more than anything for him to be there today. Sensing his mother's feelings, Engin's older brother put his arm around his mother by way of comforting her.

A shadow rose unobtrusively from the darkened corner of the noisy room and left the mosque walking down the road to a waiting car parked discreetly behind some trees. Zaheer felt the bile rise in his throat. It had been a torment sitting quietly in a corner while Safina got married to some stranger. He recalled the last time he had met her. She probably hated him since then. What was it about her that he could not get her out of his system? She consumed his every fibre, every moment. A part of him blamed himself for her alienation; he had been the one to put her on that plane and send her off. What had he been thinking? And now, he watched helplessly as she blindly committed herself to a foreigner. Why did he keep tracking her movements when he knew it was foolish to do so? She obviously had no clue about her father's condition. He had wanted so much to tell her but watching her dressed as a bride, moments away from becoming someone's wife, he could not bring himself to do it. It was best he left unnoticed. He sat in the car and asked the driver to take him back to Istanbul. He had a flight to catch to Europe in the morning.

The group left the mosque and proceeded the short distance to the house on foot. The garden had been decorated with tiny lights and metal lamps and the tables with white roses had been set up for guests and family. For a fleeting moment, Safina was reminded of the garden in her father's house. Similar lights would adorn the trees and bushes whenever there was a celebration, tables would be set up with candles, and there would be music and food and laughter. On such occasions, Bibi would forget her aching knees and would be seen moving from one corner of the garden to another, overseeing everything and giving orders to Manju Kaka along the way. She had such a marvellous skill for throwing the perfect parties, which Khodadad asked of her to arrange from time to time. Cengiz broke into her thoughts and came forward leading a short, chubby woman by the hand. "This is my wife, Nadide, and these are my princesses," he said, pointing at two adorable girls about five and six years old, hiding behind their mother's ample behind. The girls bashfully came forward holding up tiny bouquets of white rosebuds, as their mother nudged them forward to give to the bride. Engin, who had the talent of making friends with everyone, bent down and said something to the girls in Turkish and they started to giggle. He then spoke to Nadide who also smiled shyly and nodded her head, while looking at Safina. When they were alone, Safina asked what he had said to Nadide that had made her blush and smile. "I asked her to pray that we also have adorable children like hers soon. I cannot wait to have teeny weeny Safinas running around the house," he said with a twinkle in his eyes. Engin's words seem to put Safina in a wistful mood. She was reminded again that there was no one from her family on her big day and that her future children might never get to meet their maternal grandparents.

Engin was an uncomplicated yet sensitive man. He well understood that family was a vulnerable topic for Safina and because of that reason, he did not want to ever push her to talk about her people. He wanted her to feel comfortable about her feelings and close enough to him to bring them up herself. It was enough for now that his new bride easily gelled with his mother and brother and took ownership of their family without hesitation. One day, when she felt like it, his wife would share her emotions with him of her own accord.

CHAPTER 25

Renata looked at the bruises on her arm. She had been standing under the shower since almost an hour, willing the marks to wash off. But they never did. Zaheer's promises each time they made love about how it would never happen again were as hollow as his words of love, and she was a fool to believe. He was such a complicated man, she thought bitterly, to take her for granted whenever he needed her for comfort, yet he could surprise her with unexpected compassion, generosity and understanding, and always listened to her talk about herself. He knew everything about her, yet there was so little she knew about him. When she had asked him about the airline ticket to Islamabad last month, he had casually remarked it was office work. But he was forgetting that she worked for him and she knew there was no important commitment for Pakistan for which he had to rush. And then there was the box from Auguste Froschammer jewellers, tucked into his carry-all. She had opened it to find a diamond and gold bracelet in it, which obviously was not for her but for someone in Pakistan. She had quickly put the box back, afraid that Zaheer would be furious if he saw her going through his things. He came out of the shower and took her in his arms and turned her face towards him. "I will be back before you know it. Now, don't make such a sad face and smile for me," he said, letting the towel drop. Before she could protest and remind him that he had to be at the airport soon, he had her on the bed, his hands pulling her head back and kissing her neck passionately. It was times like these she doubted herself, and tried to believe the ardour she felt was real and that it was ridiculous to mistrust him. After all, he took care of her in every other way, he was just not ready to commit yet, she consoled herself and returned his passion.

Renata had been expecting Zaheer earlier but then saw the email in the office, stating he would be in Turkey on personal business for a couple days. He should have told her about this detour for no other reason than her being his assistant, if not his lover. When he showed up three days later, preoccupied and with dark circles under his eyes, she should have held her tongue rather than asked him what he had been doing in Turkey. Her question had infuriated him and he had headed for the shower without answering. It had taken her almost the whole weekend to placate him with tears and apologies until finally, he had taken her to bed. However, instead of being tender and loving towards her, Zaheer had been coarse and unkind and hurtful. He had dug his fingers deep into her arms when he held her and paid no heed to her cries of pain. In the end, he had been remorseful and rationalized his behaviour as being frustrated due to being apart from her for so many days. Renata wanted to believe him because believing was so much easier than not. She stood now, drying her hair and wondering if Zaheer was cheating on her with someone in Pakistan. After all, he came from a different culture and men from his part of the world only married someone their family chose for them.

Renata's fears dissipated when Zaheer called her into the office and told her to leave for home early. He wanted to make up for last night and would be picking her up from her apartment in an hour to take her out. Picking up her bag and coat, she left in a happy mood, looking forward to a night out with him, certain she was being doubtful for no reason.

Safina had moved into Engin's apartment and was staying back in Istanbul until Engin's contract with the hospital ended in six weeks. Virginia had refused to stay back and said it was time she headed home to Canada and was leaving in three days. The phone rang while Safina was helping Virginia pack the stuff that had to be shipped home. She had turned pale when she heard the voice on the other end and excused herself to go onto the small balcony with the cordless hand set. Safina watched Virginia through the glass door, her back hunched while she leaned on the wrought iron balustrade. Normally, she spoke while standing straight and never propped herself for support. Her body language said she was anxious as she kept looking over her shoulder to make sure she wasn't heard. Safina tried to look engrossed in packing when Virginia came in through the door. She believed there was something disturbing about the call and Virginia was keeping it from her.

"Safina, there's so much that needs to be done. I don't think I will be able to go out this evening. Besides, you two should be spending time alone instead of me tagging along everywhere," Virginia said. Engin was coming over after work to take the women out. He said they had to make the little time Virginia had in Turkey special and had planned a cruise for the evening.

"Try convincing Engin. You know he does not take no for an answer; besides, he has already bought the tickets," Safina replied, refusing to let Virginia stay by herself. She noticed that her friend's hand shook as she poured water from the decanter and spilled some on to the carpet from the glass.

"It's just the thought of travelling alone that's making me nervous," she said flippantly, noticing Safina's surprised look. Safina did not say anything but knew it was not the thought of travelling by herself that was making Virginia edgy. After all, she was used to taking trips around the world for several conferences and meetings many times a year. There was something she was keeping from her.

It was good they all had their parkas on as it was a chilly night and it was blustery on the ship. Much to Virginia's amusement, Engin kept adjusting Safina's scarf, worried she might catch a cold while she was enjoying the pampering and attention, which she had missed for such a long time. "You will spoil her rotten, Engin. What will she do when she goes back to Canada?" she said playfully. Engin looked at Safina and smiled. "We have worked that out as well. Once Safina goes back, I will join her and move to Canada in a few months. I have to take care of a few things in Germany before I can move, and when I come there, we will buy a small house and start a family," he said beaming. Virginia raised her eyebrows in astonishment, taken by surprise with the news.

When she got dropped off at the hotel, Virginia sat down at her desk and placed a long-distance call to Pakistan. This was the first time she was calling him. "*Hello ji, kaun hai?*" the person at the other end said in a language she did not understand.

"I need to speak with Mr. Babar please," she spoke. Clearly, the person did not understand English, so she put down the receiver, hoping Babar would get the message that someone had called for him and would put two and two together and call her back. It was best to just stay put and not leave the hotel until she heard from him.

"Who was that?" Mumtaz asked Manju Kaka as he was putting the phone down.

"It was a woman who spoke in English. She wanted to speak with Babar," replied Manju.

"Did you ask her name? Did you recognize the voice?" she asked, frowning. Manju shook his head in the negative.

Mumtaz left and headed for her room. Who could that have been? As far as she knew, Babar did not give the home number to any of the business contacts he made on his trips abroad. It was an unspoken rule of the house that the home number was only for personal use, and only Khodadad's lawyer or doctor contacted him on it.

When Babar's jeep entered the driveway, he could see Bibi standing by the door waiting. He hoped everything was okay with Agha Ji. "A woman called on the house phone asking for you. She only spoke English," Mumtaz said to him, narrowing her eyes and observing him carefully. "If there is something you want to tell me, now is the time, Babar. You know I don't like to be surprised," she added. Babar paled in front of the matriarch. As a rule, he tried to avoid Bibi as much as possible, and hardly ever spoke to her. He would have to tell her the truth willingly because she had her ways of getting to the bottom of things.

Mumtaz let out a long sigh. She had listened to the man without interrupting. Hearing what Babar had to say had somewhat relieved her. At least she knew that Safina was well. However, what she would do when she heard her father was ill remained a question. Mumtaz knew she was embarrassed to contact home because of her guilt and knew from her experience when Samantha left in similar circumstances, how her mother's presence was removed from the house as if she had never existed. When she motioned to Babar that the discussion had ended, he got up to leave and paused near the door. "Bibi, could you please keep this to yourself? Adam would be furious if he found out I told you," he said uncomfortably. Mumtaz did not reply and simply bade him good night.

Engin couldn't get time off from work to drop off Virginia at the airport. He had said goodbye the night before and now, Safina was taking a taxi to the hotel. She was going to miss her friend but at the same time, she did not want to leave Istanbul while Engin was still working there. When she reached the hotel, she found Virginia on the brink of a panic. She was shaking uncontrollably and was sweating profusely. Safina let her handbag drop to the floor and rushed to where Virginia sat near the desk. Something told her it had to do with the phone call she had received a couple of days ago. Upon seeing her, Virginia tried to calm herself and asked Safina to sit down—there was something she had to tell her.

"I started getting occasional calls from a stranger in the office about a year ago. He seemed to ask random questions about you, which I ignored and then the calls stopped coming. I thought it was someone who probably liked you and was just trying to get some information about you before he approached you. Then, just before Eugene's accident, another person with a heavy accent called my home number and told me about your family and that it was best I do as asked for your wellbeing. Safina, I was afraid for you and I could tell he was trying to look out for you in his own way. Anyways, this person, had a way of always finding me somehow, and would ask me about you," Virginia narrated, while Safina listened with incredulity.

"Did you ever meet him?" she asked.

"The first and only time I met him was on the plane from Toronto to Istanbul. He took me by surprise," she said breathlessly.

"Can you describe him, what did he look like?" When Virginia gave her the description, Safina uttered one word, "Babar," to which Virginia nodded.

Safina now remembered the man she saw on the plane and beach. There was something so familiar and uncanny about him, and he had gone to lengths to avoid facing her and looking at her directly. He had changed so much, certainly gotten taller and slightly more polished than how she remembered him. Safina shuddered visibly. She had always disliked Babar; hated him, rather. It was creepy to think he knew where she was or had been spying on her. But how was it possible for Babar to come and go to Turkey without her brother's knowledge? How was it that he was keeping tabs on her and to what purpose? Virginia could see Safina assimilate the information and how much it was unsettling her, and she chose to withhold the fact that their extravagant trip had been financed by Babar. He had wanted her to get away from Canada on Adam's orders and be gone from all the stress she had been going through.

Right now, Safina was more than unsettled. She was annoyed that Virginia had kept something so significant from her and not trusted her enough to tell her about it. "So, what did Babar want from you next? Did he want you to push me into the Bosporus or something?" Safina's voice had an edge when she spoke but she was totally unprepared for the answer she got.

"Your father isn't well, Safina. He is in the States getting treatment. He has leukaemia. I'm so sorry," she said tearfully.

Safina had not expected her father to come up in the discussion and hearing about him, drained the blood from her veins. The shame of her deception and her struggle to shrug off her past suddenly seemed to have grown sharp claws, which dug into her flesh while stretching it down to reveal bone and fibre. She could almost hear her skin tearing, falling away from her. Virginia saw Safina's face contorting and mistook it for the pain she thought she was experiencing about learning about her father. She did not know Safina's condition was purely because of her self-loathing and guilt complex.

They did not speak on the taxi ride to the airport. Safina had her face turned to the car's window, while Virginia looked at her friend with remorse. She felt horrible for not telling her about Babar when he had first made contact, and now it was too late. When they were almost at the airport, Virginia put her hand over Safina's in a gesture of apology. "Will you please forgive me? I was afraid," Safina spoke without turning.

"I wish I could get rid of the ghosts that haunt me," she said. The taxi stopped and it was time to get off.

"What will you do now, Safina?" Virginia asked, hoping she could make some amends by asking about her plans, but she got no reply in return and headed inside the airport, while the taxi moved on.

Safina was thankful they were keeping Engin at work at the hospital to make up for all the time he had taken off for the wedding. She had the apartment to herself and wanted to calm down before he got back later that night. To distract herself, Safina decided to cook something and pulled open the freezer to take out some chicken to bake with potatoes and serve it with garlic bread and hummus. She turned on the stereo and let Nusret Fateh Ali Khan's soulful renditions of traditional music divert her thoughts. "I did not hear you come in," Safina turned around when her husband's strong arms came around her shoulders. Engin had just got home and was touched to see his wife engrossed in putting together a salad of cucumbers, tomatoes and lettuce. He was glad they would be dining at home because he had had a busy day and did not feel like going out for food. The chicken baking in the oven looked delicious and the house looked warm and cozy. He felt blessed to have such a caring wife.

Adam and Gulrukh came home to the condo after spending the day at the hospital. As always, Mariam, the cook cum house keeper that Babar had miraculously arranged for them before their arrival in Houston had a meal waiting for them. She usually came just after they left in the morning and waited until they returned in the evenings, and after she had laid out the food on the table, Adam called a taxi for her to go back home. Mariam was a young Armenian who had moved to the States a few years ago. She had lost her husband recently and was trying to make ends meet while raising two young kids. When the agency called her about the job, she had jumped at the opportunity no matter how impermanent it seemed. Gulrukh was thankful for her presence, and on the days she did not accompany Adam to the hospital, Mariam and her went out together to shop for groceries and supplies.

Besides keeping the house spotless, Mariam was an excellent cook, who surprised them each evening with simple yet delicious meals. "Mariam, you must teach me how to make this," Gulrukh said, peering into the pot that was bubbling with soup, the aroma engulfing the whole apartment. "And I will show you how we make an amazing stew called *yakhni*." Mariam just smiled in response, pleased that her cooking was appreciated and thankful to have found such gracious employers.

The phone rang and Adam picked it up, and was overjoyed to hear Zaheer's voice on the other end. Since the time they had come to the States, he had not heard from him. He knew how close his cousin was to his father and could not understand what was keeping him away. Of course, he understood that his work kept him busy most of the time but he had hoped to have him around more.

"How is Agha ji coping with the treatment? I hope his morale is up," said Zaheer. Adam gave him a rundown of the most recent tests and informed him that his father was responding well to the medication and that his spirits were also cheerful. Zaheer promised to visit at his earliest and put the phone down just as Renata entered the bedroom door, holding a tray with fresh crepes, juice and coffee.

"*Liebling*, are you going again somewhere?" she said, sitting down on the bed with their lazy Sunday breakfast and making a long face.

"I told you I have family in the States, and I will be visiting them," he replied, picking up the glass of juice.

"But you promised this time we would go away somewhere together when you can get away," Renata said in a slightly whiney voice.

Zaheer looked into the half-empty glass and pondered for a while. After all, there was no harm in taking her along. They would stay at a hotel and no one needed to meet her.

Gulrukh spent the next couple days at home setting up the spare bedroom for Zaheer's arrival. Mariam and her went out to the Peacock Alley and bought several sets of bed linen and towels and got various ingredients for traditional cooking. They bought the choicest cuts of meats at the halal store and spices and basmati rice. Luckily, Mariam was able to locate several stores that sold Indian ingredients, which were impossible to find elsewhere. Gulrukh's excitement at having their first house guest was infectious and Mariam took her to all the places she had only heard of but could never afford to shop at herself. Taking off her scarf, Gulrukh beamed when she saw that her husband had already come home and stood watching in mock horror as the hotel porters brought in package after package of shopping.

"I will be a pauper by the time you two will be done setting up Zaheer's room. I was getting worried you were lost somewhere," he joked while the women laughed, happy that they had accomplished so much that day.

When Mariam had left, Adam and Gulrukh sat in the living room, chatting before going to bed. The fact that his father was recovering well and that Zaheer would be visiting had put Adam in an unusually good mood, and Gulrukh was thankful he was not so overwrought with worry about his father anymore. "We are lucky to have found Mariam," he said.

"When you go out shopping, make sure you always get something for her and her kids as well. We must help her as much as possible." Gulrukh never ceased to be surprised by her husband's traits, which he revealed over time and which melted her heart, bringing her closer to him. She had thought it would take time to forget she had been married once, but it seemed to her, that Adam was the first man to have won her heart so completely. He would be the last too, she reflected.

Renata's joy knew no bounds at the prospect of going with Zaheer and that too to the States. She found it difficult to contain her happiness at the office where the two took pains to be formal with each other as Zaheer had been explicit about not letting anyone at work find out about their relationship. Keeping in mind that Zaheer was Muslim, Renata packed clothes that were not revealing and a scarf to cover her head, just in case. Zaheer was being exceptionally pleasant to her and had bought her a beautiful leather jacket and boots, as well as an expensive wrist watch. She had no doubt he had been going through some sort of phase where he would mistreat her out of frustration and now all was good.

The morning after they reached Houston, Zaheer got up early and started getting ready to leave. Renata sat up in bed, surprised to see him up and asked where he was off to. When Zaheer told her he was going to visit his uncle at the hospital, Renata got up hurriedly to get ready as well, but Zaheer stopped her midway, saying he was going alone. This put a coldness around her heart and brought tears to her eyes. She had assumed Zaheer was going to introduce her to his family and they would no longer have to hide their relationship. However, Zaheer left without another word.

"Agha ji, you had us all so worried. Amma keeps asking me to bring her here and maybe I will do that on my next trip," Zaheer had been chitchatting with his uncle since almost an hour before Adam and Gulrukh walked into the room. Both men were sitting by the window overlooking the fountain. Adam and Zaheer hugged each other, while Gulrukh smiled happily to see someone from her village.

"Where is your luggage? And why didn't you let me pick you from the airport?" Adam asked his cousin confusedly, to which Zaheer replied that he had opted to stay at a hotel so as not to inconvenience the couple.

Hearing this, Gulrukh's face dropped and she got very quiet. However, Adam and Khodadad would not hear of him living elsewhere and in the end, Zaheer had to give in with a promise to bring his suitcase to their home in the evening.

Despite Adam's insistence to drive Zaheer to the hotel to pick up his stuff, Zaheer left in a taxi alone. Inwardly, he was cursing himself for bringing Renata along and when he reached their room, he ignored her puffy eyes and sour mood. "When will I get to meet your uncle, Zaheer?" she asked tearfully, to which he responded that he was moving to his uncle's house for a few days and when he returned, he promised to take her around. He left with a quick peck on her cheek and a few hundred dollar bills on the table, suggesting she go out shopping while he was away.

Mariam started putting the roast lamb with chicken biryani, kebabs and yoghurt sauce on the table the moment the buzzer announced the guest's arrival. Gulrukh showed Zaheer to his room and Adam called a taxi to take Mariam home, along with a bag full of groceries. Zaheer had noted the woman's clear skin and blue eyes with interest and casually asked who she was. Gulrukh narrated how Mariam was a blessing and was a widow who was going through a rough patch. She was a teacher by profession, but needed to complete her certifications and go to a language school before she could teach in the States. Until then, she was doing odd jobs through a temp agency and luckily, they had found her when they most needed someone. "The food was excellent. I can't believe you made my favourite lamb roast just the way I like it," Zaheer said appreciatively at the end of the meal. Gulrukh informed him she had been teaching Mariam how to prepare their village specialities and since she was an excellent cook to begin with, she was learning fast.

In the morning, the doctor told Adam that Khodadad was well enough to go home for a few days and could come when the next dose of medication had to be administered. Hearing this, Gulrukh arranged the master bedroom for her father in law and set up their own bed in the small den. Adam brought his father home by midday and once again, it felt as if they were a normal family again, with no trace of illness or stress shadowing their lives. The first thing Khodadad said when he got home was that he was sorry Adam and Gulrukh had spent the early days of their marriage looking after him. He insisted that they go away somewhere for a few days while he stayed back with Zaheer. Despite protests from both Adam and Gulrukh, Khodadad was adamant and both knew better than to argue with him. Reluctantly, Adam agreed and called a car rental for an SUV. He would leave his Mercedes in the garage in case Zaheer needed it. It was decided that the couple would take a road trip to a resort and return by the weekend in four days.

Mariam came in early the day Adam and Gulrukh were to leave and after getting explicit instructions about Khodadad and what foods to prepare for him, she started with her daily chores. She was preparing lunch when Zaheer came and sat down in the living room, which was open to the kitchen and the dining area. He had his back to where she was working but could see her moving around the kitchen in the huge mirror in the dining room. "Could I get you something?" Mariam asked after a while. Zaheer politely asked her to fix him something to eat and when she put together a sandwich for him, he came and sat on a bar stool at the counter. "I heard you are from Armenia. It's an amazing place. I was in Yerevan two years ago working with the United Nations about earthquake evacuation procedures." Mariam's face lit up to hear her hometown's name brought up. She instantly liked the courteous man and they both started chatting comfortably while she cooked. When Zaheer left at intervals to check up on Khodadad, she liked him even more for being so respectful and caring of his uncle. By the evening, Zaheer had extracted Mariam's life story and listened sympathetically about the troubled phase she was going through. He was attentive and concerned. After Khodadad had gone to bed, Mariam was about to leave when Zaheer offered to drop her home. "But, Adam calls me a taxi each night. I don't want to bother you," she said, but he would not hear of it and they both went down to the underground parking to where the Mercedes S 600 was parked. Mariam gave him the directions to where she lived and the two left for the low-income housing neighbourhood. Reaching her house, Zaheer opened the door for her, further surprising her with his manners. Within the next couple of days, Mariam was completely won over and when he asked her one night that they stop at the mall to pick up some things for her kids, she did not object. Zaheer insisted Mariam buy anything she wanted and when they came out of the building more than an hour later with two carts full of groceries and several other packages, it was already quite dark. The parking lot was almost deserted. "I didn't realize how long it took us. You really should not have done this." Mariam's sentence was cut short when a pair of hands gripped her body from behind as she was bent placing packages in the back seat. Mariam swung around to face Zaheer, too shocked to say anything, and saw his eyes gleaming in the darkness. He wasn't smiling but instead, had a glazed look in his eyes, so unlike the compassionate and warm air he always had about him. Before she could understand what was happening, Zaheer had pushed her onto the backseat on top of a package and was yanking her trousers down. The box from a jigsaw puzzle she had bought for her six-year-old daughter dug into her back. She forgot the pain assaulting her body and the picture on the puzzle box came to her mind. It was a landscape of rolling hills with two cows in the foreground and a rabbit holding up a huge carrot in both paws. The torture to her body paled in comparison to the ache she felt in her heart. She was oblivious to what was happening to her or how Zaheer deeply grazed her neck with his teeth. The physical pain did not matter but the black pit in which she was cornered seemed to get deeper and darker, engulfing her in thick murkiness. What seemed like a thousand years was over in a few minutes and Zaheer straightened up and went and sat behind the wheel of the car. Mariam curled herself on the backseat and let the motion of the moving vehicle fool her into believing she was having a dream. The car stopped and Zaheer asked her to get out and to take her things with her. Mariam's two kids came running outside when they saw the car through the window.

"Hello kiddies! Sorry we are late, but your mom wanted to get you presents and we got busy shopping," Zaheer said to the children and clicked open the trunk to reveal several bags of groceries and toys. Mariam got up from the car, too shaken to even look at Zaheer still sitting at the wheel and walked into the house, while the kids squealed with delight and unloaded the car of their goodies, oblivious to their mother's pain. Zaheer did not look back. He turned the ignition and took off in the direction of the closest bar. He was going to get hammered tonight.

CHAPTER 26

Safina lifted the receiver and dialled the number. Mumtaz picked up on the third ring. She could not get herself to respond to the familiar voice at the other end. Mumtaz spoke in Darri and the language of her village sounded sweet to Safina's ears. "Bibi, it's me," Safina whispered. Even though her hand started shaking the moment she heard Safina's low voice and she had to sit down, Mumtaz kept her voice firm and even.

"It took you this many years to call me, huh? What did you think you were doing when you left? We thought you had been swallowed by the river. And why didn't you call before? Is this what I raised you for?" the older woman wasted no time in speaking her mind. In the harshness of her words, Safina could hear the love and tenderness which had soothed her throughout her insecure childhood. She would have given anything to be able to put her head on that wide lap and let Bibi caress her with her rough hands. Both women had tears coursing down their faces, but neither was willing to let the other know about it. Bibi never gave into displaying her emotions and she got to the point. "Safina, I am trying to get either Zaheer or Babar to bring me to Khodadad in Houston. I will talk to your father and Adam and then call you there. It is time we put things right," she added. "I will no longer sit back and let your father and brother's mulish attitude dictate me. And you better ask forgiveness of them both when you see them. Allah knows how much you hurt them."

The phone call had lifted a weight off Safina's heart. At least Bibi didn't hate her. Maybe her father didn't hate her either and Adam, well, she wasn't sure about her brother. When it came to honour and tradition, Adam could be more set in his ways than their father.

The thought that circled Safina's mind was how she would tell Engin about her family and why she had been separated from them. The fact that he brought up his own childhood and family frequently in their conversations showed how much he valued familial loyalty and the bond between siblings. She had lost everyone's love over time, and losing Engin's affection was something she dreaded. Her only friend in Canada had been split from her. Samantha was her mother, yet a stranger. Bibi, Zaheer, Eugene, in fact, anyone who had remotely been close to her had been separated from her. She would have to keep the secret of her guilt locked inside her heart. Perhaps over time, Engin might understand that she led a harsh life inthe village and of her struggle to break free of the fetters that bound her to tradition.

Engin was always energetic when he returned from work; it was impossible to tell whether he had had a rough or easy day at the hospital. It was hopeless not to be affected by his joie de vivre and Safina always got caught up in his enthusiasm. When he returned that evening, he hid his face behind a bunch of yellow roses and pretended to sound like a delivery boy. "Delivery of a dozen cut roses for Mrs. Yildirim from a secret admirer in celebration of one month of blissful marriage," he spoke playfully. Taking the roses away from his face, Safina clung to him and kissed him long and hard. He was the best thing that had happened to her in her life. Aroused by her ardour, Engin lifted her off her feet and carried her to the bedroom.

Later, while drawing on his cigarette excitedly, Engin told Safina he would be able to end his contract earlier than expected, which meant that they could start planning for their future soon. They would have to start packing and selling off the stuff they didn't need and head to Germany for a few days after which Safina could resume her thesis in Canada and wait patiently for him to join her. Safina suggested she look for more permanent work so that they could buy a house soon, but Engin wanted her to complete her graduate school first. Besides, he said that he had a small house in Germany, which he planned to put up for sale and which would cover most of their expenses to settle comfortably for the time being. Safina got up and emptied the ashtray and left for the washroom to shower before they headed out to dinner. After all, one month of married life called for celebration. Or at least that is what Engin thought.

Khodadad had been coughing most of the night and called out for Zaheer several times to take him to the hospital, but failed. He walked to the guest room to look for him but found it empty. The bed had not been slept in. Khodadad sat down on the couch in the living room, hoping his nephew would show up soon but the cough was getting worse and he was having difficulty breathing.

Adam woke with a start, sweating profusely. He pushed away the bedclothes and walked towards the window and opened it to let the air in. He had a bad feeling about his father. It was almost 2 a.m. but he couldn't wait until the morning and dialled the number to the condo. There was no response. Zaheer wasn't answering his phone either. He dialled several more times, frustrated and angry at himself for leaving his father. Gulrukh had woken up at this point and suggested they call the security at the condo and ask them to check if Adam's car was parked. If not, that meant Zaheer must have gone out and hopefully, Agha ji was all right and there was no emergency.

"According to the security, my car left the garage at 7 p.m. There has to be something wrong with Agha ji. Zaheer must have taken him to the hospital," Adam said perturbed. When the hospital was called, they had no record of Khodadad being brought there and this worried the couple even more. Adam called the security at the condo again and asked them to use a master key to open the door to their apartment.

It was ten in the morning when Adam and Gulrukh pulled into the hospital's parking lot. Rushing to the Intensive Care Unit, they were met with Dr. Usman in the corridor. "It was smart thinking on your part to have the paramedics bring him here. He should not have been left alone in his condition," he said, peering over his glasses.

"What's his condition like?" I was told he was passed out on the couch when the paramedics came. I can't believe I let that happen!" Adam was pacing and cursing himself under his breath, while Gulrukh kept a hand on his arm to calm him. Dr. Usman could give no answer because his pager went off and he rushed in the opposite direction.

There were strict orders not to let anyone into the ICU and Gulrukh and Adam sat in the lobby waiting to hear from Dr. Usman. When he finally emerged from one of the restricted area doors, Adam rushed to him and asked about his father. "We thought we were going to lose him when he was brought here at 3 a.m. Fortunately, he has stabilized for now. He had a problem with his lungs and couldn't breathe, and we are currently doing tests for that. We will move him to his room by the evening. I suggest you two go home and rest for a while and be here by five," saying this, the doctor gave them a perfunctory smile and left.

It was almost noon and there was no sign of either Mariam or Zaheer. His bed hadn't even been slept in. Adam called the agency to ask about the housekeeper and they said she had called in and refused to work for them, and that they would find them a substitute.

The door opened and Zaheer walked in, with an expression of surprise on his dishevelled face when he saw Adam had returned a day earlier than expected. "So glad you're both home. The housekeeper was a con artist waiting to rob you both. I caught her trying to open the safe..." he started saying but before he could finish, Adam's fist caught him squarely on the jaw and he went sprawling across the living room. Gulrukh watched in horror at the scene taking place but was afraid to intervene and stop her husband. She had never seen him like this.

"Then why do you reek of alcohol? How could you leave my Agha ji alone in the state he is in and take off? I trusted you enough to leave my father with you. Biggest mistake I ever made!" he shouted, while Zaheer held onto the couch for support as he tried to get up. Adam was not done yet and aimed a kick to Zaheer's shin, which knocked him down again but this time, he did not bother trying to get up. Instead, he propped himself on his elbows while still on his back and grinned back at his assailant.

"Look at you! You stuck up lord of the manor! You and your father have treated me like your slave for the last time. All our lives, my poor mother and I have been at your beck and call like the hunting dogs you keep in your backyard, living off the bones you throw at us," he said, wiping the blood trickling down his chin with his sleeve. "And your sister, so ready to leave you all and begging to run away with me." Saying this, he threw his head back and started to laugh. Before he could say another word, the kick in the ribs that Adam delivered knocked him out for a long time.

Gulrukh was used to seeing violence in men. The culture in which she had grown up had prepared her to accept harshness of both man and environment. She remembered once how one of her brothers had stopped the jeep in the middle of the road, while he was driving his wife and her to their uncle's. The jeep had a small accident where two men from the other car had gotten out and sworn at her brother. Her otherwise calm brother had gotten out of the jeep and started hitting the man until he had to be pulled back by the crowd that had gathered. Gulrukh had wanted to get out and help her brother but her sister-in-law had held her back, saying it was natural for men to fight but unacceptable for a woman to ever get involved. Gulrukh's brother had a bloody lip when he came and sat back inside the jeep, but both women said not a single word and pretended as though they had not seen what took place. So, when Adam asked Gulrukh what they had to eat, she quietly warmed up some leftovers and proceeded to clear up the glass from the lamp that had broken when Zaheer knocked it off the table when he fell. "I will be going to the hospital in an hour. You can rest and make sure to throw out the linen from the guest room," Adam said without looking up.

"We are leaving tonight. Pack up," was all he said when he slammed the hotel room door shut with a bang. Renata had looked up from the magazine she had been reading and had planned to give Zaheer the silent treatment when he showed up, but one look at his swollen jaw and the blood on his collar had startled her and she got up suddenly to go to him. "Just stay away from me! Stay away!" Zaheer screamed, while holding up a hand to keep her off. This triggered her and she lashed out at him in German, giving vent to the pent-up anger of the past two days. A resounding slap which missed her cheek and landed on her ear sent her reeling across the room. This was too much anger for one day, Zaheer thought, and headed for the shower.

CHAPTER 27

Engin and Safina had spent six days in Berlin together where she got to meet several of his friends and people he had worked with. She always knew her husband was an agreeable and liked by everyone sort of person, but she was not prepared for the host of people who came to congratulate them at their small house or on the reception Engin's brother, Ertugrul, had arranged for them. It was not only the doctors he worked with that came or his college mates; his neighbours, many of his former patients, players from his football team, coaches, teachers from his high school, Farah's co-workers all wished the new couple well. Compared to him, Safina could count the people she called as friends on the fingers on one hand. Was she unpopular? Or did she give off an unwelcoming vibe which distanced her from the people around her? she wondered.

Virginia met Safina at the airport. Despite her objection, Engin had insisted and called for her to pick up his wife when she arrived in Toronto. Now, spotting her friend standing patiently in below freezing temperature and peering over the crowd looking for her, Safina could not help but feel remorse at how she had treated her. Virginia had been a friend who had not asked any questions but wordlessly looked out for her. The two women hugged each other tightly and the bitterness from their last meeting seemed to melt.

"I hope you are not thinking of moving back to that hole you were living in," Virginia said, manoeuvring through rush-hour traffic. "Your room at my place is yours until you and Engin decide where you want to live. Starting tomorrow, I'm hoping you will start work at the university and get your degree out of the way at the earliest." Strangely enough, it felt exhilarating to be back in Canada. This was the only other home she had known besides her village in Pakistan, even though both were starkly poles apart.

"Did Babar call again?" Safina asked to which she got a silent no.

"I will tell you if he does, rest assured," replied Virginia.

The next few days were busy for Safina as she had to catch up on work that she had missed. It felt good to be back in university and she was mildly surprised and pleased to see so many of her colleagues came over to congratulate her on her marriage. It appeared she was not so invisible, after all. Safina had gone down to the cafeteria and when she came back, Virginia was on the phone. Something told her it was a call from Babar and when she placed Virginia's cup in front of her, she mouthed, "It's him!" to her. Safina asked for the phone to speak to him herself.

"Babar, this is Safina," she said. There was a pause on the other end and then she heard Babar speak in Darri. Without wasting time, he got to the point.

"Agha ji's condition has gotten worse. I am taking Bibi to him in two days, I thought you should know about this," Babar's words sucked the air out of Safina's lungs and she perched herself on the desk for support, holding the receiver with both hands.

"Is my brother aware you have informed me about Baba?" Safina asked, hoping he would say yes. There was a long silence where she could tell Babar had done this without his knowledge. So, it meant, her brother had still not forgiven her, and perhaps, neither had her father. Despite her aversion to the man and the sneaky way in which he had stalked her, she was grateful to him for taking the risk to inform her and she said so to him before ending the phone call.

Khodadad held Gulrukh's hand in both of his. Adam had just given him the news that he was going to become a grandfather. Gulrukh suddenly felt shy with her new-found status of mother-to-be. This baby would make so many people happy; besides Agha ji, both her parents would be overjoyed at the news. She knew that the moment they found out, they would sacrifice goats as thanks and distribute money among the poor. But she looked at her father-in-law and her heart contracted. The episode at the condo where he had passed out had affected him badly. Had he been brought to the hospital in time and given proper care, his lungs would not have suffered as much. Dr. Usman had been tight-lipped about the incident, knowing well that Adam was not to blame, but it had put the progress they had made light years behind.

"Adam, I would like to be the one to tell Sherbat Murad he will hold a tiny baby in his arms soon," Khodadad beamed with pride and pleasure. "And Bibi is going to be overjoyed. She has missed having children around to spoil with her cooking. Oh! This is such a happy day for me. May Allah let me hold my son's child before I go," he said. It was uncommon for his father to express emotion like that, but Adam understood how significant the arrival of a child meant for Khodadad. It warranted the continuance of the Khanzada lineage.

Bibi came out of the arrivals door swinging her outsized handbag and chiding Babar about something, while he looked as if he had gone through hell and come back. Adam could not help but smile looking at them. Bibi's entry into the States had been done in her true militant style and he could tell Babar had endured her without complaint through the long flight. She hugged her nephew but not before delivering a withering glare at Babar, who appeared to shrink inwardly in his heavy frame. Despite the circumstances she was coming in, Adam could feel the lightness in his heart at seeing her. Bibi had a way of making things right, and he already felt she had taken some of the pressure off his mind.

Gulrukh had prepared a feast with the help of the new Bengali lady they had hired as a helper. There was another young woman, an oriental, who came in to clean up and help Gulrukh with her shopping and errands, and who now gaped open-mouthed at Bibi staring at her bare legs under the skirt, while marching through the house inspecting the standard of her cleaning. Satisfied, Bibi went to her room to freshen up and sat down at the table to eat. "So, when did Zaheer leave? I hope he looked after his uncle well," she asked during the meal. "I haven't heard from him in a while. I don't know why he has to be so busy all the time and take responsibility for all the work at his office. One would think he has become the director of a company. He doesn't seem to have time for anything else." Her comments went unanswered with Gulrukh ladling more rice onto her plate and asking if the food was all right. Bibi was a shrewd woman. She noted in silence how abruptly the conversation at the table had gone quiet, while Adam sat clenching his glass so that his knuckles stood out white. So, it had started, she guessed with a sinking heart. Her husband's mental illness would come to haunt her one day. She had dreaded this moment all her life. There was no doubt in her mind that her son had disgraced her; otherwise, Adam would have said something regarding his visit and would have filled her in about how he was doing. Suddenly, she lost her appetite and announced she was tired.

"But Bibi, you haven't even tried the korma yet," Gulrukh protested, but Bibi had already gotten up and left the table to go to her room.

Tired as she was from her journey, Bibi could not fall asleep. She kept tossing on the mattress which was too soft for her and seemed to sink with each breath she took. Her mind was occupied with her meeting with Khodadad the next morning. She prayed she could keep her nerves and not let her cousin see the pain she felt. The room suddenly felt warm and she got up to go out on the balcony off the living room to get some air. She could hear muted voices in the room outside and was glad the newlyweds were up. Perhaps she could sit with them for a while and tire herself a bit more. The mention of Zaheer's name stopped Bibi in her tracks. "Believe me I tried to convince her to come to the police station to file a complaint, but she is terrified of the shame it would bring on her. I think she feels Zaheer will come back and hurt her children," Adam was telling Gulrukh. "I cannot believe this happened to her while she was in our care," he continued. Bibi could hear Gulrukh's soft sobs. "Bibi must never find out about this, you understand? It would kill her. I will do whatever I can to look after Mariam and help her in every possible way. Don't you worry. She is my responsibility," Bibi did not want to hear more.

She padded back to the bed and tried to stifle the moan that was rising in her chest. So this was the reason why Adam avoided any mention of her son's name. She felt ashamed and hurt. All these years, she had prayed the ghost of mental illness which ran in her husband's side of the family would not come to haunt her son. Now, after years of believing God had spared her shame and misery in her old age, her husband's sickness had come to manifest in Zaheer's life. She had inferred from Adam's words that Zaheer had exhibited sadistic behaviour while on his visit to Houston recently, which she knew of so well from the time she was married.

Khodadad had been bathed and had insisted on being dressed in his white *shalwar* suit with *qameez* for his cousin's arrival. He had been asked to refrain from wearing any kind of fragrance but cajoled the nurse to let him spray on his favourite cologne just this once. When Bibi arrived with Adam and Babar in tow, he was sitting by the window, watching the fountain spout its magnificent jet into the air and cascade down in a mist onto people enjoying the outdoors. "Look at you, sitting shamelessly watching those women getting all wet under the water! And here I thought you would have a hundred tubes attached to your body with a television to your side counting your heartbeats," stormed Bibi into the room. Khodadad smiled and his eyes crinkled, and the sunlight caught their blue, making him look, for a moment, like the Khodadad of another time. The fact was, Bibi had pushed away all thought of Zaheer and willed herself to taking care of her cousin. There wasn't anything that she could do for her son, but right now, Khodadad needed her more than anything else. She swallowed the hard lump that came to her throat when she laid eyes on Khodadad and willed her eyes to stay dry and her voice firm. She could tell the trauma her cousin's body was enduring. If it was the Creator's will to take him from her, she would make sure he went happy, with no regrets and no loose ends. It did not take long for Mumtaz to take on her role, by default, as captain of the ship. Since there was no Manju Kaka to boss around, the next best substitute was Babar, and she lost no time in snapping orders at him. "I suggest you keep a notepad handy. I have a list of tasks for you today," she ordered while he stood trying to cower behind Adam. "Every week, arrange for two crates each of apricots, peaches and apples from the family orchard to be delivered to the house. I will juice the fruit for Khodadad to drink instead of the chemicals they give him here. Replace the water in the refrigerator with bottles of *Aab e ZamZam*—holy water from Saudi Arabia—and make sure all the nurses here know that I will not adhere to any visiting hours and will come and go as I please." The list went on. Adam rolled his eyes while his father wiped tears of mirth falling down his face. He had missed Bibi so much.

CHAPTER 28

After the phone call with Babar, Safina had sat on the sofa in Virginia's office, holding her head in both hands. She did not speak or cry but sat there for a long time. Virginia left the room to give a lecture and when she came back, she found Safina sitting in the same position. She sat on the sofa next to her and laid a hand on her arm. "Good grief! You're burning up!" Safina's eyes were glazed when she raised her head and her cheeks glowed feverishly. Alarmed at the state she was in, Virginia grabbed Safina by the shoulders and pulled her to her in an embrace. Perhaps it was the touch of a human, or maybe it was the frightened look on Virginia's face, that made Safina crumble and she let out the flood of emotions that had been locked inside her for so long. She sobbed uncontrollably, the tears soaking up Virginia's blouse. When her tears ceased and she felt lighter, Virginia cancelled the rest of her day, grabbed her keys and they left for home.

"I'm ordering pizza for dinner. Why don't you shower until it arrives and then we can sit and eat while you tell me what that was all about," Virginia suggested. Safina was too spent to argue and did as she was told and when she came down, the pizza was waiting on the coffee table along with a bottle of Tylenol.

The sun was barely out by the time Safina finished. The women had sat there through the night with an endless supply of coffee, while Safina told her complex life story and Virginia listened without interrupting. By the time she was done, her fever had subsided and she felt light with relief for sharing her burden. "You have gone through a lot at such a young age, and I thought I had it the worst with Kevin leaving me so suddenly, and then Eugene disappearing from my life," Virginia said, looking into her empty cup. "The question is, what do you want to do? I don't see what you can accomplish by just letting things be the way they are. You will never know how your brother or father might react to you until you go and find out for yourself," she added.

"My father can be very inflexible, he completely shut out my mother when she left us and my brother, well, he's another story," said Safina.

"Illness such as your father's changes a lot in a person, dear. You may be surprised to see a different reaction to what you are imagining," responded Virginia. What she said made sense and gave Safina a kind of hope of expiating herself of her mistakes. She remembered what Suleiman Bey had said to her outside the mosque about unburdening her heart. Right now, that was exactly what she needed to focus on.

The telephone rang several times but there was no response. Safina calculated the time difference again to make certain there would be someone to pick up her call. "Perhaps they have already left for Islamabad to take the flight to Houston. I suppose I will have to wait until Babar calls again. Did he say which hospital my father was in?" Safina asked hopefully, to which she was told Babar had left no such information. They would just have to wait patiently to hear from him.

Mumtaz finished her morning prayers and waited for Babar to show up from the hotel he was staying at and take her to the hospital. It had been more than a week since she had arrived in Houston and she had been spending most of her mornings at the hospital with Khodadad. She would come back during midday and then Adam would take her place. Adam was also trying to manage the business as best he could as there was work only he could take care of. He had made a quick five-day trip to Europe to see some of his clients and then set up a temporary office nearby. Meanwhile, Babar was doing the running around with Mumtaz and keeping in touch with their trade partners in Pakistan.

"I have prepared the thermos with the juice which you need to get from the refrigerator and the broth, but before you do that, sit down and dial that woman's number. I need to speak to Safina," she said to Babar when he walked into the apartment.

"You know I can't do that. Adam is in the other room, what if he hears us?" Babar said, unable to think straight before having his strong cup of morning tea.

"Do you think I'm stupid?" Bibi retorted. "Adam's not home! He got called away on business just after you left last night. He didn't want to bother you and will be back sometime in a day or so." Babar knew Adam would be furious if he ever found out.

Safina picked up the phone as she was closest to it. She had just been talking to Engin and was in a happy mood. Engin had finally managed to sell his house at a good price and had even got a call from the Mt. Sinai Children's Hospital in Toronto for an Orthopaedic surgeon's position that was vacant. He was hopeful to get the post and move to Canada within a few weeks. Virginia was pleased to see Safina's face light up and the two were discussing her plans for where they would live when the phone rang. Mumtaz could hear laughter in her niece's voice when she answered and she hated to spoil the moment by what she was about to say. "Safina *jaan*, I am here in Houston. When can you come?" she asked. "No, he is still the same, but I feel he would feel better if he saw you. He is excited he will be a grandfather soon, so he's in a good mood. Babar will book your ticket and pick you up from the airport. Here, speak to him," and she handed the phone to Babar, who felt a bit revived after his cup of tea. Safina gave him the details about when she could travel and hung up. She was finally going to come to terms with her family.

Zaheer paced his apartment in a black mood. That day, he had been told to pack up and leave the office without any fuss; otherwise, he would face consequences. His erratic behaviour at the office was getting worse and he was finally told he could no longer work there. Moreover, his German visa would become invalid in a week. He had considered going through a fake civil marriage with Renata to be able to stay back, but even she had suddenly decided to shut him out of her life. Strangely, it was he who was trying to sweet-talk her instead of her pleading with him. His mind would blow if he didn't find a solution quickly. He did not want to return to Pakistan and struggle to find his worth. He would be a nobody there—a failure. With Adam calling all the shots, and he being the docile, submissive cousin waiting for his next pay check—too inadequate to support the lavish life style he was accustomed to—he would never be able to have the independence he sought. Calling his cousin was therefore out of the question and his mother was probably in Houston by now, babysitting his tyrant uncle. The only option that came to mind was Safina. He would need to calm himself considerably to charm her. He knew what to say to melt her and convince her that he sacrificed their love because her father and brother had threatened him all these years. She had to believe that he loved her and that her marriage to that Turkish fellow was an impulsive mistake. He thought of using Samantha for this purpose, but that would not work. Samantha had seen him in one of his foolish outbursts when he was in Canada last. She had shouted at him and threatened to go to the police if he didn't leave.

Safina was by herself at the house packing when the doorbell rang. Virginia had promised to get back from work early to drive her to the airport. It had taken a lot of courage for Safina to come to a decision. What was the worst that could happen? Her father would refuse to see her, shout at her, or worse, ask her to leave without forgiving her? She was prepared for all that. What troubled her was how her brother would react. He was more compelled to take honour and pride to another level, and might even pressure her to return home. He was heartless, as far as she knew.

She opened the door to see Zaheer standing in the gusty, cold wind. His face looked ashen and he seemed to have aged considerably. "How did you know where I live?" was all Safina could think of to say to him. It amazed her how easy it was for everyone to track her whereabouts.

"Won't you ask me to come in?" Safina hesitated for a moment before letting him enter. Zaheer looked worn out and ill and Safina went to get him some tea. When she came back, he had removed his jacket and was sitting on the sofa with his head thrown back. He took his time, then began to tell Safina how he had been threatened by her father to leave her alone all these years. He had been afraid for his mother and for Safina, who would have had to bear the brunt of her father's wrath if they had gotten married. Safina listened with incredulity at where the conversation was headed and asked Zaheer to stop. She did not want to be reminded of the past; she was married and very happy and she told him so.

"But you must understand, all my life I have only loved one woman. Believe me, I have tried to fool myself into thinking other women could fill your place, but it was not so. I was there for your wedding, Safina. I wanted to stop you from giving yourself to a stranger, but I couldn't. I just couldn't. You are the only one I want to be with and I think, deep down, you want this too. We were made to be together," he said with a catch in his voice. Safina stared at him, sorry that his heartache had reduced him to such a state where he was willing to put his pride, inheritance, and familial ties at stake only to be with her. She tried hard to put herself in his shoes and understand the depth of his misery, and how it must have taken courage on his part to bare his soul to her. When Zaheer reached out to hold her hand, she did not object. It felt like the most natural thing to do. Encouraged, Zaheer edged closer to her on the sofa and touched her face and looked deep into her troubled eyes. Safina turned her face away from him and tried to get away. The man sitting in front of her only made her feel pity and disappointment in him. She had always known Zaheer to be upright and proper. In the past, she would have easily given up everything to be with him, but he made sure either of them did not cross the line of propriety and trust, no matter how attracted they were to each other. The desperation she saw in him, and the way his eyes ran over her, made her feel uncomfortable, and slightly revolted.

"You know perfectly well that I'm married now, Zaheer. It's time to move on for you as well, and," Zaheer cut her off and held her hands tighter.

"I don't see the doctor around. If he is so in love, where is he? How can he leave you here by yourself?" The conversation had gotten way out of hand and she was infuriated at how strangely her cousin was behaving. This was so unlike him and totally unacceptable. She had to get away from him and tried to pull her hands away but before she knew it, Zaheer was holding her in a tight grasp, his one hand tangled in her hair and the other trying to pull her closer to him. She suddenly knew why her father had kept her away from him. It was a parent's instinct—his gut feeling—that had prevented her from getting married to Zaheer, and the image of Khodadad flashed before her eyes. With unexpected strength that coursed through her body, she pushed the nauseating face away from hers and tried to get up from her seat. But Zaheer was too quick for her, he had grabbed her arm and in a flash, had her body pinned to the wooden floor with the weight of his own. He tried to turn her face towards him with his free hand while Safina squirmed in his grasp. However, Zaheer's actions were unexpectedly cut short when a resounding thump to his head knocked him out for good. Safina, who had clenched her eyes, opened them to see a startled Virginia standing above them, brandishing the cast iron skillet mid-air.

Virginia pushed away Zaheer's inert body lying on top of Safina who was too shaken up to move. Both women looked at him sprawled on the wooden floor and wondered if he was alive. "What on earth is your cousin doing inside the house, Safina?" Virginia asked, her eyes staring at the man. "What did he want from you?" Safina could not find her voice to answer and tried to get up on shaky legs. Zaheer was starting to moan and on instinct, Virginia reached for the cell phone in her pocket to call the police, but before she could dial the number, he opened his eyes and winced when he gingerly felt the weal swelling fast on the back of his head. "There's no need to call anyone, Virginia. Please, just listen to me. I don't know what overcame me. I really don't. Look at me Safina," he said, but Safina was standing near the kitchen counter, far out of reach and ready to pull out the sharpest tool she could find. She could not believe the man she was willing to give up everything for could stoop so low. Continuing in a pleading voice, Zaheer tried to rationalize his action by proclaiming how emotionally he was shattered after losing Safina. "I cannot get over the fact that we will never be together. Not now, not ever. And after what happened just now, I know you will not ever think of me as a friend. There is no need to call the police. I will leave you to your life Safina and never bother you again. Just think of my mother and her love for you and try to forgive me if you can," he said beseechingly.

"What you tried to do just now accounts for physical assault in this country. Do not, for a moment, think you can just molest someone and walk away! Safina, do not let him talk you out of this," Virginia hissed with the pan still in her hand. In the end, it was Safina who decided to let Zaheer go. She thought of Mumtaz Bibi and what it would do to her if she ever found out that Safina had handed her son over to the police. The shame alone would kill the woman. Zaheer had come to reclaim his love for Safina but left with a wounded pride and an ugly welt on his head.

Looking back, he tried to say something to Safina but her face was turned away, and he left without a word.

She was after all her father's daughter and had inherited his persevering spirit. The episode at the house did not deter her from going on with her plans, and as dazed as she was by the trauma she had just endured, she stepped on the plane, resolved to follow through what she had set out to do.

CHAPTER 29

"**D**o you remember how much Safina used to love these peaches?" Mumtaz said while pouring fresh juice from the thermos. "Viola would argue that the peaches in Provence were better than these and Safina would get all worked up and go around the house with a long face. She used to spend hours sketching using fruits as her models," she said, while she noted Khodadad's expression from the corner of her eye. "I remember once how you took the kids to the orchard and they planted those cherry saplings you brought from Europe. Safina would go several times a week to check on her plant, while Adam couldn't care less. She was always like that—sensitive, with a nurturing heart." Khodadad quietly sipped the juice through the straw. "She had that favourite horse, what was it called? Ah, I remember, you named him Bijli. Oh, how that girl would ride him!" she continued.

Mildly annoyed at Mumtaz confusing the horse's name, Khodadad spoke, "It was not Bijli. Her favourite horse was the one we got from Peshawar, Baadal, the one who had the white star between the eyes" he said, correcting her. "Safina used to sneak apples in her coat for him. Once, when I asked her what was making her pockets so heavy, she replied, 'Baba, these are just extra bandages in case Baadal hurts himself.'" By this time, Khodadad was laughing and continued reminiscing about the equestrian exploits his daughter had had. By noon, both Mumtaz and Khodadad had dug up the most bizarre adventures they remembered of the kids' childhoods, so that when the nurse came to check up on him, she found Khodadad laughing with tears streaming down his face, while he helplessly watched Mumtaz mimicking someone in a high-pitched voice. After that,

Mumtaz started bringing up Safina's name frequently and it did not sound unnatural at all.

"I know you miss her," she said one evening while Adam was also in the room. "I know you would like to see her and hold her." Upon hearing this, Adam got up and left the room and Gulrukh followed.

"Why doesn't Bibi understand that it was my mother and sister that brought this illness on my father? It was the shame and pain of their betrayal that did this to him. Has she forgotten already how the family suffered because of her selfishness?" Adam said through clenched teeth. Gulrukh laid a hand on his shoulder and gave it a light squeeze.

"If Agha ji can forgive your sister, so can you. Right now, you are the one who is suffering. Maybe it is time you let go of your anger," she said in the soothing voice she knew always comforted her husband.

Luckily, she had slept through most of the flight. The nasty episode with Zaheer had shaken her more than she was willing to admit. Virginia had been silent through the ride to the airport and her knuckles stood out white as she gripped the steering wheel tightly. She was appalled that Safina let Zaheer walk out of the house without doing anything. "You wouldn't understand, Virginia. Mumtaz Bibi has been the person holding our family together for all these years. I cannot send her only living child to prison when she's the one who is helping me reunite with my family," Safina pleaded, secretly not convinced she had done the right thing in letting Zaheer go. It was some consolation to think that his injured pride and the enormous bump on his head, would probably keep him in insufferable agony for a long time as a painful reminder of his offensive behaviour.

The aircraft circled Houston and came for a smooth landing on the strip. For a fleeting moment, Safina thought of Engin and how she would have to explain her abrupt departure from Toronto, but she knew Virginia would handle him when he called.

"Does Baba know that I'm coming?" Safina asked Babar when he received her at the airport.

"Bibi wants it to be a surprise," he answered.

"And what about my brother?" she asked hopefully, and was told her brother was out of town. Babar took her directly to the hospital, where Bibi had insisted Khodadad wear a crisp *shalwar* suit instead of the standard blue gown for the patients that day. Before they got out of the car, Babar hesitated, then pointing to her neck, asked if her husband had done that to her.

"You should cover it with a scarf before you go in," he said wincing. Safina looked confused and lowered the mirror behind the sun shade, and was shocked to see bruises where Zaheer had tried to grab her by the throat. "No Babar, it was not my husband. Engin is in Germany at the moment," and saying that, she left the car without further explanation. Hell would break loose if her family found out Zaheer had come near to raping her, and she could not let Bibi know about this—ever.

Babar left the hospital building after pointing out her father's room to Safina. He still cared for her deeply. His boyhood obsession with her had turned first into a feeling of rejection and misery at her abrupt disappearance, and later into pity for her and for the path of disgrace she had chosen for herself. It was no secret in the village that Agha Ji's daughter had followed in her mother's footsteps and left her father humiliated for the second time. Babar's constant interaction with the locals made him realize how unsuitable and unlikely a match with her would have been. She was not cut out to be the wife of a traditional tribal, who had nothing to his name. To think she would ever find him appealing and worthy was just a pipe dream and Babar let go of that delusion.

Safina had been mentally preparing herself for her meeting with her father and was inwardly relieved that Adam would not be around. She opened the door and saw Bibi had knitting needles in her hand and Safina could see she was nervous as her hands shook slightly. Her father had his back to the door but turned his head when he heard the door open. "Khodadad, look who's here to see you," said Mumtaz, and Safina did not wait for him to register. Instead, she dropped her handbag and rushed to cling to her father. She wept, she sobbed, and Khodadad let her empty the sadness from her soul and caressed the head resting on his lap. He had wasted too many years of warmth and love and affection, which he could have had with his daughter.

The nurse entered to find a stunning, young woman talking to Khodadad and holding his hand, while the bossy woman, who the hospital staff had nicknamed 'The Dragon Lady' sat opposite them, wiping her face of tears. "Angie, meet my daughter, Safina. She flew in all the way from Canada to come see me," Khodadad said with pride, looking at his daughter. "Safina, Angie should have been named 'Angel' because that's exactly what she is. She's the gentlest nurse at this hospital, and also the prettiest," he added with a wink. The nurse blushed and asked Safina a few polite questions about how she was doing and left smiling, eager to share the news with her co-workers that Mr. Khanzada had a normal, beautiful woman in his family and not all of them were as intimidating as the one that hovered over him night and day.

The women left in the evening for the condo and were met with Gulrukh at the door who welcomed Safina with the utmost warmth and showed her to her room. She asked Gulrukh when her brother would return and was told he would be back in two days. "It will be fine, Safina Baji, don't worry," she said, laying a hand on her arm, "I know Adam loves you very much. He carries a picture of you in his wallet," she said meaningfully. Upon hearing this, Safina felt some hope that her brother did not hate her, after all.

The next two days were spent visiting the hospital and catching up on all the stories of the village that Safina had missed. The family was disappointed to hear that they could not be part of Safina's wedding but it was enough for them that she had married a caring man with strong family values who cherished her. "And to think all these years I had been saving that Burmese ruby set to go with your wedding outfit," Mumtaz interjected with a pout.

"Bibi, you know what you have to do when you go back. You must give Safina the Bursar gems and all the jewellery you have kept for her, and you must invite Engin to the village. No, wait, invite his entire family for a visit. They should come and stay for a long time. Tell Adam to show them around Pakistan. Maybe they could plan a trip to Swat Valley and stay at our cottage there," Khodadad continued talking along the same lines during which Safina and Mumtaz had gone very quiet. He spoke as if he had convinced himself that he would not be returning with them and was delegating his responsibility as host to his cousin. Safina also made time in the evenings to get to know her sister-in-law and was pleased to learn that she was a gentle yet resilient young woman, who had practically set off in her bridal dress for a foreign country before giving anyone even the chance to object. It was assuring to know she would be the pillar on which her brother could lean in times of difficulty. The fact that she would soon be a mother had brought the two women close and one afternoon, they left excitedly with Babar to do some shopping for the baby.

The women entered the house laughing and chatting animatedly, while Babar carried in several packages and looked thoroughly washed out. He had hoped his shopping forays had ended after the trips he had made with Bibi prior to Adam's wedding. However, he came back wiser that afternoon after learning that babies needed more clothes than he had ever owned in his entire life and that there were over a hundred types of creams and powders that kept the baby's skin soft rather than the warm olive and almond oil mothers in the village had relied on for centuries for this purpose. It took several seconds for everyone to register that Adam sat in the living room, feet propped up on the ottoman, watching them with blazing eyes.

Adam saw his sister and noted she had gone very thin. She looked a lot like their mother but in a different way. Where he remembered his mother as small and with an impression of fragility and sweetness, Safina had an air of confidence and worldliness about her. She looked straight back at her brother and slowly came forward. The two stared at each other for a few moments, until Safina broke the silence by calling out her brother's name and holding out her arms to him. In that moment, she did not care about being rejected, all she wanted was to hold her brother who was a spitting image of her father and hold him tightly. Adam did not need his name to be called out twice, and getting up spontaneously, caught his sister's hands and pulled her in for a hug. It seemed so natural to let the bitterness and anger evaporate, while they held each other for a long time. Safina kissed her brother's face, not at all surprised he had grown to look just like their father but in a more rugged, fierce kind of way. He had the same hands and eyes and looked very handsome with his gold flecked hair and blue eyes. Had she known the reunion with her family could be so simple, Safina would have come to them ages ago, she thought with regret. So much time had been lost in assuming the worst.

The next morning, Dr. Usman was in Khodadad's room when Safina got there. The doctor seemed pleased that the patient was showing substantial progress despite the setback he suffered a few weeks ago, and he no longer needed an oxygen mask to assist with his breathing. "I think it would be a good idea if you took your father home for a few days but make sure there is no repetition of what happened last time and there is someone with him constantly," he said. This was the greatest news the family had heard in a long time and Safina quickly arranged for her father to be taken home. Mumtaz felt an uneasy tug at her heart. Her son had been with Khodadad when he fell sick the last time. What did the doctor mean when he said something about leaving him by himself? Was Zaheer not with him? Was this the reason why everyone seemed to skirt around the topic if his name came up? If her son had anything do with Khodadad's condition getting worse, she would never forgive him.

The family had just had an incredible meal of lamb stuffed with saffron rice and Kofta curry, eggplant and lentils along with crème brulee and a variety or salads and barbecued meats. Gulrukh and Mumtaz had cooked up Khodadad and Safina's favourite things and the conversation around the table had been light—a reassurance that they were once again together, and that their sourness and resentment was a thing of the past. Khodadad's suggestion that Safina and Engin should soon be given a proper tribal wedding was met with full approval from Mumtaz and Adam, and Babar was asked to bring out his notepad to take down notes. "I wonder if we can get Viola to come as well," Adam was suggesting when the phone rang.

"It's for you," said Babar, handing Safina the receiver. Virginia's voice at the other end sounded concerned but upon hearing the cheerfulness in Safina's, she let out a sigh of relief.

"I was worried because I didn't hear from you. I hope your father is doing well and that thing with your brother..." Safina laughed at her unease and told her all was well between her and Adam. "Good, I just thought I would let you know, your husband just called and I told him you were in Houston with your folks. I hope that's okay." Safina listened, unsure whether she should spring her family on him so quickly.

Since everyone was in a jovial mood and were being open with each other, Safina told them who had called and that her husband, who until then had been unaware of her family, knew now from Virginia that she was spending time with them. "Call him. Now. You must talk to him. Wait, call him and tell him your father wants to speak with him," Khodadad said eagerly. "I would like to have a word with my son-in-law." And Safina did just that. She had been fearful of how Engin would react, but he surprised her. He was overjoyed she was with her father and he hoped to meet them one day. Khodadad wasted no time. Within minutes of talking with Engin, he had convinced him to get on a plane and join them. Engin was arriving in four days.

Safina lay in bed that night, thinking how much her life had changed suddenly. Everything was moving so fast. Had Babar not called Virginia, she would never have been reunited with the people she loved the most. The tightness around her heart had disappeared and now, when she looked in the mirror, she did not see the emptiness in her eyes; rather, there was a sparkle to them, conciliation and peace. This was precisely what she had prayed for at the mosque in Sogut, to right the wrongs of the past and come together with her father. It didn't even feel odd that her mother was not part of the conversations, or that no one mentioned Zaheer's name, it still felt like a complete, average family. And now, her father wanted to meet her husband. She must have done something wonderful to have pleased the gods she mused, and fell asleep.

CHAPTER 30

Keeping in line with ancestral tradition, Khodadad had insisted on giving his son-in-law a welcome fit for a king. The adjoining apartment had been taken over on a short lease and the next two days were spent in a whirlwind of decorators, caterers and jewellers coming in and out. Khodadad and Mumtaz sat in the living room poring over catalogues and deciding on colour schemes and upholstery, while Safina spent the day with Gulrukh at an Indian fitter's who had promised to stitch a beautiful deep red with gold embroidery silk *shalwar qameez* suit with a chiffon scarf for her. There was not enough time for Mumtaz to head back to Pakistan and bring back any of the family jewellery; therefore, Khodadad had personally gotten in touch with his contacts in Amsterdam and had a spectacular rubies and diamond necklace complete with tear drop earrings and bracelet sent for Safina. Adam feared that all the excitement would wear out his father but looking at the radiance on his face and his animated discussions with Mumtaz regarding the preparations and which often ended in argument, Adam kept his concerns to himself. The pair was being their old self and both deserved this happiness.

Safina came back after a long day of shopping and found her father and Mumtaz beaming. "What's going on? Am I missing out on some fun?" she asked suspiciously. Adam, who had been on the phone when she entered, put the phone down.

"They are saying it could be done. I will see to it in the morning and finalize the details," he said to his father. Safina looked even more confused, wondering what her family was up to behind her back. Adam told her that their father insisted they hold a small reception for her and Engin and for that purpose, the wheels had already been put into motion. He had just now hung up with the caterers and banquet hall people.

"But, we should ask Engin first, don't you think?" she said, looking around at everyone. "I'm sure he would like his family to be here and I would want very much for Virginia and Suleiman Bey to be part of all this."

Mumtaz was unable to hold her excitement any longer. She told Safina that she and her father had thought of everything. They would invite everyone Safina wanted to call and have a proper family event. This was too much for Safina to process. First, Engin had been invited, or summoned, she would call it. She knew how impossible it was for him to drop everything and come right now. However, he had agreed to do so without protest. Then, her family expected Virginia and Engin's family to do the same. It seemed unfair to disrupt everyone's plans to suit theirs and Safina said so. "You're both doing this in such a short time and so out of the blue. The magnitude of the kind of event you're all planning requires time and a host of other things to consider, like people's schedules and their commitments..." she said exasperated, but Khodadad cut her short.

"Time is what I don't have, my darling. Things would have been different if..." but before he could complete his sentence, Safina rushed to her father's side and buried her face in his shirt, sobbing uncontrollably. She had callously forgotten that her father was sick, and even in his failing health, he was trying to bring some essence of fatherhood into her life and acknowledge her husband with honour and love. She felt ashamed for thinking about how quickly everything was being planned and how her friends would react to the suddenness of being invited. In the end, these things did not matter. What mattered was letting her father feel that he had done his duty to his daughter and let his kindness erase the painful years of separation they had endured.

The next day, Dr. Usman called Adam into his office. He understood that Mr. Khanzada had been reunited with his daughter after years of separation and that he was in high spirits; however, he warned Adam that all that restlessness and exertion might take a toll on his already waning health and they would have to put him back on heavy medication. He recommended that the patient be brought back to the hospital so that he could rest. When Adam passed the doctor's message along to his father, Khodadad flared up and refused to listen to another word. Adam knew there would be no point in pursuing the topic but quietly suggested to Mumtaz to keep the level of excitement and activity to a minimum.

Despite Safina's feeble attempts to keep everything low key, the guest list reached over a hundred people. There was Engin's family, Suleiman Bey, accompanied by Cengiz, as well as Virginia and a few of their colleagues from the university. There was a slight commotion at the hospital when several of the hospital staff received the light pink invitation cards and then Khodadad had Babar draw up a list of the people who were their business associates and lived around Houston. "Is there anyone you would like to add to the list?" Mumtaz asked, peering over her glasses. Safina thought for a moment and told her about Hilal. Viola and her husband were already going to be there and there was no one else she could think of. Babar was given the task of co-ordinating with Cengiz and arranging for Hilal's visa and travel arrangements. Mumtaz sighed, and continued going over the menu list. She had half-hoped Safina would say she wanted her mother to be present. Perhaps it was for the best, she thought. It would not serve any purpose and would only put a damper on Adam's spirits. She had dared not bring up Zaheer's name and was not surprised no one did either. It was almost as if her son never exsisted, she thought with a sinking heart.

Safina couldn't help but giggle when she saw how nervous Engin was in anticipation of his meeting with her father. They were both sitting in the back seat of the car while Babar drove them from the airport to the condo. "...and when he said, I want you here, there was nothing I could say. I mean after all, he is the father of the bride," he went on talking in a light banter. Babar observed them in the rear-view mirror. There was no way he could have given Safina those bruises he had noticed when she had arrived in Houston. Engin obviously loved her enough to be here with her and there was something wholesome and open about him. Babar had dealt with enough thugs in his life to know that Engin was not one of them. Safina's body would not be leaning so close towards him the way it did right now and she wouldn't have that glimmer to her eyes if her husband was the aggressive type. The couple he drove were in love and cared sincerely for each other. It was enough for him to know she was loved by a caring man.

On the day of the reception, Mumtaz had put a ban on Safina and Engin seeing each other and Farah had completely supported her. The two women had been drawn to each other since the day they met; Mumtaz's hard-hitting approach to everything was complemented with Farah's gentle yet practical nature. "But we're already married, Bibi! How can you ask us not to even talk to each other today?" Safina sounded almost like a school girl, pouting and cantankerous. Mumtaz and Farah exchanged disdainful looks and Safina knew there was no way going about it. She would just have to do as asked and play along with their irrational stipulations. Engin had been given a starched white *shalwar* suit with a waistcoat and a ceremonial bandolier with brass studs to wear. On his feet, he wore the most intricately embroidered Peshawari sandals made with soft kid leather. Khodadad added a turban and completed the outfit. Dressed as he was in traditional attire, no one would have guessed he was of Turkish origin and did not belong to some village of northern Pakistan. Safina walked down the large hall supported by her father and brother on either side, while Mumtaz and Farah stood to one side, pleased to see their efforts had made this day a success. Babar had somehow managed to get hold of a Russian troupe that gave a colourful performance like the ones they had in their village on festivities. Dressed in white with red cummerbunds and swords in their hands, the dancers enthralled the audience with their presentation performed to the rhythm of drums and foot stamping, while they brandished ceremonial rapiers in the air. The evening concluded with a sumptuous spread of cuisines from both northern Pakistan and Turkey and platters of fruits and dried nuts flown in from the Khanzada orchards.

Dr. Usman took Adam to the side. He looked worried. "All this is very good, Adam and I give you one hundred percent for putting together such a fantastic evening, but I must warn you; this is coming with a heavy price. Mr. Khanzada does not look well at all. I can't let him go home tonight, he's coming straight to the hospital from here," he said, leaving no room for argument. Adam had not had the time to notice his father much, and when he saw him sitting with Suleiman Bey engrossed in conversation, he was taken aback at how pale and feeble he looked. He was obviously making a lot of effort to hold himself up in front of the guests so as not to embarrass the family by showing how weak he felt. Adam went and sat next to his father, and holding his hand, quietly motioned to him that they were leaving. Adam left with his father unobtrusively and drove to the hospital. His father did not protest this time. He was thankful for the evening and felt blessed to have both his children with him, and looking back at the crowd occupied in the merrymaking, he let himself be led to the car.

Adam had stayed with his father through the night. As predicted by Dr. Usman, the excitement of the past few days had taken its toll on Khodadad's health and he had to get assistance for his breathing. There was a nurse who came in every few minutes to check on him. When Mumtaz was told by Babar that Adam had left specific instructions for no one to come to the hospital that night, she debated whether to defy his orders and join him, or to do as told. The family sat in the apartment all night, unable to rest easy and dreading the worst. When Adam came home early the next morning, he found his sister cuddled in his aunt's arms, while Engin lay sprawled on another sofa. Everyone was fast asleep and he assumed they had stayed up waiting and worrying through the night.

"How is Agha ji?" Gulrukh asked coming out of their bedroom, holding her prayer beads. Adam nodded his head in dejection, indicating that his father's condition had worsened. Gulrukh took him by the hand and made him lie down and left to get him tea. When she returned, she found Adam fast asleep. The house help arrived and Gulrukh got busy with preparing lunch and juicing fruits for Khodadad. Engin woke with a start when the phone rang. It was from the hospital and Dr. Usman wanted the family to be there. It was time.

When life left Khodadad's body, all the people who mattered to him were by his side. He had taken off his breathing mask, insisting he wanted to speak to everyone and took his time to thank each person for the meaning they gave to his life and asked to be forgiven for any wrongs done to them. Despite their stoic efforts to not show emotion and appear strong, there was not a dry eye in that hospital room. Lastly, Khodadad held both his children's hands and made them promise to be each other's support. It was eleven p.m. when the doctor declared him dead. Babar had been given the charge by Adam to start the arrangements for his father's body to be transported to Islamabad and after two insufferable days of grief and condolences, the family left on the first flight to Pakistan, with the casket holding Khodadad's lifeless body in its luggage hold.

The stress of the past two days combined with their loss had robbed the family of all energy, and soon, Safina fell asleep sitting next to Engin. It was a long flight to Pakistan and she had a pounding headache. Engin had suggested she relax for a bit and let her rest her head on his shoulder, and she did just that, sliding into a fitful sleep.

The air suddenly seemed to thicken and engulf her, making it difficult to suck air into her lungs or to see where she stepped. She was in the village again and trying to find her way to the house through thick fog. Small sounds reached her ears but it was impossible to discern what they were. The fog grew thicker and seemed to seep into her clothes, crawling over her skin and giving her goose bumps. She wanted to scream but the sound did not come out. She wanted to call out to her father as he would know how to rescue her. Baba had warned her to stay away from the woods, but she had disobeyed him and now she was lost. She groped unsuccessfully in the dense air hoping her father would find her. Just when she lost hope and let herself fall, a hand caught her arm bringing her back on her feet. Despite the murkiness, she could tell it was Adam, and not her father who caught her.

The flight attendant tapped on Safina's shoulder, holding a glass of water and a pill. "I'm so sorry to have woken you up but your father insisted I give this to you right now. He said your head hurts," and saying this she handed Safina the glass of water and a painkiller. Engin and Safina looked at each other, completely flabbergasted.

"Did you just say her father asked you to give my wife a painkiller? How can that be possible? Could you describe him for us, please?" Engin asked the attendant.

"Oh, it was a tall man with very blue eyes, and he wore loose white clothes," she answered, puzzled by the query. Hearing this, Safina felt the goose bumps on her arm rise. She could sense her father's presence; the dream was his way of letting her know that she need not be afraid and that he had entrusted her to her brother. Looking at the passenger, the attendant couldn't understand what she had said to upset Safina. She was white as a sheet.

"Is there a problem? I'm sorry, I didn't know who the man was, but he did say he was your father and..." Engin interrupted her, holding up a hand, and explained that Safina's father had passed away and was in the luggage hold of the aircraft that they were in right now. He was being transported to Pakistan for burial and that is where the whole family was headed.

Even in his death, Khodadad had looked out for his daughter and felt her grief. Just then, Adam walked over to where Safina and Engin sat. "I had the strangest dream a minute ago. Baba was with me, I could feel him," he said and was met with three faces that turned to him speechless, and with a look of incredulity.

Samantha tore open the envelope. It was sent through registered mail and carried Pakistan's postmark. She bent to pick the newspaper clippings that fell to the floor. There was one from a magazine in the U.S., which had the picture of Safina sitting next to a man—a wedding photo, no doubt. At the bottom it said: Safina Khanzada, daughter of philanthropist Khodadad Wali Khanzada and Dr. Engin Yildirim's wedding reception in Houston. It was an indiscriminate photo of the couple seated at a table, smiling at each other. Another face in the picture was that of a young man who had his head turned to the other side, presumably talking to someone. The young man was a replica of Khodadad's when she first met him. Samantha's heart contracted involuntarily. The boy for whom she had left everything had grown into a man. The soft boyish features had matured into a fierce and chiselled face. The aquiline nose and widow's peak, like that of his father's, and the firm jaw came together to structure a proud and striking appearance. She looked carefully to find some trace of herself in that face, but found none. The other few clippings were from newspapers and magazines, some more pictures of Safina and her husband and the last one of Khodadad. The caption read: 'Generous charity donor and rare gems trade mogul dies after one year long battle with cancer.' The article below talked about how anonymous the deceased preferred to live; his private life a mystery. He was the recipient of several Pakistan's medals of honour and a few from around the world. His contribution to relocating and supporting orphans and widows from the Taliban conflicts was notable, as was his involvement in promoting education and health care in the rural areas of the country. He was also a generous benefactor for research in mental health treatment and was succeeded as tribal chief of the northern regions of Pakistan by his son and heir, Adam Wali Khanzada. That was it. It was almost as if the newspaper clippings were about some foreign family, unknown to her; there was no connection to her, no mention of her link to those names. Nothing.

Zaheer had been in the airport lounge in Dubai, waiting for his connecting flight to Islamabad when his eye fell on the magazine the lady sitting next to him was reading. He had almost snatched the magazine from her, staring at the picture of Safina looking breathtakingly beautiful in a red dress. Her husband was smiling into her eyes and she was returning his smile. The family had gone to pains to make Dr. Yildirim look like a tribal, but it was such a sad attempt. Tribal men, such as those from the Khanzada line, did not smile so much, he smirked. Over the next few days, Zaheer would feverishly look for newspapers or magazines with any mention of the Khanzadas. He started lingering in the bookstores of Islamabad which carried foreign newspapers and would grab as many copies as he could of the ones that interested him. When Virginia had unceremoniously thrown him out of her house and threatened to call the police if he didn't leave, he had been humiliated beyond words. His world was crumbling around him and he could not do anything about it. The medication didn't work; it never had. Besides, he was sick of playing the good boy part all the time; there were times everyone had to let their guard down and let nature dictate their actions. All his life, he had to prove he was better than anyone, had to work the hardest, and be the sympathetic ear and the shoulder to cry on. What was there for him in return? Hand me downs of the Khanzadas. "I have put the Islamabad orchard under your name, I have set aside funds for your water project," his uncle would say to him superciliously, and he would have to look grateful beyond words, kissing his hand in gratitude, indebted for life. What his uncle forgot to mention was that the Islamabad orchard was useless. It required a team of costly horticulturists to keep the exotic plants thriving in unfavourable climates. Trees of that orchard were not meant for a warm environment. The support he got for the water project was an insignificant amount compared to the magnitude of the project he hoped to spearhead. It was an insult to receive the cheque he received and for which his mother kept reminding him he should be thankful for, and everything else his uncle had done for him. Had fate not played her cruel hand and let his father live, he would have been the tribal chief today, instead of being the orphan protégé who had been taken under Khodadad's wings. On an impulse, Zaheer had taken the clippings and put them in an envelope. Let there be some smoke in dying embers, he had smiled inwardly and dropped the letter marked for Samantha Pridmore into the letter box.

CHAPTER 31

Safina put the last of the boxes into the truck and dusted her hands on her jeans. Sorting, discarding, and packing twelve years of your life lived in one house took time and energy and right now, she had neither. Engin and her were leaving for Ghana in a week and she had spent the past month getting rid of all their old stuff, selling off most of the furniture and packing the things she would need later into cardboard boxes to be transported to Halifax where Virginia lived a retired life with her botanist husband and his two kids from his first marriage. She looked for her friend going into the backyard and found her sprawled on the deck chair with her sun hat over her face, fast asleep. One would think her coming all the way from Halifax with the promise of helping her wind up their six-bedroom house would have lessened Safina's workload. In reality, all Virginia had done for the past two weeks was play with Safina and Engin's two children or spent lazy afternoons taking naps by the creek that ran behind the house. Exasperated to see her deep in slumber, she went indoors to tackle the last of the closets that needed sorting. The house had a bare look with most of the furniture already sold off. The hand-knotted silk rugs Adam had so generously gifted them when they first moved to the sprawling house in the suburbs of Toronto, were rolled up and stacked near the kitchen, ready to be loaded into the truck. Passing through the kitchen, Safina's heart melted when she noticed two casserole dishes with the foil still on them resting on the hot plates. While she had been packing boxes in the garage, Virginia had quietly prepared lunch for all of them. Not only that, there was garlic bread and a dish of mashed potatoes sitting in the warm oven. Sighing, Safina made her way up the wooden staircase and into one of the spare rooms. The room was a particular favourite of Safina's. It was where she did most of her work, preparing lectures for the coming day and sometimes sketching by the window that overlooked the brook. This is where she kept all her personal belongings, which had been put away because they brought back memories that could still upset her. There were pictures in a drawer of her mother when she was beautiful and young, some of her in the village with Zaheer, as well as her old sketch pad. In the closet, she found her old Swiss Army backpack which she had with her when she made that fateful journey from the village to Islamabad and then to Canada. Safina pulled out the faded bag and rummaging inside one of the pockets, when her hand touched something small and hard. It was the tiny, blue box which she had left in the bag so many years ago. Even now, it was painful to bring back those days. She sat down on the loveseat and lifted the lid off the box to reveal the sparkling earring with a teardrop diamond clasped in silver and gold claws. It was an astonishing piece of fine craftsmanship and she remembered seeing it when she had opened her father's private closet so many years ago. She remembered she had only brought one earring with her to Canada, perhaps losing the other when she left her father's room in haste. The box had remained forgotten all these years in the bag and looking at it now, she wondered if she should return it to Adam and Gulrukh. They might still have the matching piece somewhere. "What are you doing here by yourself, dear?" Virginia said, startling Safina out of her reverie.

"I must have forgotten to put this away in the locker with the rest of the jewellery. It is much too valuable to be stored with the rest of the things. Perhaps you could keep it with you?" Virginia could tell when Safina was having one of those moments where she would drift off into the past and come back gloomy and quiet. Evidently, the contents of what she was holding had put her in that state. Taking the box from her, she promised to keep it safe until Engin and she returned to Canada in four years.

Zaheer paced the hard earth, grinding his teeth. The incompetent lawyer had just informed him that his mother's legacy left no room for him to sell off the land he had acquired on her death two months ago. What's more, he could only inherit the land if he decided to make the village his home and would revert to the Khanzadas in case he ever tried to sell it. He had lost his cool in the solicitor's office, shouting at him incoherently and threatening to contest Mumtaz Bibi's will. However, there was nothing that could be done as his mother, shrewd as she was—even in her death—had abandoned her only son and played into the hands of her adopted family. The will might as well have been carved in stone, with no loopholes he could have used to his benefit.

The truth was, Zaheer could not compromise on the extravagant lifestyle he had gotten used to and which his uncle had indulged him with. After Khodadad's death, Adam had made sure nothing besides what he had inherited from his uncle's will came his way. There were no monthly cheques for his upkeep, he drove a modest car, and lived in the apartment Khodadad had left him. The orchard had long been sold and the few million rupees which had been left him for his water scheme and had supported him for a while, had been spent. He was now out of work, had no contacts he could approach and to make things worse, his mother had died. In the past, he had often played the card of the neglected son and Mumtaz would occasionally transfer some money into his account. Whether Adam was aware of these transactions, he couldn't tell. But, he knew Adam would never allow for any of the land to come under his name. Now, Mumtaz was gone and there was no hope of any cash coming his way. In addition, he had sold off most of the jewellery he had surreptitiously pocketed when he had come to see his mother once at the Margalla Hill house. She had cried all the time he was there, burying her face in her scarf and for a moment, he had almost felt remorseful for how she suffered. Instead, he had lost his temper, something that happened too often now, and accused her of never being a mother to him. He had been left between the cold walls of a boarding school as a kid, lived without a family, and never knew a mother's touch. How could he grow up and have a regular life when everything in his life had been anything but normal? The entire sum of his father's heritage to him was a mental disorder, which manifested itself in all aspects of his life and left no room for him to do much else.

CHAPTER 32

Zaheer now went through the contents of his wardrobe, looking for that balled up tissue in which he had kept the earring. More than a year ago, he had taken the jewellery from his mother's room, he knew behind which book she kept the key to the safe, and had opened it to clear out the valuables. There wasn't much he found there, she had probably moved most of the stuff to the village, except for a few bundles of cash, both in sterling pounds and rupees and some jewellery. He had crammed the money into the long pockets of his winter coat and discarded the boxes and put the jewellery in the front pockets of his trousers and jacket. When Mumtaz came looking for him after completing her evening prayers, she was told by the caretaker that Zaheer had already left.

The corpulent jeweller with the brown stained teeth sat behind a scratched glass counter top in the shop reeking heavily of incense. The tiny, inconspicuous shop was located in the back alley of *Anaarkali* bazaar in Lahore, known for its black-market activities. The man had looked at the pieces before him, holding each one against the light and scrutinizing them through a lens. "These are exceptional pieces and I won't ask where you got them from but you do realize selling these will be tricky as the owners have probably notified the police. I will only be able to give you a fraction of their value," he had said, his beady eyes mentally appraising the items and calculating the fat profit he would make. Had he not been in desperate need of cash, Zaheer would have waited to find another buyer. The jeweller had picked up the tear drop diamond with a sharp intake of breath and held it gently under the light. "This is a rare piece; definitely worth more than all the stuff you brought here put together. I will give you three hundred thousand rupees for the pair."

Zaheer had looked at the man with disgust. He knew it was worth much more than what was being offered. "There's just the one. I don't have the other earring," he had said, his throat suddenly going dry. The man in front of him had scratched his huge belly that was pressed against the glass counter and smiled to reveal pan and tea stained teeth. His expression said he had made a kill. Zaheer had looked at him, the bile rising in his throat and told the jeweller that the earring was not for sale. The trader knew when he had overstepped and had pushed the seller too far and now altered his tone. "No need to feel offended, sir ji," he said obsequiously. "What I meant was, I can pay you half of that for one earring and when you get the other one, you will be paid for it. Just a moment," and saying this, he shouted to the back of the room at a nonexistent shop assistant, asking him to hurry up with the cup of tea, "can't you see, *sahab* is in a hurry?"

When no amount of insistence could convince Zaheer to leave the single earring with him, the jeweller reluctantly counted the money to pay off for the other pieces on the table. Picking up his cash and the earring folded carefully in a square of white tissue, Zaheer left the stifling shop with his head lowered and coat collar pulled up against the biting January cold of a Lahore evening. After that, Zaheer had often wondered where the matching earring could have gone. His mother had been so scrupulous about keeping valuables in a safe place, so how could she have lost it? He then recalled a conversation between his mother and his uncle where his mother was being instructed to get rid of anything that belonged to Samantha. His uncle had given the earring to Mumtaz and when asked why it was not a full pair, he had stood there and with a pained look, said that Safina had rifled through his closet before she left. She had dropped one on the carpet and the other one was probably with her.

The taxi dropped Zaheer off in front of the traditional style house, over run with maple ivy. The house was surrounded on three sides with tall red maples and birches and the front had been renovated to look like the house in the village. Safina must have taken pains to replicate the look. There was a cherry tree to the left with a swing hanging from the branches and a rickety old bench underneath. Walking over the cobblestone path leading up to the front door, Zaheer found a duplicate reproduction of the main door to the village house. It was a carved, mammoth structure with two doors and brass knockers inlaid with semi-precious gems. He was sure the inside was also modified to resemble the house of her childhood. Before he could ring the bell, the door opened suddenly to reveal a petite blonde in a bright yellow jogging suit standing in front of him. "I thought it was my yoga trainer," she smiled to reveal perfect white veneers.

"I'm sorry. Isn't this Dr. Yildirim's house?" Zaheer asked. He was informed by the woman that Dr. Yildirim and his wife had moved away and that she and her husband had leased the house from them for a few years. There was no more information that the woman could provide him and gave him the name of the lawyer who had dealt with their rental lease. That was the best she could do and bade him good day. Frustrated that his plans to patch up with Safina had been thwarted, albeit temporarily, Zaheer headed to the nearest main street. He would have to figure out his next move.

Virginia had just dropped off her husband's two teenage twins at the train station. They were heading back to their universities after their Christmas break. She had been drawn to their openness about their mother's death since the first time she met them many years ago. They had been young girls back then, and despite the trauma suffered at the loss of their mother in a brutal road accident, they were a close knit, wholesome family. The children had raised no objection when their father, Dr. Ralph Flynn, announced one day that Virginia and he were getting married. In fact, they had welcomed the addition to their family and made her feel wanted and loved, something Virginia had missed since she lost her own parents and brother. The children had spent four years in the Flynn house in Halifax while still completing high school, and had now moved in different directions where their universities were located. After the twins left, Ralph had decided to retire from his position as Head of the Department of Science at Dalhousie University and sell the rambling old house to relocate to a remote suburb of Halifax. Initially, Virginia had been a bit sceptical about moving away from the city, but looking at the tiny stone cottage with its brick chimney and gabled white windows, she had fallen in love with the house. The cottage was surrounded with ancient trees and came with fifty acres of farming land. She understood why her husband was drawn towards it; he always talked about retiring and running his own farm, where he would experiment with foreign crops grown in a modified temperature controlled environment. After two years of persistent hard work and many hundred thousand dollars later, Ralph had realized his dream and grew vegetables and grains indigenous to South America. While Virginia spent her days writing for historical journals, Ralph could be seen working in the big barnlike structures with artificial lighting, automatically adjusting temperature or walking through the outdoor fields inspecting his harvest.

Virginia noticed a car parked in the driveway when she turned the bend towards the house. It must be one of the people come to collect the order which had to be shipped to Vancouver, she thought. However, the man leaning against the car did not look like one of the men who came to pick up vegetable supplies. The man was dressed in a suit and looked strangely familiar. Driving closer, Virginia brought the car to a stop and coming out, walked to where he was parked under the cluster of trees. If he had changed over the years, it was only to look more handsome, Virginia thought with some disgust. The deep blue eyes, so common to Safina's side of the family, sparkled in the early winter sunlight. Zaheer's dark brown hair was now speckled with grey and he had an athletic, middle-aged lankiness about him. She wondered what brought him to her doorstep in such a remote area. "How did you find this place and what are you doing here? Please leave before I call the police," she said unceremoniously, while trying to locate the farm help Ralph employed out of the corner of her eye.

"And good morning to you as well," he replied, revealing even, white teeth. "Won't you invite me inside for a cup of tea? It's freezing here and I've been driving for a long time. I think I have a lot of explaining to do," he asked Virginia, continuing to smile. The sincerity in his voice made Virginia weigh his words and finally, she asked him to come in. After all, what harm could he do? Joel was working close by behind the house, and if there was any trouble, she could always shout out to him.

Virginia listened to what he had to say, stroking the tiny beagle in her lap. He spoke about his battle with schizophrenia, which he inherited from his father's side of the family and over which he had no control, but thanks to medicine and a remarkable counsellor, that was a thing of the past. He was sorry for what had happened at her house in Toronto and wanted to make amends with Safina. He knew she would understand and would also make her friend see what he had suffered all these years. Zaheer's remorse sounded genuine. What's more, he appeared to be doing well in life, his health seemed good and not once had he displayed any sign of inconsistent or unpleasant behaviour. "I only want to make amends, Virginia. I don't want anything but to apologize for actions over which I had no control," he said earnestly, "she is family, after all." Virginia prevaricated, unable to decide. After the near-rape incident in Toronto, it was understood that Safina never wanted to hear Zaheer's name. However, listening to him sitting there, Virginia could see how the man had suffered all these years and wanted nothing more than to ask forgiveness.

"Tell you what. Let me ask Safina and find out what she thinks. If she wants me to give you her number, I will. I cannot do so without asking her first," she said matter-of-factly. Zaheer nodded and said he completely understood. After all, his cousin probably hated him and wouldn't want to hear his voice out of the blue. He thanked Virginia for her understanding and seeing that she had warmed up to him, started to make small talk about the farm and showed interest in the latest book she was working on. He came to learn that before she left, Safina had been working on a book about the tribal cultures of the world but right now, had put that on hold. Once she returned and Virginia shipped back her things, maybe she would take it up from where she left off.

When he was about to leave, Zaheer paused at the door. "I don't know if Safina will agree to speak with me or not. There's something I've wanted to give to her before I return to Pakistan. I believe it belonged to her mother," and saying this, he pulled out the earring, now in a small silk pouch instead of the tissue it had been in, and handed it over to Virginia.

As she emptied the contents of the pouch onto her palm, the older woman let out an involuntary shriek of surprise. "Oh you found the other one!" she exclaimed excitedly, holding up the earring between forefinger and thumb and sitting down suddenly. "Safina will be astounded when I give her both of these instead of one," she laughed, so happy to imagine the look of surprise on Safina's face when she opened the box to discover the missing twin. Zaheer tried to look just as pleased, and graciously thanked Virginia for her time and for listening to him. He left after she promised to call him at the hotel he was staying at, the moment she heard from her friend.

Zaheer had had enough time sitting in Virginia's tiny living room, its walls lined with shelves groaning with the weight of books and knick-knacks, to observe the layout of the cottage. His guess had been correct. Safina had the missing piece. He had presumed correctly that she had left her things with her friend, perhaps also the rest of her gems, which Adam must have given to her after their father's death. He did not want to wait for the doddering old professor to return before he got what he wanted.

The house was dark except for a light upstairs. He waited for exactly half an hour in the biting cold until that light also went out. Moving along the side of the house and keeping clear of the snow, Zaheer made his way to the back of the house. He had unlocked a rear window earlier that day when he had excused himself to use the tiny washroom. Climbing in was easy but the moment he stepped in, the beagle, alerted by the creaking boards, came scampering down the wooden staircase. "Come here, Petsy. Good girl," he called out to the startled dog, and offered it a biscuit that he pulled out of his jacket. The dog whimpered for a second, then came and rubbed itself against Zaheer's leg. Zaheer made his way upstairs, and looking through the door left ajar, found Virginia asleep on her side, the light from the moon giving her heaving frame an uncanny look. He opened the door wider and moved inside. The tiny box on the dresser was what he was looking for. Picking up the box, Zaheer removed the lid to feel its contents, and reassured that Virginia had matched both earrings, he fumbled for the drawer handle to look for the rest of the items. Just then, the beagle decided to start yapping and nipping at his trouser leg. The light went on and Virginia, dazed, looked at him in horror, standing in her room.

He did not want to kill the dog but its incessant barking and tugging his pant cuff between its teeth was infuriating him. Before he could tell what he was doing, he had pulled the ornamental dagger off the shelf near him, unsheathed the silver casing and slit open the nuisance from the throat. Virginia, whom he had forced down the stairs and pushed onto the recliner, screamed when the dog let out a single yelp and lay on the floor, unmoving. "I did not want to do this, you know. But I've always hated pets inside the house, and she was being very annoying. She ruined a very expensive pair of pants," he said menacingly. He asked Virginia for the rest of the jewellery which he was sure Safina had left with her, and listening to her denials, threw the dagger to the side and tried to reach her throat. The woman got up suddenly and lost her balance, knocking her head on the coffee table. Zaheer looked on in terror. This was not going as planned. He would have to kill her before he left. A light went on in the barnlike structure outside and Zaheer froze. He had to leave but he couldn't before he made sure Virginia was dead. He got down on his knees and turned the face around to feel her pulse. She was breathing. Another light went on outside. He was panicking and didn't know what he was doing. He had come near to killing her, what was he doing? He removed his leather glove and patted Virginia's cheek, trying to revive her but found no response. She had stopped breathing and a trickle of blood traced a dark path across her forehead. Steadying his hands, Zaheer turned Virginia over to look at her face and despite the near darkness in the room, he could tell she was dead. There wasn't time to go back upstairs and look for the rest of the jewellery. The lights outside went off. When he reached his car parked further up the road behind a grove, he paused to look back at the house. The lights went on in the barn again and after a few seconds, turned off. He felt in his pocket for the earrings and finding none, he let out a hollow laugh, amused at his own fear of being caught. He remembered turning Virginia's face towards himself and bending down to check her breathing. The box had fallen out of his pocket and lay open, the earrings spilled onto the carpet, glinting in the moonlight streaming through the window. Being the state he was in, he left without picking up the earrings and in his fright, had completely forgotten that Virginia had mentioned the state-of-the-art lighting and heating system in the barns, which kicked in when required of their own accord. It had been daylight when she had told him, so of course, he hadn't noticed. Perhaps it was best he got rid of the earrings—let Safina find them and go to hell wearing them, he thought with a twisted smile and turned the ignition.

Zaheer spent only enough time at the motel to change into a suit and collect his travel documents. Driving the rented car, he reached the airport just when dawn was leisurely breaking and abandoning the car with the keys still in the ignition, he made his way inside. "You can take the flight to London Heathrow and then find a connection to Islamabad, sir, but even then, there are no available seats until tomorrow, I'm afraid," the girl at the counter was telling him.

"You have to understand, it's my wife. I've just been told she might go into labour soon. I must get to Islamabad as soon as possible." The young woman had looked at him and noted the expensive suit and manicured nails. Sighing, she clicked some more buttons on the computer.

"I might be able to put you in business class on the London flight. Is that okay with you?" Zaheer almost jumped over the counter to kiss her.

He waited in the passenger's lounge, impatient for the flight to be announced. How long before someone found Virginia? he wondered. The flight from London to Islamabad was not until four days. If the police connected the dots, it was only a matter of time before they knew it was him who had broken into the house. He had made sure not to leave fingerprints and he had rented the motel and car with a fake ID, but still, he wasn't sure if he had left any clues. He was not willing to admit that she was killed because of him; her death was caused by her knocking her head on the table, he reassured himself. Zaheer spent four terribly long days in a shabby hotel waiting for his flight or for the police to show up at any moment. When it was the day of his departure, he had to have enough alcohol to steady his nerves and get on that flight. Only when he would get on the plane to Pakistan would he be able to breathe easy, he thought. Surprisingly, he was very calm; anyone looking at him, his raincoat casually draped over his arm and holding a rolled-up copy of *The Times* in hand would have thought him to be some executive travelling for work. He made his way quietly to the passenger's lounge and waited.

The plane landed at the Benazir International Airport in Islamabad and Zaheer looked out the window half-expecting police cars to be waiting on the tarmac. Finding none, he took unhurried steps and left the airport unobtrusively.

The drive to prison always brought back bitter memories. Images of a young boy being dragged by the arm, the clang of metal doors swinging easily on well-oiled hinges, the musty, disinfected smell hopelessly trying to veil the odour of sweat and fear chased each other in Krenos' mind. He had sworn as a kid to fight against evil, to be blameless; untarnished. He didn't know his pursuit for good and the desire to combat crime would invariably bring him to the same sound and stench he abhorred as a child.

Flynn sat waiting in Krenos' office, with the blue box sitting on the desk. He had not waited to meet him at the police station but insisted on seeing him without delay and had driven all the way to the prison where Krenos was going to be that day. One look at the earrings and Krenos knew there was more to the story of the random intruder. Flynn explained that before his wife's death, he had only just seen the earring once. What he couldn't remember at the time was that his wife had shown him only one earring saying that the matching one had been lost by the owner. Along with some books and notes, Virginia had been safe-keeping the earring for her friend, Safina, who was working in Africa with her husband. Whoever came to the house that night had brought the missing pair and forgot to take it with them. As implausible as the story sounded, Krenos knew there was a probability to it. He took the box and its contents into custody and reopened the file of the unsolved mystery of Dr. Ambrose's death.

Zaheer breathed in the fresh spring air. He felt happy to be alive after that narrow escape from being caught, and that too on foreign soil. He was out of harm's way in Pakistan. Soon, he would get back the reins on his life and start fresh.

Finding women who fell for his charms had never been difficult and he had finally decided to settle down with one. Asmah was the only daughter of a textile tycoon who had died recently, leaving his daughter as sole inheritor of his massive wealth. The widow and daughter lived in one of Islamabad's exclusive neighbourhoods and hardly ever left house on account of the tragedy that befell them—that is, until Zaheer walked into their lives. Seeing Asmah's father's death as a God sent opportunity, Zaheer sold his posh apartment and rented a small house in their neighbourhood. Soon, he had made his way into the grieving family's house and into their hearts. It was not unusual to see him sitting with the widow and her daughter, trying to ease their sorrow by his enchanting personality and sympathetic ear. Often, the three would be seen in public together, dining at fine restaurants or going to the movies or even going for long walks on the many trails around the beautiful city. Before long, the visits took on a deeper meaning and Asmah and he got engaged in a quiet ceremony. "I don't think I can wait that long, Asmah. I find myself thinking about you all the time I'm not with you," he had said to her one day, dazzling her with his sad, blue eyes. Asmah, who was an only child, had never felt wanted by any man. Where the girls at the exclusive American School of Islamabad where she had studied had easily found dates and enjoyed the attention of boys, Asmah's austere looks and almost sad, unadorned features inhibited her classmates from approaching her. The only reason she got invited to parties, and that too rarely, was because her classmates' parents would insist to add her name to the guest list, knowing her father was one of the wealthiest and extremely influential men in the country. The moment Zaheer entered their lives, Asmah had felt her heart tug whenever he looked at her. She started taking an interest in what she wore and even ventured to the salon to get her hair styled. It was a nice feeling to know her efforts did not go unnoticed when Zaheer stopped midway between a conversation with her mother one evening and looked up to notice her appreciatively walking into the living room. His gaze paused on her, taking in the new designer kurta and flattering hairdo framing her face. His eyes said he was pleased with what he saw. This was the first time a man had looked at her admiringly, and Asmah's mother noted the change in her daughter's demeanour with satisfaction. Not only did Zaheer make Asmah feel special, he had equally charmed the dead business tycoon's widow. Whenever Mrs. Tahir had to go see the lawyers or deal with any of the mundane, tiring legal work, Zaheer was always there to accompany her. The fact was, the vacuum left by the late Mr. Tahir was filled with their debonair, helpful saviour whose selflessness and kindness was not lost on the grieving women. Both mother and daughter had come to depend on Zaheer to not only help them with any official work, but to also make their days and most evenings lively. When he left their house late that evening, Zaheer felt euphoric. Asmah's mother had agreed to get them married within the month and before long, he imagined he would be sitting behind a desk as the CEO of a sprawling multi-national company. All those visits to the lawyers had given Zaheer a pretty good idea of the magnitude of the widow's wealth. It was a matter of time before he would be one of the richest men in the city, if not the country, he mused with pleasure. He could not wait to see the look of shock and surprise on both his cousins' faces when they read about his catch, and regret the way they had underestimated him all those years.

Turning into his street, Zaheer did not notice the unmarked cars parked outside his house. Before he could bring his Audi, an engagement present from the dead businessman's wife, to a stop, the door to his car was pulled open and he was dragged roughly from his seat. One of the special force police officers yanked the surprised man by the collar and handcuffed his wrists behind his back. Another officer turned him around to face the several cameras that suddenly seemed to have appeared out of nowhere, blinding him with flashes from their cameras.

Adam had watched enough, he thought. Sitting in the backseat of the car parked not far from the scene in progress, he had watched Zaheer being led away through the on-looking crowd and host of journalists. Before he was pushed into the back of the police pick-up van, Zaheer had looked across to where the Range Rover stood. The tinted black glass of the window rolled upwards, but not before he caught a glance of Adam watching him being led away.

The Special Force officer spoke into his walkie-talkie. "Yes, the perpetrator has been arrested and is being transported to the station. Yes, it's confirmed it is him, you can inform Krenos in Toronto. Over."

CPSIA information can be obtained
at www.ICGtesting.com
Printed in the USA
LVHW011348010819
626156LV00004B/688